To my brother Billy
and his wife Margie

Love William

BEYOND THE GARDEN

A Novel

NOLAN M. ROBINSON

ISBN: 978-1-4834-1298-6 (sc)
ISBN: 978-1-4834-1297-9 (e)

Library of Congress Control Number: 2014909718

Because of the dynamic nature of the Internet, any web addresses or links contained in
this book may have changed since publication and may no longer be valid. The views
expressed in this work are solely those of the author and do not necessarily reflect the
views of the publisher, and the publisher hereby disclaims any responsibility for them.

Any people depicted in stock imagery provided by Thinkstock are models,
and such images are being used for illustrative purposes only.
Certain stock imagery © Thinkstock.

Lulu Publishing Services rev. date:07/10/2014

For those whom had worked at the Willowbrook over the years

CHAPTER 1 ━━━━━━━━━━

"Some people pray to their Lord and others pray to their Savior. But Ruben does neither."

Those words were spoken about the young man that was working the far end of the bar. This was his domain for the evening. This is where he greeted the customers with a smile, sometimes sincere and sometimes not. But he was always professional. Even though on the surface he did not appear that he belonged wearing the classic bartender uniform with his rust colored sideburns and long hair that was tied back of his head. The long sleeves covered his tattoos. Although he had an edge about him, he was still a good bartender. He knew most of the regulars; not all by name. But he did know what they drank and how much they tipped.

Those words were spoken by the bartender who was on the service station. His name was Grant. He was a tall and thin man with wavy hair that had nearly all turned white. He wore wire rimmed glasses on his long face. Usually he would end a sentence with a smile. For many years he had worked as a bartender in the restaurant and a small nightclub that was Anna's Garden, but every one called it The Garden.

"He doesn't believe in God?" Nicole demanded to know. She was the black cocktail waitress for whom Grant was filling her order. She was very attractive with small facial features that gave her the appearance of someone too young to be a cocktail waitress. She wore her hair short, her lipstick a bright red, extensive amount of jewelry and spike high heels.

"No, Nicole. That is not what I said. I said that he might feel that it is not important if God exists or not. People don't have a choice in what they believe. And he believes that one shouldn't count on someone that might or might not exist. He believes that one should count only on themselves."

"That's crazy. Everyone knows that there is a God."

"Not really. You might know what you want to believe, but that is not necessarily what you do believe in. And that, my friend, depends only on one's own experiences. A person has no choice in what they believe in. His belief in God depends on his own experiences."

"That is bull shit. Of course there is a God, Everybody knows that there is a God," she said as she picked-up the tray of drinks. She walked past the customers that were sitting at the bar. She leaned over the counter so Ruben could hear her over the music of the blues band. "You don't believe in God?"

He smiled at the unexpected question. "Well," he laughed, "What brought that on?"

"Do you believe in God or not?"

"I've never seen any proof that he exists. But once I got a quarter from the Tooth Fairy. So, I do believe in the Tooth Fairy." With a disgusting look, Nicole turned and walked towards the cocktail tables.

Another bartender approaches the bar, carrying two empty liquor bottles. His name was Seth. He was entering middle age. His once athletic body had begun to take on some extra weight. His square face was clean shaven with some gray hair on his temples. He had on easy going disposition.

"How's it going?" Ruben asked as he took the two empty bottles and replaced them with two unopened ones.

"They haven't dropped the salads yet. I have a feeling that they are on the talkative side."

"Why? Everyone giving a toast?"

Seth smiled in agreement.

"You in the hole?"

No. Davy is stuck down there."

"That is a good place for him."

"Yea. I'm sure, whatever he has, he is entertaining them."

"What kind of party you stuck with?" Ruben asked.

"It's some kind of Latin thing. They're speaking mostly Spanish. You should have it," said Seth.

"I'm only one-fourth Mexican. The only Spanish that I know is adios you ass hole." They both smiled at the joke.

"Yeah, that's about all that I know too. I used to play ball with lots of them, but I never picked up much of their lingo."

Three men came weaving through the tables towards the bar. The big man in the front was wearing an expensive suit. He was being followed by a young baby faced blond-haired man in blue jeans and a silk shirt that had the top buttons undone. In the rear was a small man with a goatee wearing khaki.

"Gentlemen," Ruben said as he placed napkins on the bar, guiding them to where he wanted them to sit.

"I'll have a Manhattan," said the man who was obviously the leader, as he sat down at the middle place. "And make it as if it was your own."

"Give me what you have on tap," the blond-haired man said with an arrogant smile. "And give Lenny one of those girly drinks,"

The man with the goatee gave him a disgusting look. "The house Merlot will be fine."

"I'm Dick," the well-dressed man said as he held out his big hand. Ruben hesitated a moment before they shook hands.

"I'm Ruben."

"This is Lenny," he motioned to the man with the goatee. Then he put his hand on the other ones shoulder, "And this young stud is Max."

A lovely and shapely young waitress, who had long and wavy blonde hair that surrounded her innocent looking face with sky blue eyes came from the dining room. Her name was Hope. She was carrying a slice of Devil's food cake with a lit candle on it. "Happy Birthday, Ruben" she said as she leaned across the bar for a thank you kiss.

Being somewhat embarrassed, he gave her a peck on the lips. "Thank you, Hope," he said as he was putting the cake beneath the counter.

"Hey! Birthday Boy," Dick said. "You can't put it away that fast. You got to make a wish and blow out the candle. Isn't that right?"

"I think that I know what he will wish for," Max snickered as he sized up Hope.

Ruben placed the cake back on the counter and relit the candle before he blew it out.

"Well," Dick wanted to know, "What did you wish for?"

Grant had walked to Ruben's end of the bar to join in on the conversation. "Yeah, Ruben, what did you wish for?"

"Nothing."

"Nothing?" Dick mimicked him. "You had to wish for something."

"Fairness."

"Fairness? Justice?" Dick snickered. "Sorry, my young man. But that won't happen in your life time.

"Say, this calls for a shot. Give us your best tequila, and whatever your poison is."

"Sorry, but we aren't allowed to drink on duty," Ruben replied as he poured the shots. "Do you want salt and lime?"

"We don't need any training wheels." Dick answered.

"So," Grant asked Dick, "If you don't believe in justice then what would you wish for?"

"First thing, who in the Hell wants justice? If there were justice then we could all be in jail. No thanks. Just give me money and I'll buy any damn thing that I want."

"I think that I would wish for love," Max said as he smiled at Hope.

"Hell," Dick laughed, "If you have money you can buy all the whores you want."

"No. That is not what I mean."

"I know what you mean," Dick replied. "But I can tell you that true love is like justice, a myth."

"And what would you wish for?" Grant asked Lenny.

"I guess love and justice," he said as he smiled at the little joke that he made.

"Shit, I know what you would wish for," Dick said. "What every dam artist wants, fortune and fame. Anyway, fame."

"Now, that you put it that way, it would be nice to have a painting or two or three hanging in the Art Institute. Even better yet, in the Louvre. They can take down that painting of that fat woman without any eye brows, and put up one of my master pieces."

"Well." Grant proclaimed, "There you have it. The trilogy of man's desires, love, respect and security."

"What are you? Some kind of a damn philosopher?" Dick scorned.

"Are you a real artist?" Hope asked Lenny. "I would love to have my picture painted. But I don't have any money."

"That might not be any problem," Lenny said as he studied her. "We are always looking for beautiful models. Give me a call if you are willing to do what it takes, we will pay you."

Lenny handed her a business card as Seth asked Dick, "Are you the owner of the Get-A-Way?"

"Yeah, that's me. Do you have a boat?"

"Mine is much smaller. You might have seen it, Spirit? It's docked close to yours"

"I'll keep an eye out for it." Dick said as the maître d' led the three men to their table in the dining room and Hope and Seth returned to their stations.

Grant asked Ruben. "Why didn't you have a shot? After all, you only turn twenty-three once. I'm sure that they wouldn't mind."

"I'm particular who I drink with."

"Well, look who is here," Dick said as Hope approached their table.

"Hey," Max said with a loud voice. "Where is my piece of cake? You do know that it's my birthday too. So, where's my piece of cake or a piece of something else."

"It's true what they say," Lenny said to the embarrassed waitress, "there are more horse's asses than there are horses."

"My name is Hope. And I'll be your server," she said as she glanced at Max, fearful of another off color comment. She handed them menus.

"Well," Dick said, "What do you recommend?"

"Everything is good," she replied.

"Young Lady, you do know that that is the worst possible answer you can give? Don't you know?" Dick questioned her.

For a moment she was still. Then she asked Dick, "What do you have a taste for? All of the sea food is fresh. My favorite is the crab cakes," she continued. "The catch of the day is sole. All the steak are prime. The biggest and the best cut is the porter house."

"I'll have that," Dick said with an approving smile. "Make it on the rare side."

"I'll have the sole," said Lenny.

"I don't know what I want," said Max. "What else you got good that I might like?"

"I'm sorry, but we don't serve fried bologna."

Dick and Lenny broke out in laugher. The people at the nearby tables joined in at Max's expense. With a soft smile, a smile that asked forgiveness, Hope said, "We have lamb."

He pondered the lamb then he shook his head.

"The Chicken Florentine is very good."

"Okay, I'll try it."

She wrote down their orders. As she walked away she glanced back at Max.

"I like that girl," Lenny smiled. "She knows how to put Max in his place."

"That she did," Dick said. He leaned over the table and the others joined him, so no one could hear them. "Maybe we can use her in our first movie."

"You said that Roxy would be the first," Max protested.

"Lenny said that she might not be that photogenic." Dick explained

"What in the hell are you talking about?" Max said angrily. "She's pretty. She's lots prettier than that God damn waitress."

"No one is saying that Roxy isn't pretty," Dick said. "How well will she photograph? Who knows? Maybe we can use both of the girls. Little girl on girl action. To make the business successful we will have to have lots of performers. After all, this is a new venture for all of us."

CHAPTER 2 ━━━━━━━━━━━━━━━━━

Towards the end of the evening the kitchen help came to the bar for their night cap. Then they carried their beers to a nearby table. Most of the dining room waitresses had already left. Seth and Davy had finished their party and joined the others at the bar.

"Do you want a 7 - 7?" Ruben joked.

"D-Don't be an a-ass hole," Davy answered. He was a thin freckled faced man with burgundy color hair that lay flat on his forehead. He wore a diamond stud in one of his ears. "Gave me a b-beer."

"What's the joke?" asked a customer as he got up to leave the bar.

"There's an old bartender joke, '7-7' was invented by a man who stuttered," Grant replied.

Four Latin women from Seth's party had come into the lounge and were sitting at a cocktail table, bringing with them their drinks from Seth's party. Three were in their middle ages. The fourth one was younger, late twenties or early thirties. She had honey color skin with long wavy black hair. On her cheek was a scar. It was not noticeable to most people, but it was still visible. She was different from the others. It was the way she looked at Seth-not as if she was flirting with him in a childish manner, but in a way to let him know that she was attracted to him. Seth smiled at her and she returned the smile. "How is it going, Angela?" he said softly, so the others would not hear. They had exchanged names when he served her at the party.

"Fine Seth," she answered before she rejoined her companions. She sat at the opposite side of the table from the bar, so Seth could see her.

On the other side of the room Hope was helping Nicole clean off the cocktail tables. "I think that Ruben is cute." Hope commented.

"You have the hots for him?" Nicole teased.

"No! No. Not really. I just find him attractive. That's all."

"And you want him to jump your bones," Nicole laughed.

"No! That's not what I said."

"Boy am I surprised," Nicole said sarcastically. "And I'm sure everyone here will be too."

"All of them know?"

"Only the ones that isn't blind."

At the bar Davy asked in a loud voice "Hey, does any w-one know who won the game today, the Sox or the Cubs?"

"The Sox, of course," Ruben smiled.

"Tonight a guy in the washroom th-thank me for washing my hands. I-I told him that I always like to have clean f-fingers when I-I pick my nose," Davy said to humor the others.

The band leader thanks the people for coming. He tells the audience to give themselves a hand. The few that were still there clapped as they slowly begin to leave, the musicians started to break down their instruments.

"I don't un-understand why people clap for th-themselves. It makes about as much sense as clapping in a movie. L-like the actors will be able to hear you."

"I clap at the movies," Nicole said as she set a tray of dirty glasses on the counter.

"I rest my case."

"You're just an ass."

"But I'm a cute ass," Davy laughed.

"I cut someone off tonight," Seth said. "And he wasn't even drunk."

"Then why did you?" asked Grant.

"Because he wanted me to. They were doing shots and he was making a face, like it was hurting him. So, what the hell, I cut him. The ones that were bullying him into taking the shots didn't like it. But the hell with them."

"I cut off a guy tonight too. Not be-because he was drunk. But because he w-wasn't tipping." Davy laughed at his joke as the others smiled.

"I have to get up early," Nicole said to Ruben. "Can you take Hope home?"

"No problem. It will be my pleasure."

"Do you have the time for a night cap," Grant asked with a knowing smile. "What will it be?"

"A Zin will do. But I'll have to punch out first."

"Go ahead and punch all of us out too," Grant said as he poured a glass of white Zinfandel, then he put a straw in the glass for her.

Yvette was the other cocktail waitress. She was a tall slender woman in her mid-thirties. Her dyed brunette hair was in a bob cut. As she set her tray of dirty glasses on the counter Davy asked her jokingly "Did you m-make enough for an m-motel for us tonight?" "In your dreams."

With a big sigh he said, "Guess w-we w-will have to do with the ba-back seat."

"I will have a gin and tonic," she said to Grant.

"What will my fellow traveler have?" Ruben asked Hope.

"I don't know. I don't really drink."

"How about a boiler maker?" Ruben asked.

"What is a boiler maker?"

"It's a shot of bourbon with a beer chaser. Is that something that you would like?" Ruben asked jokingly.

"No, no! That would be way too strong. How about a wine cooler?"

"I think we can do better than that. Tell me what you like?" he asked. "Do you have a favorite fruit or ice cream or candy even?"

She paused for a moment "My favorite ice cream is… dream sickle."

"Dream sickle it is." Ruben made the drinks as Grant washed the glasses. The other two bartenders went behind the bar to make their own drinks. Ruben served Hope and took a beer for himself and walked around the counter and sat down on the stool next to her. His legs rubbed against hers. It made her feel awkward. She wondered if he realized that their legs were touching. And if he did, and if she moved her leg, would that offend him. She decided to pretend that she never noticed.

"This is really good. How did you make it?"

"Oh, I can't reveal that. It's a trade secret. If I tell you then I would have to kill you."

"I guess that I w-will have to go home to an empty house," Davy said with his head hanging down.

"Isn't your wife there?" Yvette asked Davy.

"I don't know. Th-this morning I found the key to her chastity belt on the n-night stand."

Yvette distorted her face, trying to keep from laughing.

June, the owner, brought to the bar the roses that were from the dining room tables. She handed them to Seth. "I'd like some roses too," Nicole asked.

"These are for special people," June answered her.

"I'm special, aren't I?"

"Yes, you are," said Seth as he handed her a rose and gave one to Hope. He offered one to Yvette. She politely refused. "I don't remember anyone ever giving me a rose before," Hope said to Seth. "Thank you very much."

"Thank you too," added Nicole.

"You are most welcome. And thank you too, June."

"You're welcome," she said. "By the way, Ruben, there's one of the lights out in the office."

"Do you work there during the day?" Hope asked.

"Yes, I'm the Jack of all the trades," he said as he examined her face for approval or disapproval.

"And master of none," added Davy.

Nicole looked at Ruben then at Seth and asked "Do you believe in God?"

"I guess so. I'm a Catholic. Not a good one. But I am Catholic."

"And how about you?" she asked Grant.

"Do you want to know if I believe in an afterlife? The answer is no. What is most strange, since in my previous life I was a Hindu."

"Very funny," she said sarcastically. Then she turned to Yvette and asked, "Do you believe in God?"

"What's with the survey? You trying to determine if God exists based on the number of people who believe in Him?"

"It just that Ruben does not believe in God."

"And you're sending Hope home with that heathen?" Grant laughed.

"What I believe or don't believe is none of your damn business. You should decide what is right or wrong on your own. Not what they teach you in church. It is immoral to let others do your thinking for you. But thinking for yourself takes guts. Something that most people don't have. And that is why they have religions. And they are scared to be free thinkers.

They might have to question their own belief. And that might make them lose their security blanket."

"You questioning the morality of your champion?" Grant asked Nicole with a smile and a wink.

"You don't believe in Heaven or Hell," Nicole asked Ruben.

"Heaven, Hell and the Garden of Eden is all a creation of man."

"Not even Garden of Eden?" asked Hope.

"Some people feel that the Garden of Eden is more of a psychological thing than an actual place," Grant said. "We have a built in inferiority complex. It goes back to when we were infants. We were small and weak and our parents were big and strong. So, they must have come from a better place and time. And that is what I believe is the origin of the Garden of Eden, much like Heaven."

"You saying that Heaven is really Garden of Eden?" asked Hope. "And that is what we want is to return back to the Garden of Eden?"

"Pretty much, but we can never return."

"If it's all the same with you, I'm going to keep my security blanket for a while," said Seth.

"Tomorrow is Sunday, so I have to get up early to go to church," Ruben said mockingly.

"Hey, does anyone know who w-won the Sox and Cubs game?" Davy asked for the second time, with a smile.

"Don't be an ass," Yvette told him.

"You want him to give up his most dominant characteristic trait?" Grant joked.

"It's time to hit the road," Ruben said to Hope.

"I guess so," she replied.

As the two went beyond ear shot, Grant said, "If I wasn't so old, so ugly, was rich, and didn't have bad breathe and if I had an I.Q. above room temperature, I would hit on her myself."

"I know what you mean," Yvette said. "She can do much better then Ruben."

CHAPTER 3 ━━━━━━━━━━━━━━

Ruben held the door of his ten year old Ford Mustang as Hope slid into the passenger's seat. He tried to conceal his pride as he climbed in behind the wheel. Next to him, sitting in his car, was the most attractive lady that he had ever known. And now he was taking her home. She was like a goddess, someone that he felt was out of his reach, someone that would not give him a second thought. Now she was in his car and he was going to take her home. He looked at her in the soft light as he started the engine. He let the clutch out to quickly, making the car lurch foreword and die. It was something that had not happened since he first learned to drive a stick. The embarrassment give him a sinking feeling, as if it had brought him back down to reality. He was not someone in her league. As they drove along the city streets the street lights would cast it glow onto the goddess next him and then she faded back into the shadows until the next street light. He knew that it could be his only chance that he might ever would have with her. Not knowing what her reaction might be, he reached across and took her hand. To his delight she did not pull it away.

They were still holding hands when they pulled up in front of the apartment building. "That's the one," she said. The windows on the second floor apartment had a dark grayish shine that gave it a cold empty look. It was the place that she spent her lonely nights. At first it was not that bad, for she was excited with the possibilities that lay ahead of her; the possibilities that never came her way. So the nights turned into weeks, then into months. Sometimes there were nights that she felt so removed from family and friends, so isolated in the endless city, which she would lay in bed for hours with tears in her eyes. She would imagine what it would be like sleeping with a man. Ruben had caught her eye and he had become the primary figure of her fantasies. Now they were in front of her apartment.

It was the time for her to decide to fulfill her desire or spend another night alone in the empty apartment. He squeezed her and pulled her next to himself. She let him kiss her. It was the first time in a long time since she kissed anyone, and never like this. She was filled with excitement as their two bodies pressed up against each other. Of all of her twenty-one years her emotions had never been as strong as they were on that night, and with that man, of all men. No, her parents would never have approved of him. But then who would they approve of? Anyone?

"Are you going to invite me in?" Ruben asked with the look of a lost puppy.

"I don't know. The apartment is in just a mess. Maybe another time."

"When everything will be the perfect? Will that never be?"

"Maybe just for a minute. I have to get up in the morning," she said as he hopped out of the car to open her door. "I have to go to church," she said to herself.

The small apartment was only furnished with inexpensive furniture and second hand things. The bone white walls only had photos of her family and a calendar with a picture of a country church. "This is it. It isn't much," she said as they entered the apartment.

"You going to show me rest of you apartment?"

"This is it. That is the kitchen," she motioned to the other end of the room. "And this is the living room. And that's the bathroom."

"And this must be the bedroom," he said as walked toward a closed door.

"No!" she cried as she tried to cut him off. But it was too late. He pushed through the door to view her unmade bed. She felt a little embarrassed and somewhat defenseless. Again they started to kiss passionately. She did not notice that he slid off his shoes and his hand was under her blouse. Not until he unsnapped her brassiere was she aware of what he was trying to do. She pushed away from him, but she gave little resistance as he pulled her back. She squirmed as he slid his hand over her breast. They continued to kiss for a moment. Then he pulled her blouse over her head. She tried keep her breast covered, but he yanked the brassiere out of her hands and dropped it to the floor. "No," she said halfheartedly as he disrobed. She looked at his naked body and it made her feel less self-conscious. For some reason being intimate with this man seemed to be right. She did not fight him as he removed her shirt and panties. "I never," she said softly.

"You never what," he asked as he lay on top of her.

"Nothing."

CHAPTER 4 ━━━━━━━━━━━━━━━━━━━━

The old priest stood at the altar, on that foggy morning. He took a deep breath as he put his trumpet to his lips and blew. The first note hit the far end of the empty church and vibrated back. The music flew through the windows and onto the lawn and over the cemetery and then throughout the city. The city that is built by the lake. With its skyscrapers that cast their long shadows over the streets, avenues, boulevard and the alleyways, which went far beyond the city limits, into the many surrounding towns, making them extension of Chicago. To the north there are such towns of Evanston, Northbrook and Lake Forest. To the west lay Oak Park, Bensenville, Carol Stream and Naperville. To the south are towns with the names of Oak Lawn, Palos Hills, Blue Island and Whiting, Indiana. That is only a few of the towns and villages that is a part of the area that is known as Chicago. A city of immigrants, where its citizens eat things with the names of pierogi, burritos, egg foo yung, mezza, sushi, spanakopita, paella, hummus and dam alu, along with fried chicken and steak. They play football, basketball, baseball, sixteen inch softball and soccer, along with tennis and golf. There are the haves and the have nots. Some live in mansions and some crowded into old apartment buildings. But they all remember, or think that they remember, how things were like in the past, a time when things were better, real or imaginary. And at the same time they dream of the future. The lucky ones believe that their dreams will come true. The others live with less hope.

The old priest played a song, then another. Both were songs that foretell of the Day of Judgment, the day that they will have to answer for what they had done, the deeds that they did to others. And they will have to bear the consequences for their actions. When he finished, when he felt that he had expressed all that he was feeling, all that he was able to express with his musical instrument at that time, for he was approaching exhaustion. He had gone to his physical limits, he had no more to give. A nun clapped. "Very Divine, Father."

"Thank you for trying to humor this old man."

"No. Really. That was quite a good."

"Playing the trumpet is my only vice. It's is a reflection of my vanity."

"But, isn't music a gift from God?"

"That is what I keep telling myself."

As the priest was putting the trumpet back into its case he noticed a man carrying a bouquet of roses. "Who is that man?"

The nun went to the window and looked out. "I don't know. About every week he brings flowers to the cemetery. Sometimes he comes in, but not often."

"I know. Usually he sits in the back pew. He is a strange man, in the sense that he never takes communion."

"Maybe he is not of our faith."

"Or maybe he feels that he is not worthy to take communion with us."

"Not worthy? No Father, surely he knows that everyone is worthy in the eyes of the Church."

"Knowing and feeling is two different things. We all have our demons. Some are greater than others."

"And, Father, you think that his demons are that great?"

"I have no way of knowing, but he is always bringing flowers to place on a grave. Why? Is it because he loves them or is there more?"

"You must go and talk with him."

"But it's getting close to time for mass," the old priest said as the congregation began to fill-up the pews, and then he give the nun conceding smile.

In the cemetery Seth stood in front of the family plot. There were three graves with a space for another, his. He divided the roses into three equal parts and placed them on the graves. First on his wife, Grace, then on his son, Nelson, followed by his daughter, Crystal, who was buried next to the plot that was reserved for himself, as if he and his deceased wife would guard over their children throughout the remainder of time. He stood there a long time, mumbling some words and began to tremble as his legs gave away and he fell to his knees, as tears run down his face. At first he wiped away the tears, then he let them flow freely.

He felt a hand on his shoulder. He looked up. At first he could not make out who it was because of the sun. "Father Rafael," Seth said as he got up and wiped the tears from his face. "I'm sorry. You caught me at a bad time."

"Tears are a sign that we have a soul. We are the only thing in God's creation that sheds tears. We should be proud that God gave us that ability. It shows that you care. And it shows that you are a good and loving man," said the elder priest.

"No, Father. I pray to God that that was true, but it's not."

"My Son, would you explain why you feel that you aren't a good and loving man?"

Neither spoke, but stood there looking at each other. Then Seth said, "Because a good father should always protect his family. That's his responsibility. To protect them, not to kill them."

"You saying that you killed your family?" the old priest asked, half afraid of what the answer might be.

"Yes. I did. I killed my family."

"How? If you don't mind me asking."

"How? By my careless and reckless driving."

"Why were you driving that way?"

"That is a question that I ask myself over and over, every day of my life, and probably will until I die. The simple truth is that I was pissed off. Because I had to trade my baseball glove for a paint bush. My whole life I had but one dream. That was to pitch in the majors. As a kid, it was for the Sox. Then I was drafted by the Angels, then my dream was to wear their uniform. I was living the American dream. I had a good and loving wife and two wonderful children. And a dream of making it to be a major leaguer, my immortality. But, I guess that I wasn't good enough. I made it to triple A, and that was it? Then one day they told me that it was time, 'to move on', that I would never make it to the big league. So that was it. All of those years of hard work was for squat. I had a wife and two kids and the only thing that I could get was a job painting houses. One night, I think it was just one of those days. You know what I mean? Nothing seemed to be going right. And it was raining. And I was driving too damn fast. I lost control of the car and it slid under a truck. As a bad joke by God, I was the only survivor. My wife and my two kids were killed." He choked-up for a moment and he wiped away the tears before continuing on. "And I, the one who killed them, was still alive. I should had been the one who got killed, not my family. They were innocent. 'They didn't do anything to deserve their fate'. Those were the exact words the judge used. 'They didn't do anything to deserve their fate.' And I agreed with him. He said that my knowledge of what I had done would be a burden that I would have to carry for the rest of my life."

"That is a heavy burden for one man to carry. You must ask for forgiveness. And let God remove your burden, and return to His grace."

"Forgiveness? Forgiveness? Just who in Hell do I ask? My wife, Grace? My son, Nelson? Or would you have me to ask my little daughter, Crystal? I would love to, but they can't forgive me. They are dead!"

"You can ask God."

"I didn't kill God. I killed them."

"No, you didn't kill God. But you did kill his children. You must ask His forgiveness. I'm sure that He will grant it to you. And your family will do the same. Let God lift this burden from your shoulders. Let us pray."

"Pray to God? I'm sorry. But He won't answer my prayers. It's as if I'm dead to Him. I would sell my soul to have them back. If I had one wish it is that I would be like Orpheus. And I would ascend into the land of the dead and retrieve them."

"Be careful what you wish for. If you ascend into Hell, you might not ever get out." the Priest said.

"Would it matter?"

"Have you lost your faith?"

"No. No. I realize that God is my creator. And I am subject to His laws. I try to live life the best that I can. But still I feel that God has banned me."

"The question is not that God has banned you, but have you banned Him. He is still there. He is still your father. Like the Prodigal Son, you must return to the church. Not for His sake, but for yours. You must let Him be part of your life. Let Him guide you. Without Him you are as a ship without a rudder."

CHAPTER 5 ──────────────

Removed from the others department store employees, Hope and Nicole sat at a table in the employee's lounge, with their fast food. "Did the Nazi yell at you, for being late?" Nicole asked.

"Of course. He always needs someone to yell at. It made that little creep feel important. So, that's my good deed for today, letting him feel important."

"Talking about good deeds, tell me, how did it go Saturday night?"

"I should be mad at you. Matter-of-fact, I am. Leaving me at The Garden like that."

"Yeah, like you didn't want Ruben to take you home," Nicole said, "So, did you?"

"Did I do what?" Hope replied.

"Oh, you poor little innocent thing. You don't have any idea what I am talking about. Do you? Did you two do the big nasty?"

"Well, we did sleep together. But we didn't have sex."

Nicole broke out in laughter. A moment later Hope joined her. Most of their fellow employees turned towards the laughter. Hope leaned, towards Nicole, preventing the others from hearing and whispered, "I won't be able to drink virgin pina colada anymore."

"Were you a virgin?"

Hope smiled with a look of embarrassment.

"Oh, my God, girl, you were a virgin, weren't you? Twenty-one years old and you never had did it before. That's hard to believe."

"Well, how old were you the first time?"

"I sure in Hell wasn't twenty-one, that's for damn sure." Nicole looked at her friend and asked, "Is he your boyfriend or what? Was it a one night stand or you an item?"

"I don't know. I hope so. I never had a true boyfriend before. Oh, there're lots of boys I dated. But none of them was serious."

"So, is this serious?"

"I don't know. I hope so. I do like him a lot."

"What kind of protection are you using?"

"None."

"None! Are you crazy? Do you want to get knocked-up by a guy that you hardly know?"

"I know, I know. But I was always told that only bad girls needed birth control."

"Well, you're not a good little girl any more. You better get something soon. You should know that. You was a nurse. Wasn't you?"

"Only for a short time."

"So, in that nursing school they didn't teach you how babies are made?"

"I know, I know. I'll go on the pill or something."

"What happened? If you don't mind me asking?"

"What do you mean? 'What happened?'"

"You know, why aren't you a nurse anymore?"

"That's a good question, why I'm not a nurse anymore? I'll tell you. After graduation they assigned me to the terminal children's ward. That was Hell. It did not matter what you did, they all were going to die. Every last one of them. Nothing you could do about it. They were all going to die. Every morning, when my shift was over, I would go to bed and stay there until it was time to go back to the hospital. You can't imagine how depressing that was. Sometimes I would cry myself to sleep. I always had this dream of helping people. But when the time came I wasn't able to do it. Regardless of all the years of training and bragging to everyone that I was going to be a nurse in the end I couldn't. No I wasn't going to become another Nightingale. I thought that I was going to save the world. Yes, that was what I was going to do, save the world. But they assigned me to the terminal children's ward. How could anything be worse? Spending all night with dying children. Nothing you could do, they were going to die. Then, one day the burn unit brought in a little boy, an innocent little boy. They said that he was beyond hope. And we were supposed to give him morphine and watch him die. I couldn't bring myself to go back to work. And that is why I'm not a nurse."

"I'm sorry," Nicole said, not knowing what to tell her friend. "I don't know, being a nurse still must still be better than working here for minimum wage."

"Say, what did Grant mean by Ruben is your champion?" Hope asked to change the subject.

Nicole smiled. "I never had a guy defend me before. Specially a white man. Boy, I thought he was going to kill that bastard. He threw him up against the wall. I tell you girl, that poor bastard turn white as a sheet. Ruben is no one to mess with."

"What happened?"

"What happened? Well I spilled beer on this guy. He jumped up yelled at me, calling me the "N" word. Then he took off, without paying his tab. Well, Ruben caught him by the door. Let's say he paid his bill plus a good tip. I tell you, girl, after that no one ever messed with him. No, he isn't someone you want to get mad at you."

CHAPTER 6 ━━━━━━━━━━━━━━━━━

The Garden customers were made up of the people who occupied the city. Many of them were immigrants. Unlike where Hope was from in Wisconsin, where the population was families that were farmers since before the Civil War. But the patrons of the restaurant, for the most part were a mixture of the native Chicago ones and the ones that came from somewhere else- from another part of the country or from another country all together. Some of them had pronounced accents. If they had a strong European accent when Hope heard them she would assume that they were from Poland, and not from one of the other many countries which they had migrated from. Grant had told her that the drinks that the people ordered have lots of bearing on what ethnic group that they belong to. Also what social class they were a part of, or which one they would like to belong to.

Five jubilant, well dressed young patrons that appeared to be professionals, who were out for a good time came in. They were led by the maître to a six top in Hope's station. "My name is Hope," she informed them as she passed around the menus and the wine list. "I will be your server tonight."

"And I am Al," one of the men said in a mocking manner. "This lovely lady is my wife, Nance. Pay attention, because you will be tested on this later."

"Don't be an ass," his wife admonished him.

"No, this is important," he joked. "She told us what her name was, so we should tell her ours. It is common courtesy. We have to introduce ourselves. This is Barb. Her husband, Bob, is using the little boy's room. And this is Mary. She is the wife of this big guy, Danny, Danny McGee." He noticed that Hope did not have any reaction to the name of Danny McGee. "Are you a football fan?"

"The Pack." Soon as the words were out of her mouth she knew that she might have alienated her customers. She quickly added, "I also like the Bears."

"So, what are you? A cheese head?"

"Give the poor girl a break," his wife said, trying to stop the harassment of Hope.

"Would you like something from the bar?"

"We probably will have wine," Mary said as she looked over the wine list. "Bob drinks wine, doesn't he?"

"Yea, he is an old wino from way back," Al joked.

"Let's hold off on the wine until we decide on what we are having."

"How about appetizers?"

"What do you recommend?" Nance asked. She appeared to be the one in charge.

Hope attempted to say, 'Everything is good', but that was no longer in her lexicon. "If you like seafood, both the shrimp cocktail and the mussels in a marinara sauce are very good. The shrimp cocktail is made with fresh shrimp."

"Hey, guess who is the bartender?" the third man in the party said as he approached the table. "Danny's old friend, Ruben Garcia." They all laughed except one- the big athletic looking man. Hope wondered what was the inside joke.

"He just got lucky, that's all," Danny defended himself. "He broadsided me when I wasn't looking. The damn coward. In a fair fight I would have beat him to a pulp."

The man, who evidently was Bob, laughed, "Nothing like rewriting history, is there. Don't forget that we were there. And I don't remember it that way. That little guy kicked your ass."

"You want to step outside and see who is the bad ass?"

"You guys are acting like you're still in high school," Barb admonished them.

"He just got lucky, that's all. He caught me on a bad day. I would kick his ass nine times out of ten. He just got lucky."

"Sure," Bob replied to Danny in a sarcastic manner.

"Why did they get into a fight?" Hope asked, knowing that she was out of place, intruding in on customer's conversation.

Al, the man who was not part of the argument told her, "Because Danny was making fun of Ruben's father."

"Yea," Bob added, "We were going to have career day and Danny told Ruben that his dad should tell the class what it's like to be a jail bird."

"They say that it's not how big the dog is in the fight, but how big is the fight in the dog," Al said. "And Ruben is a pit bull. He's going to kick your ass or you're literally going to have to kill him first. He's one of those guys that goes crazy in a fight. You know what I mean? He just goes wild. You can see it in his eyes. With him it's kill or be killed."

After the kitchen was closed and the last of the diners had either left or moved into the lounge, the waitresses added-up their receipts-doing the math to determine how much they made in tips, and how much to give the busboys. Still in her waitress uniform Hope went and sat at the bar-knowing that it was against rules. But she knew that no one was there who would object. Ruben offered her a drink and she requested a dream sickle. That night he was working with Davy. Nursing her orange cream drunk and waiting for Ruben to get off, she looked at the rows of bottles of liquor on the shelves, which were lined-up in front of a red velvet background which was bordered with a frame of a bygone pictures or a mirror. The bottles of the spirits were all different shapes and sizes. One was a tall thin bottle that was filled with a yellow liqueur, the one beside it was shaped to look like a monk. There was one that was in a tall square green bottle. Most were round but some were square. They were in opaque or clear bottles that showed the fermented liquor that they incased. Some people preferred to call them spirits because they can transfer a person into a different being, one that is less restrained.

She observed the contrast between the two bartenders. Ruben, the more muscular one had sideburns and long hair that was pulled back into a cue, was polite but more reserved, more professional, but some could find him to be a little intimidating. As for Davy, with his burgundy colored hair and his child like face which was covered with flecks, was Ruben's counterpoint. Grant once told her that Davy might appear to be someone to whom everything seemed to be a joke, because he was always smiling and laughing and exercising his quick wit. The reason was because of his speech impediment. He felt a strong need to prove his intelligence by showing off his ability to come up with a joke at the drop-of-the-hat.

When Yvette asked him if the martini was a dirty martini his replied was, "It's so so dirty that I'm a shamed of myself." Or he might say that the one with the ice was the lumpy one. Or as he was shaking bitters into an old fashioned he could tell the customer that they used to have the bitters in pill form but it was too hard for the people to swallow. On occasion he will push the envelope too far, but those were rare. He had the ability to size-up someone at first glance, by the way they wore their hair or how and what kind of clothes they were wearing. He told her that it wasn't hard to tell if someone was trying to give a false impression.

"How?" She asked partly out of want to know and partly to see if he really could size-up someone that quick.

"I once had th-these two ladies come in here. Th-they told me that th-they were beauticians. And I told th-them that one of them did their customer hair the way that she thought was best and the other one did it th-the way that the customer w-wanted it done. One of th-then told me that I had it ba-backwards. About a week later th-they came back and told me that I was right. How? Easy, the one th-that was dressed immaculately, with every hair in place I knew that she w-was a per-perfectionist, so she could do her customers hair the way she thought it should be done. Her friend was the opposite, she dressed in loose fit-fitting clothes and her hair lo-look like she was caught in a w-wind storm. She w-was secure in herself, she was the t-type of a person that knew t-which her work did not reflect on her as much as on her customer. If a guy wanted an o-one night stand, something th-that I would n-never do, he would hit on the o-one that was more care free."

"I'll keep that in mind," Hope laughed. "So if you can tell what someone likes by just looking at them then tell me what I am like."

Davy slid his hand into his shirt and started moving his fingers to mimicking his heart pounding. "You are like," he was trying to come up with a good line, "Mary Poppins, you are per-perfect in nearly every way."

"Perfect in every way?"

"Well, your taste in clothes might be p-prove on."

"You don't like my uniform? I wore just to match yours."

Ruben walked to the other end of the bar to see what they were laughing about just as he heard Hope saying, "So, am I the type of a girl that you think would be a one night stand?" Soon as the words came out of her mouth she saw the disapproving look from Ruben.

CHAPTER 7 ━━━━━━━━━━━━━━━

Terkel's Diner was not a true diner. It was one of many grills, an Italian beef stands, which are found throughout the Chicago area. Their specialty is Italian beef sandwiches, which is a sandwich that is made of thinly sliced roast beef that is marinated in Italian seasonings and served on a slice of French bread- usually served with hot peppers or with sweet peppers. The sweet peppers are bell peppers that have been roasted with olive oil and Italian seasoning or cooked in the marinate. Also they serve gyros, hamburgers and hot dogs which some of the locals call Red Hots. The customers of these small restaurants were a reflection of the city. All races and nationalities and all class levels patronize these restaurants, but the primary customers are the working class. It has been said if you want to see the real people of Chicago you should to go to an Italian beef stand.

After a movie, Hope and Ruben stop in at the grill. They study the menu that was hanging over the grill as the two cooks debated if American or Swiss cheese belong on a patty melt. Ruben interrupted them by saying, "I tell you what. You give us one of each for free and we will tell you which one is the best." They look at him with disgust. "Hey, she's a dairy farmer from Wisconsin and I, obviously, have good taste," he said smiling with pride as he put his arm around Hope. "So, what do you say?"

"You want a patty melt?" asked one of the cooks displaying a lack of humor.

"No. I'll have the Italian beef dinner." Glancing at Hope he commented, "It's good here."

"What's an Italian beef?" Hope asked.

"It's the Chicago sandwich. Try it."

"But I don't know....I'll try it."

After being served they sat at one of the few tables and Hope unwrapped her sandwich. "This is all wet and sloppy."

"Hey, a good Italian beef is like sex, it should be wet and sloppy."

Being somewhat embarrassed, she still found herself laughing. "Were you surprised that it was my first time?" she whispered.

"Yea, I'm. Most people have eaten an Italian beef before."

"No, you know what I mean."

"Yea. I think so. There're not that many twenty-one year old virgins running around here. I know because I've been looking. I will walk up to a lady and ask 'Are you a virgin?' And they will slap my face. So, I assume that they aren't."

"How old were you the first time?"

"Well, it was the other night with you."

Hope slapped Ruben on the shoulder. "Quit being funny and tell me."

"My first time?" he said with a smile as he stared into space. "Bonnie, Bonnie McKay. That was her name, Bonnie McKay. The lovely Bonnie McKay. I was still fourteen, the summer that I turned fifteen. She was a neighbor. She was a little older than me. Two or three years older. My Dad was on trial. And, I guess, my Mom never wanted me to be alone. So, Bonnie was sent over to keep me company. And that is what she did. Oh, yeah, that was what she did. She kept me company alright. She tickled me. She wouldn't stop, so I tickled her back. I hit her tits, and she acted like she never noticed So, I grabbed them. And I will tell you that she had some good ones alright. She went, 'Oh,' and acted like she was surprised. Then she grabbed my crotch. And that was it. She said that if we was going to wrestle we should go to my room and take off our clothes so we wouldn't ruin them. That was what she said. 'So we wouldn't ruin our clothes.' She was right, we didn't ruin our clothes."

"What ever happened to her?"

"Bonnie? Heaven knows. After Dad was convicted, we had to sell the house in Oak Lawn and move into the city. Hard to tell what ever happened to her. She might have become a hooker or a preacher's wife with a house full of kids. You never can tell how someone is going turn out."

"You said that your father was convicted. What was he convicted of?"

"Manslaughter."

"Manslaughter?"

"Yeah. Manslaughter. He killed a man in a bar room fight. His misfortune was that the man was a cop. And the judge threw the book at him. He got the maximum, just because the man was a cop."

Hope squeezed Ruben's hand. She was tempted to tell him that she that was sorry, but she knew that it would sound patronizing. "The other night there were these diners said that you got in a fight with one of them, when you were in high school."

"You must be talking about Danny McGee. He was there the other night, long with some others buddies. Did they tell you that I kicked his ass?"

"More or less."

"He had it coming to him. I took him down a notch or two. That bastard had it coming to him. But I was the one that got expelled."

"Not him? Only you?"

"Yeah, that's the way it goes. They said that because I had been in other fights, but, shit, he had too. He was nothing but a God damn bully. By beating the hell out of him I was doing a public service. The truth of the matter was that he was the big football star and his old man had political connections, and I was nothing. That's the way it goes. The haves and the have nots. If they want to screw you there's nothing you can do about it. That's the way it is"

"You sound like you accepted the roll of the underdog."

"Do you think that I'm a loser?"

"No, that's not what I mean, not at all."

"Then what do you mean?"

"Sure, you were dealt a bad hand, but that doesn't mean anything. Only that you have to try harder, that's all."

"Yeah, I know. Someday I will make it, someday I'm going to be successful. I don't know how, but I will. I will have that big house in the burbs and a big car to go along with it. You wait and see."

"I'm sure you will."

"You know Gus?"

"Froggy?"

"Yes, Froggy. You do know he don't like that name. Anyway, he owned a place like this, before he got The Garden. He said that if you work for yourself then no one can fire you."

"So, was he fired once?"

"Yeah, when he was young he jumped ship. All that he could speak was Greek. He got a job in one of those Greek restaurants on Halsted. The way they always did it is that they would get someone fresh right off of the boat and put them in the kitchen, washing the dishes. Then they would put then on the line or if they learned to speak good enough English they would make them a busboys, and then into waiters. Well, one day when Gus was a busboy one of the customers asked for more water in the finger bowl. He told her that she wasn't suppose to take a bath in it. And the bitch got him fired. I guess that she must not have had a sense of humor. So he got a job in an Italian beef stand. From there he went on to The Garden. Sometimes he talks like he expects me to take it over. I think that he is crazy."

"Why do you say that," Hope asked. "They don't have any kids, do they?"

"No, but I don't know. I don't know anything about running a restaurant. But sometime I do think about it. Maybe that's the way to go." Ruben said more to himself then to Hope.

"How come the name is Anna's Garden, not The Garden?"

"I guess that was the name of the daughter of the original owners. It was a restaurant with a garden. They must had been some kind of romantics, growing their own food for the restaurant."

"What happened to the garden?" She asked.

"Well, over time they added the banquet room and enlarged the parking lot."

"Too bad, I think that it would be nice if it had stayed the same."

"I afraid that nothing ever stays the same," commented Ruben.

Later that night Ruben and Hope drove northeast on the Stevenson Expressway to Lake Shore Drive. They exited by McCormick Place, a large complex which it held trade shows and conventions. "That's where they have the Auto Shows," Ruben commented.

"I know. Isn't that where they also have political conventions?"

"Yeah, that's what gives Chicago its' nickname The Windy City. All those long winded politicians."

Going north to their right, laying between them and Lake Michigan, was Soldier Field, a large stadium with Greek style columns. "That's where the Bears play. They are our city champions. Although almost none of them are from this area, we still go into a state of depression when they lose. But we are happy when they win. Especially if they beat that evil team from the north," Ruben laughed.

"I didn't know that the Bears ever beat the Pack," Hope replied.

They turned right and went between Soldier Field and another large structure with Greek style columns. "That's the Field Museum," he said.

"I know. That's where they have all of the dinosaurs and all of the stuffed animals."

"Weren't those dinosaurs hanging out with Adam and Eve in the Garden of Eden?"

"Very funny," she said sarcastically, looking away from him, hiding her smiling face.

"Yeah, I think so. It is in the Bible, isn't it?" laughing at his own joke, he turned left and when they got to the Shedd Aquarium he turned right onto a peninsula that has the name of Northerly Island, previously the home of the small airport of Meigs Field The boulevard on which they drove was about a half of mile long. In its center were three monuments. The first one was of Thaddseus Kosciuszko, the famous Polish General who fought in the American Revolutionary War. The second one half way down the boulevard was a monument to the Czech painter Karel Havlicek. At the end was the Polish Astronomer Nicolaus Coperincus, which stood in front of the Adler Planetarium. To the east, over Lake Michigan, the sky revealed the stars which the planetarium replicated. They drove about halfway back on the tree lined boulevard before they parked the car. The two young lovers got out and walked across the grass to the concrete steps that led to the water. The surf was gently lapping against the embankment.

"It's nice here, isn't it?" She said, more as a statement then a question.

"Is this the first time you've been here?"

"At night? Yes."

"Sometimes I like to come here, by myself, when no one is around, that I know anyway, to get away from it all, you know what I mean? My little retreat." The skyscrapers looked like a large cluster of giant boxes that were filled with diamonds and were studded with rubies and spangled with sapphires.

"It's beautiful, isn't it?" she proclaimed.

"That it is," he replied. "From a distance, everything looks better, especially at night."

"Sometimes I think that you are a little on the negative side."

"What? Me?"

"Yes, you."

"I will tell you what happened once. This is a true story. I saw this rainbow, and I looked to see where it ended, where the pot of gold is. Guess where it ended?" She shrugged her shoulders. "Right there. Right on the top of those skyscrapers. So, that is where the money is, the real money. Sorry, it's not at The Garden or at that department store where you work. It's over there, in those skyscrapers. I'm afraid that for now it's out of my reach. You might say that I am being negative, but no, I'm afraid that I'm just being a realist."

"So, you think to be successful you have to be a big time executive?"

"No. But those and the doctors and the other professionals are the ones that live in those big houses in the burbs. Not the ones that punch the clock. You said that I think that the deck is stacked against me. Well, it is. But it doesn't mean that I'm going to throw in the towel; that's for damn sure. I'm working on my G.E.D. When I get it I'm going on to college. I don't know which college or what I'm going to major in, but I do knew it will be something that I can make lots of money at. Yes, someday I'm going to make it, I'm going to make it big. You just wait and see."

CHAPTER 8 ━━━━━━━━━━━━━━━

As Father Rafael started the Sunday morning sermon, Seth slipped into the church. He always felt out of place here, and that is why he always sat on the last pew on the rare occasion when he did go inside of the church. Some of the congregation greeted him with a smile. It was the first time that he had been in the church since he had the conversation with the priest. On that day as he was placing the flowers on the graves of his family then he heard the choir singing. Their voices beckoned to him. For some reason, he answered their call. He did not know why, but there he was, an outsider sitting among their midst.

"The sermon today is from the writings of Saint Paul to the Romans. At that time the Roman were persecuting the Christians for their faith. And as a folly of human nature, these Christians wanted revenge. If someone hurt us, especially if we feel that it is unjust, we want to hurt them back. But Saint Paul said no. He wrote, 'Revenge is mine, said the Lord.' That is something that is very hard for us to grasp. Oh, we say that we understand the concept that Jesus was saying when He told us to turn to the other cheek. And we all say that we are good Christians, and we follow the teachings of the Church. But, do we? Or do we not? In our hearts don't we all want revenge? Don't we want that person to hurt the same way that he made us hurt? We demonize our enemies. We dehumanize them. We make them unworthy of our mercy. We want them to suffer the same way we and our love ones suffered. Do we not? But Saint Paul said no. Not for our enemies benefit, but for our own selves. God is a merciful God. He doesn't want to see anyone to be filled with hatefulness. Because hate is a cancerous thing. It will destroy us. It will make us lose our perspective on what is right." Father Rafael looked towards Seth as he continued. "Sometimes the person that we are the angriest with is ourselves. Our self-hatred can stifle us, in many ways. And that is not the will of God. If it's not good for us to hate others and then it's not good for us to hate ourselves. Especially it is not good for the ones that we love and those that love us."

After the service, when Father Rafael was shaking the hands of the departing congregation, he told Seth that he wanted to talk with him. After the last ones were leaving he said, "Let's go back inside. These old legs can only stand for a limited time. And I'm afraid that my legs have reached their limits." Father Rafael smiled as he guided Seth back to the pew which he came from. "I'm glad that you found it in your heart to join us today. Hopefully you will become a regular."

"Maybe. But I'm not going to promise anything."

"Very well. But that's not the reason that I asked you to stay behind. The other day, when we talked, I got the impression that you needed to unburden yourself. Today's sermon was on hatred. I spoke of how hatred can destroy people. And I feel that it might be of a special meaning for you."

"You think that I am self-destructive?"

"Destructive? That might be little a strong, but I do think that you are denying yourself of happiness. I think that it might be time for you to move on with your life."

"And forget about what I did? I wish that it was that easy."

"Guilt can be a harmful thing."

Seth smiled as he said, "I thought that guilt is the number one tool of the Church."

The elder priest returned the smile. "Our propose is to guide our parishioners in the ways of our Lord, through the teaching of the Church. Everyone needs guidance. And that is our mission. Not guilt. Although, I must admit, sometimes we do use it, maybe a little too freely, but you can't condemn us for that?"

Seth smiled.

"Because if you do, then you will have to condemn yourself. Am I not right?"

After a long pause Seth said, "Are you telling me to be unfaithful to my wife?"

"I'm telling you to be faithful to yourself. I did not know your wife. But I assume that she was a loving woman and a good wife and mother. Am I not right?"

"Yes. You're right. She was."

"If the table was turned, wouldn't you want her to find happiness?"

"But she didn't kill her husband."

"No. This is true. But on the other hand, there is nothing that you can do to bring her back. Is there? It is time for you to move on. Life is short, too short to be consumed by regrets. That is something that I do know about."

CHAPTER 9 ━━━━━━━━━━━━━━━

"Russ, is that your boy?" a man in an orange jump suit said to a man with a crew cut.

"Yea, that's my son, Ruben."

"Well. He sure as hell looks like you, except for the hair. My son looks like the mailman," the man said as he laughed at his own joke.

Russ walked to the window that divided the two rooms. He sat down in a booth and picked-up the phone and said, "Hi, Son. It's good to see you."

"It's good to see you too, Dad," he replied.

"Where is your mother? Is she here?"

"She had to work, she's coming Sunday."

"Well, if she has to work, she has to work," he said with disappointment in his voice. "Thank you for the card and the money. I always can use the money, so, tell me what have you been up to, now days?"

"The same old, the same old. Still working at The Garden. Still sharing an apartment with Mom. I guess that's about it."

"Yea, I know what it is like, having to share living space with others." He smiled then asked, "Tell me, is there someone special in your life?"

"I don't know what you mean."

"Yes, you do. Do you have a girl friend?"

"I have lots of friends that are girls."

"You know what I mean. Do you have that one, that special one?"

"Are you getting at that age that you are thinking about if you're going to have grandkids or not?"

"Not really, but you do know that after all this is a penitentiary? And as you probably know that it gets its name from the word penance. So, we are supposed to spend our time here repenting for the evil that we have done. I don't know about repentance, but we do have a hell of a lot of time to think. And to be truthful with you, yeah, I do think about if things are going alright with you. After all, you are my son. "

"Yea, things are going okay," Ruben smiled. "There is one girl that is a little special."

"So, does she have a name?"

"Hope."

"Hope? That a good old fashioned name."

"She's an old fashioned girl."

"So, tell me about this old fashioned girl of yours."

"There's not much to tell. She is a farm girl from Wisconsin. She's very pretty. No, she's beautiful. Some think that she is much too pretty for me."

"Don't cut yourself short. You're a good looking guy. But I do know how you feel. People said that your mother married beneath herself. It turns out that they were right, didn't it? I told her that she should divorce me after they threw me in here. But she won't. It's probably a good thing for me, but not for her. I don't know what I'll do if she wasn't out there for me. Go mad? Probably. I don't know."

"Mom does say that she don't have many friends."

"Nobody wants to be a friend with someone whose husband is a jail bird. That's for sure. They are afraid that it might rub-off. That's why I say that she would be better off if she divorced me. But what is good for one is not necessarily good for the other."

"Why are you here?"

"Hell! You know why I'm here. I killed a man in a fight. That is it. Simple as that. No more."

"I know that. What I don't know is why you got into a fight with a cop."

"Well, someday I just might tell you."

"How about today?"

Russ removed his glasses and rubbed his face. "Well, I guess you're right. The simple truth is, I was defending you mother's honor."

"Mom's honor?"

"Yeah, your mom's honor. Simple as that, Wallace was a bastard. That was why the son of bitch became a cop, so he could bully people around. He was a damn coward. That is what he was, a God damn coward. And he liked to take advantage of young ladies and then he would go around and brag about it. Well, your mother was one of them. You wanted to know, didn't you? Well. I'm telling you. That God damn scumbag took advantage of your mother. That's right. It happened before we started going together. But it didn't make him stop bragging about it.

"That night he was with some other cops. He must've figured that they would help him out, if he needed it. Well, a man only can take so damn much. Like I always told you, a real man only fights with his fists. So, I hit the bastard. I hit him hard. Hard as I could. He hit the floor like a pound of wet liver. Blood was all over his face. He got up and he charged me. He tried to tackle me. But I sidestepped him and ran his head into the bar. Breaking his nick.

"At that moment, not only did his life end, but so did mine. I was thirty-six years three months and seventeen days old. You mother was thirty-eight years eight months twenty days. You were fourteen years two months and six days."

Chapter 10

Hope unlocked Ruben's apartment door and looked in for the first time. She felt strange as if she was intruding in a place that she did not belong. Even though Ruben gave her the key and told her to meet him there, she still felt that she was trespassing. Every home has a smell. This one had the odor of beer and cigarettes with an underlying smell of mildew. The furniture was old and out dated. It was a place to stay if you had no other place to go. She set down her over-night bag and removed her jacket. Surveying the apartment, she saw over flowing ashtrays and a sink that was piled up with dirty dishes. She felt it was her duty to clean the apartment. First she emptied the ashtrays and then she started washing the dishes. She never heard the key go into the door, nor when it opened. Sensing that she was not alone, Hope turned to find a middle-aged woman staring back at her. The woman had dyed orangey-red hair in a beehive and with heavy make-up on. "Who in the hell are you? And what are you doing here?" she said coldly.

"I'm Hope," she replied, holding out her hand. But the woman did not reciprocate.

"So, what are you? A house cleaner or one of Ruben's whores?"

The harsh words stopped Hope cold. "I'm a friend of Ruben's. You must be his mother?"

"How did you get in?"

"He gave me a key. He told me to meet me here."

"Oh, he did, did he?" the woman said, looking at the overnight bag, then she gave her a disapproving look before she hurried off to a bedroom.

Hope stood there with her mouth open. She had never before faced any one that was that rude. She was caught completely off guard. This was Lucy? The mother of Ruben, the man she had been falling in love with.

Maybe that was not Ruben's mother? And she was in the wrong apartment? She knew that she was at the right place. The key fit the door and a picture on an end table was that of Ruben. She was in the right place and that was his mother. She questioned if she should resume washing the dishes or not. It might offend Ruben's mother. And watching television was definitely out of the question. So, Hope quietly sat on the couch and waited for him.

It seemed to be an eternity, sitting uncomfortably on the old couch before she heard a knock on the door. She jumped up and greeted Ruben with a kiss. "It's good to see you, Honey" she said as she hugged him.

"Been waiting long?"

"Not long," she intentionally under estimated the time that she had been waiting.

"Is Mom here?" he asked as she motioned toward the closed door. "Mom!"

The door opened slowly and Lucy came out. "I didn't hear you come in." She gave Hope an insincere smile.

"We are off to Hope's farm, in the land of the Cheese Heads."

"And they will call you a Fib," Hope said with a nervous laugh.

"Are we….Are you going to eat something first?" Lucy asked.

"We will grab a bite on the road," Ruben replied.

"What will I eat? I guess that I might find something to eat. I don't know what."

"There're T. V. dinners in the fridge."

"A T.V. dinner?" she said with a disgusting look on her face.

"It won't kill you," he said as he fetched a bag from his room. "It's time to hit the road

The middle aged lady who was wearing a floral apron, paused from setting the table to look out the window and noticed an old car that was driving up the lane. "They are here," she said as she turned to her daughter. "My lands, Desiree, you are still in your pajamas"

She laughed at her mother. "You just now noticed how I'm dressed. I always clean house in my P. J's." She was as beautiful as her sister, but not as innocent looking as Hope was. Her blonde hair had a large wave in the front and short in the back. Her trade mark was long dangling earrings.

"Well, get yourself upstairs and put on something decent," she said as she looked at herself in the mirror. She quickly ran a comb though her shoulder-length graying hair. Then she hurriedly put on lipstick.

The car was greeted by an aggressive border collie. Hope hopped out of the car and yelled at the dog, "Sport!" Not knowing what to do, the dog ran back and forth, between Hope and the man who was still sitting in the car. She grabbed the dog and he started to lick her face. "You are a good dog, aren't you? Yes, you are. You're a good dog."

"Well, look who's here," said a boy in his early teens that came from the direction of the cornfield. "It's my little sister." The boy hurried to stand next to Hope, letting her know that he was now taller than she was. She surprised him with a hug. For a moment he was embarrassed, then he hugged her back.

"I missed you, Andy."

"Well, I guess that I missed you too."

"You made it just in time for supper," Hope's mother said as she hurried to embrace her daughter. Her eyes widened for a moment when she saw the long-haired tattooed man in a Jack Daniel's tee shirt.

"Mom, this is Ruben," Hope said with pride.

"Welcome to our home."

"Thank you Mrs. Adamsen,"

"Oh, call me Evelyn."

"Well, Evelyn, I see where Hope gets her good looks from."

"I see that we have a real sweet talker here."

Ruben smiled, not knowing if she was being complementary or she was mocking him. Behind her, he saw two men walking towards them, talking to each other. Behind them were the dairy barn and silos, beyond that lay the green fields of the gently rolling hills of Wisconsin. It was obvious that the two men were Hope's father and brother. The elder one, had the appearance of a man who had spent his life working outdoors in the weather, and the younger one was walking in his father's footsteps.

Hope ran and threw her arms around her father.

"How's my little Bunny?"

"Did you miss me, Daddy?"

"Yes, I sure did. Every time I had any heavy lifting to do, or a real dirty job, I thought of you."

"Oh, Daddy," she said, trying to act like she did not enjoy being teased. "I want you to meet Ruben."

"Glad to meet you, Sir."

"The pleasure is mine. But you don't have to call me Sir. Gene will do," said the big man with a graying beard with a firm hand shake.

"I'm Chuck." the younger man said. He was the spitting image of his father, without the beard. "I assume that this is not your first time in Wisconsin?" Gene asked.

"Matter fact, this is the first time. I have never been behind the cheese curtain before. Actually, this is the first time that I've been on a farm."

"Hopefully, it won't be your last," Gene said.

"Well, is someone going to introduce us," Desiree said with a sensuous smile as she walked down the porch step, bare footed.

At supper Ruben felt as if he was in a Norman Rockwell painting. The picture of the Adamsen family setting around the dining room table. In the center of the table was a stuffed turkey, surrounding it was all of the side dishes: mashed potatoes and gravy, corn-on-the-cob, green beans, cranberry sauce and homemade biscuits. The aroma from the food filled the room. It was a place in which he felt that he did not belong. But, never the less, that was where he found himself. He was given a place of honor. At the end of the table, not at the head of the table, where Hope's father sat, but at the other end. It seemed to him that there was an order to the seating arrangement. Gene was seated at the head of the table, he was flanked with his wife, Evelyn, and on the other side was Chuck then Desiree, Andy, between his mother and Hope.

All of the family stood up. Hope took his hand. Then, to his surprise, Desiree grasped his other hand. Then he noticed that they all bowed their heads. In a sober voice, Gene prayed, "Let us gave thanks to you, the Creator of the universe, for all the good that you have bestowed upon us. We know your will, for you speak to us through your words from the Bible. You gave us your laws and your will, with the knowledge that you are a just and loving God. And we want to give special thanks today, for having us being blessed with Hope, who returned home, and with her friend, Ruben. May he feel welcome in our house, for he truly is. In Jesus Christ name, our Lord and Savior, we pray. Amen."

The other members of the family follow with an, "Amen." Then they started passing the platters of food around the table. Each taking what was thcir share, then giving the platter to the one sitting next to them. Slowly Ruben began to feel his self-consciousness slipping away and he became more relaxed. "Do you always eat like this?"

"No," Andy replied quickly. "Usually we don't use silverware. We just take a hand full of food and jam it in our faces."

"Andy!" Evelyn said firmly. Then in a softer voice she asked Ruben, "What do you mean by that?"

"I don't know. It's as if this is like a holiday or something. Everyone sitting around the table at the same time, eating a big meal. You know what I mean?"

"Your family doesn't gather around the table for dinner?" asked Gene.

"Not for a long time." The room became silent. He added, "This is real nice. It's like Thanksgiving. I don't know why you ever left home," he teased Hope.

"That is the nicest thing to say," replied Evelyn.

"What line of work are you in?" asked Gene.

Ruben glanced at Hope, than he answered, "Maintenance."

"Did you go to college?" asked Andy.

"No. You can say that I had on the job training." He did not want to lie to then. But, at the same time he never wanted to reveal that he was a bartender nor that he had been expelled from high school for fighting either.

"He's our guest. So, quit asking him all those questions," Evelyn demanded.

"But if we don't, then when how will we know if his intensions are honorable or not?" Desiree laughed.

"Monkey!" Gene scolds her.

"Monkey?" Ruben asked. "Your nickname is Monkey?"

"She has a long tail," Andy teased her.

"When she was small, she always liked climbing in the old Oak tree," Evelyn said.

"Just like a monkey," Andy added.

"So, Gene builds the girls a tree house."

"Did you hear that?" Desiree said to her younger brother. "Daddy made it for 'the girls'. You're not allowed in it."

"Try and keep me out."

"On second thought, you are so clumsy, you probably will fall on you head and break your neck. Be my guest."

"Now children, let's be civil. You don't want Ruben to think that you fight all the time, do you?" Evelyn pleaded.

"You're right," Desiree said with a mocking smile. "Ruben, you do know that we have the perfect family? And we live in perfect harmony."

CHAPTER 11 ━━━━━━━━━━━━

Three Latin ladies entered The Garden lounge. Seth smiled as he remembers the one with the scar on her cheek. "Angela? I see that you made it back" Seth said to her as she approached the bar.

"Yes I did, Seth," she said with a slight Caribbean accent.

"So, you remember me. I am flattered."

"You remembered my name," she said with a smile.

"But, aren't all Spanish women named either Angela or Maria?"

"I'm not from Spain. I'm Dominican. I'm from the Dominican Republic. And my friends are Mexicans. They aren't Spaniards either. We are Latinos"

"I'm very, very, very sorry that I called you Spanish. Will you ever be able to find it in your heart to forgive me?"

She laughed and said, "In time, may be. But it probably will be a long, long, long time."

"So, in time you might be able to forgive me?"

"Maybe in time," she answered him with a smile and with her head tilted to one side.

The world seemed to have gone away for a moment, at time it was only those two, him and the beautiful bronze lady that was giving him a big smile. It made him feel like he was a shy little boy who was going to get his first kiss. He had to fight the urge to jump over the counter and give her a kiss. It would had been so wonderful, but he didn't. Instead he wrote down his name and telephone number on a napkin and handed it to Angela. "In case you find it in your heart to forgive me, give me a call."

"It's not proper for a lady to call a man."

"Well, I don't want to go against appropriate behavior, do I? But I don't have your number," he said as he handed her the pen and a napkin. "Here is our stationery."

"If I give you my number, what will you do with it?"

"I will cherish it as one of my most valuable possessions."

"So, in other words, it will be just something you will keep? It's won't be anything that you will ever use?"

Seth looked at her and said, "I will use it."

She smiled and wrote down her name and number and gave it back to him. As she was walking away she turned to give him another smile.

"Oh, those Spanish eyes," Yvette said, teasing Seth.

"We were told that we should be friendly to the customers," Seth replied as he gave her a gin and tonic for a night cap.

"And that is what I call being a loyal employee."

"For the record, she not Spanish. She is Dominican."

"So, are you going to give her a call?" Yvette asked.

"You were ease dropping?"

"A good employee has to know what's going on. Right?" Yvette said mockingly.

"You are definitely a good employee."

"A Dominican?" Grant said as he carried his drink from behind the bar to a stool in front of it. "Be careful. She might be one of those hot blooded Latin women."

"Yes. And if you do her wrong she will be out for revenge. So you better watch your ass," Yvette added in a teasing manner.

"Oh, yeah. You ever heard of a woman scorned? And that goes double for the Latin women," Grant said light heartily. "You do know that women aren't as noble as us men are. They aren't as understanding as we are."

"Yeah, I know how noble you men are. About as noble as swine," Yvette argued. "You're always trying to find a good excuse to get into a fight. Just to prove your manhood. You would rather fight than have to compromise."

"Hey! I'm a lover, not a fighter," said Seth.

"Who in the Hell are you trying to kid? You were a professional ball player, were you not? And sports are just a substitute for war, isn't it? It's a way to show off your masculinity, in hopes that some poor innocent girl will get excited over you."

"You are saying that men play sports just to get laid?" Grant joked.

"Yes, you can say that."

"Well, maybe I should take up playing football," Grant said. "Does anyone know of a senior football league?"

"Playing ball is the same as fighting in a war?" asked Seth.

"Or the promise to be willing and able to defend the helpless women and children against the evils of the world, if need to be," Grant added. "Back in the prehistoric days, the men had to defend the cave from the saber-tooth tiger. Now we defend our turf, or whatever that maybe. Street gangs defend their area of the city. Schools or cities, use their sport teams. Country, it's the military. It's all the same. Men used to fighting off the saber-tooth tiger. And now we all doing basically the same thing in hopes to get laid."

"Well, in that case, maybe I should go and find someone to beat-up," said Seth.

"You know that you guys are really swine? Don't you?"

"But, don't forget, that women are the reason for our swinism," Grant said.

"I thought that you weren't allowed to make up any more words?" Yvette questions him.

"The only specie other than us where the female have climax is the orangutans, and only where they share the same habitat with tigers. So, you can come to the conclusion that women use their sexuality to manipulate men to fight their battles. Whereas men are far too noble to take advantage of the, so called, fairer sex."

"Grant, you must have eaten lots of green apples, because you are fill of bull shit."

"Just for the record," Seth said, "I have never been in a fight."

"Never?" Grant asked. "Of all those years that you played ball, you never once was in a rhubarb?"

"Oh, sure, I was in rhubarbs alright, but I always was able to find someone on the other side that didn't really want to fight either. So, we would grab each other by the arms and we would push each other around. It did look like we were fighting. But no, I've never been in a real fight.

I don't know how well I would do in one. So, Grant, do you want to go for a couple of rounds, so I can find out how well I would do in a fight?"

"And the winner will get laid?"

"If you two are going to fight just to get laid, don't look my way," Yvette laughed.

CHAPTER 12 ━━━━━━━━━━

In the middle of the night Ruben walked out of the farm house and sat down on the front porch. He lit a cigarette as he seen Sport coming around the corner of the farm house. He patted his leg to motion for the dog to join him. Cautiously the Border collie approached the stranger, the man that the family welcomed into their midst. The man held out his hand and the dog sniffed it, then he licked it. "Good dog," Ruben said softly as he started petting Sport. He remembered his own dog that he had to give-up then they moved from their house in Oak Lawn, so many years ago. For the first time in his life he felt like he knew what he really wanted. If there were a heaven on Earth then this must be it. Hearing someone behind him, he turned and was greeted with a kiss from over his shoulder by Hope.

"You couldn't sleep either?" she asked.

"Not with Andy impersonating a locomotive. So maybe Desiree should move in with him and we'll sleep together? Sounds like a good idea to me."

"I'm sure that Daddy would kill us both."

"No, no. We will assure him that nothing happened. That we are just two honorable young people who happen to be sharing the same bed. That's all."

"Let's go for a walk," she said as she pulled him up to his feet. Hand in hand the two strolled around the farm. Stopping to steal a kiss now and then or to gaze at the stars and the nearly full moon. They were surrounded by the sounds of the night. She told him tales of things that took place on the farm. The time that Chuck fell through the ice on the pond, when the cows got out, the winter that Andy became snow blinded and nearly frozen to death, and the Halloween that Desiree soaped their own car windows.

"So, this is the famous tree house?" Ruben asked as they approached the back of the house. "Let's check it out."

Hope led the way, up the wooden ladder, that was boards that had been nailed to the tree. She climbed inside and pulled Ruben in after her. It was a little house with two openings, the door and one window on the opposite side. It was comprised of a small table with romance novels and two small chairs. On the floor was an old mattress.

The tree house began to sway. "Is this safe?" Ruben asked.

"What do you mean?"

"It's old and it is moving."

"Don't worry. Daddy built this," she said as she embarrassed him. Then she pulled his shirt up and over his head. It was the first time that Hope was the aggressor. It took Ruben by surprise.

"Here?" he said as he looked toward the house.

"Why not? No one will know. They are all in the house sleeping."

He smiled as he gave in to her desires. Afterwards the two lay naked in each other arms until they fell to sleep.

"What have you two done?" a loud angry voice demanded to know as a bright light shined on their naked bodies. Startled, the two stared into the blinding light. At first, Hope did not recognize her father's voice. She had never seen him that angry before. They covered their bodies as her father left their presence. In the early morning light they looked at each other and felt ashamed. Looking out the tree house they saw the family gathering in front of the tree. Not wanting to face them, the two hesitated to climb down. Ruben started to go through the tree house door. Then Hope gently pulled him behind herself. Slowly she climbed down on the old wooden boards that were nailed to the tree and Ruben followed her.

"I will not tolerate such ungodly behavior," were the words of the angry man. In the stillness of the morning, the words were magnified. "You must leave and never come back," he said to Ruben.

"If he goes so do I," Hope said in a deviant manor as she stepped in front of her father. Without warning, he slapped her. The blow knocked her back into Ruben. Her face turned red as her eyes filled with tears that streamed down her cheeks. She bit her lips to prevent from crying out and she began to shake. She never felt the wrath of her father before.

Quickly, Ruben stepped between Hope and her father. "If you want to hit someone, hit me," he said with clutched fists.

Hope ran into the house. Her mother turned angrily to her father and demanded to know, "Why did you do that? They are only human. They were only doing what is natural." Then she followed her daughter into the house.

Hope was jamming her clothes into her overnight bag. Afterwards, she looked around the bed room, the room that she had shared with her younger sister, where they would lay in the bed and tell each other secrets and their most private thoughts. Now those times were done. They would always be in her past, never to return again. She felt as if she was an outsider looking in on someone else's world, one that did not belong to her anymore.

As Hope was crossing the living room, to get Ruben's things, her mother came through the front door and embraced her. "I'm sorry. He shouldn't slap you. Are you alright?"

"No! I'm not. He hit me. He hit me in front of Ruben."

"He over reacted. I know. But he still loves you."

"He has a funny way of showing it."

"I know. He shouldn't have slapped you. But, you must understand, things have not been going all that smoothly for him, or for us. I didn't want to tell you this, but now I think that I must. The bank won't give us the money that we need. We might lose the farm."

Hope stared at her mother with mixed emotion. Evelyn looked at her daughter with sympathy as she said, "I don't know how to tell you this, but we are not going to be able to give you the money for your school loan anymore."

"I don't need your money. I'll manage some way. Don't worry about me," she said as she left the house and got in the car with Ruben. As they drove off, she did not look back. She stared straight out the front window, not making a sound until they came to Route 12. Then she began to cry uncontrollably until they reached the Illinois state line.

CHAPTER 13 ━━━━━━━━━━━━━━━━

"I don't know what I'm going to do," Hope said to Nicole as they drove away from The Garden in the rain. "I don't see any way I'm going to be able to make it work. I'm not making enough to get by."

"I hear you talking Girl. It's tough, I know. Some weeks I wonder if I'm going to have enough to eat on. Working two damn jobs and still not making ends meet. That really sucks."

"Daddy isn't going to help me out anymore."

"He's has been helping you?" asked Nicole as she was trying to see though her fogged up window shield.

"He was paying my student loan for me. But no more. They say that they can't afford it."

"Do you think that they can or can't?"

"I don't know. Maybe they can or maybe they can't. I don't know. It's hard to say." Hope replied as she watched glaring lights passed by.

"Why would they lie to you?"

"Because they caught us."

"What! Your parents caught you? You saying that they walked in on you?"

"No. Well, yes. It was the same as them walking in on us. We made love in the tree house, and Daddy found us."

"And you had a falling out?"

"You could say that. Before we left, Mom told me that they were about to lose the farm, and they would not be able to help me out any more."

"Do you really think that they might lose the farm?" Nicole asked.

"I don't know. I hope that they won't. But, on the other hand, if they keep it then she might have been lying to me. But I don't think so. Still in the big picture it doesn't matter, does it? I still don't have enough money for my student loan."

"Well, girl, I just don't know what to tell you. Have you given it any thought of what you might do?"

"Do you remember that artist that was at The Garden the night of Ruben's birthday? You know, the first night that he took me home?" asked Hope.

"No. I don't recall any artist. What did he look like?"

"Oh, you must have seen them. Those three men that were at the bar when I gave the cake to Ruben?"

"No. I didn't see you bring him any cake. I'm sorry. I must have been working the floor."

"Well, anyway, one of them is an artist, and he told me that he would pay me to be a model. I don't know how much he will pay, but it might be worth looking into."

"Do you really want to get naked in front of a man that you hardly know, who will be painting a picture of you for all to see? What would your religious parents think?"

"He might not want to paint me in the nude. Right now, I don't really care what they think." Hope defended her plan.

"And how about Ruben?" Nicole quizzed Hope. "Do you really think that he wouldn't care if you posed naked? And I don't buy that you don't care what your folks think either."

"I know, I know. But what am I can do? I have to do something, don't I?" Hope responded.

"I don't see how that should be the way for you to go," Nicole advised her.

"Maybe he won't want me to be naked. Not all paintings are of nudes, right? And if he wants me to take off all of my clothes I will tell him no way."

"Hope," Nicole shook her head, "listen girl, I don't think that you should. But if you're going to then you better watch your ass." She laughed. "But don't let him look at it."

"Very funny," smiled Hope as they pulled up in front of her apartment building. She turned to Nicole and told her. "Thank you for driving me home."

"You know that you don't have to thank me every time I drive you. You pay more than your share for the gas."

"But you are still going out of your way to pick me up and drop me off. You are a good friend. You do know that you're are my best friend? Sometimes I think that you might be my only friend."

Nicole took hold of hand and said, "I always see you as a close friend too."

"Guess it's now or never," Hope said as she pushed open the car door, letting in a gust of cold wet wind rushed in. In one hand she held her purse and shoes while in the other hand covering her head with her vest as she ran towards her apartment building, splashing in the water along the way. After she managed to open the door the soaking wet blonde waved back to the car, where the young black lady softly said, "You're my best friend too."

CHAPTER 14 —————————

"How is everything going?" The foreman asked as he entered the large room where Seth and two other painters were working.

"These damn walls are soaking up the paint like a sponge. We're going to need lots more paint," replied one of the painters called Stanly.

"Okay, I'll send more over. Do you need anything else?"

"Yeah," Jake, the other painter, said with a hint of a southern accent. "You can get us some steak sandwiches and some beer."

"I think that bologna is more like it. We didn't get that Broadview job."

"What the hell? Do you have anything else lined-up?"

"Not yet. But we do have some irons in the fire. We are waiting to see if they accept our bid."

"What happened with the Broadview job?" Seth asked.

"We were undercut by Good Earth Painters. We can't compete with those damn wetbacks, that's for sure. First it was the black and now it's those damn wetbacks."

"That's for damn sure," Stanly said "How in the hell are we supposed to make a living? They work for peanuts. Shit, a guy can't make it on three or four days a week. I guess we're supposed to live off of rice and beans, and live in an apartment with three other families."

"Send all of them back where they came from, back to Mexico or India or where in the hell that they came from." Jake stated

"Poland?" Seth smiled as he looked at Stanly.

"You know what in the hell I'm talking about, I'm talking about those damn illegals that come over here to go on welfare or to take our jobs. That is what in the hell I'm talking about. Send every one of those damn asses back."

"You are right," the foreman added. "I got my tax bill. I don't know how in the hell that I going to be able to pay for it. Most of it is going to pay for the public school. Hell, my kids don't even go to public schools. I don't care if they close the damn things down."

"And the County Hospital?" Seth said sarcastically.

"Yea, County Hospital."

"And the Police Department?" the foreman looked at him suspiciously as Seth continual. "And the Fire Department?"

"Don't be an ass." the foreman said coldly before he left.

"It sounds like you love with those damn illegals. Are you a damn wetback lover?" Jake said. "Maybe you should go and work for Good Earth."

Both of his co-workers turned their backs to him. He wondered if he had gone too far and crossed the line. He never felt that his lack of not being prejudiced towards people of other races or ethnic groups should be held against him, but in the back of his mind he always knew that it might. Now he realized that if he did not appear to share their feelings he could be ostracized to the point that his job might even be at stake. What would the repercussions be if they knew that he was thinking about going out with a Dominican woman? And if he did have a relationship with Angela would they not someway fined it out, sooner or later. These were his thoughts as he spread the white paint over the rough surface, giving it the illusion of being smooth.

On his way home Seth stopped at a fast food restaurant. As he was eating his gyro and fries he noticed the table that was close to his was occupied by four fair skinned high school girls. They were all laughing about something. He was not able to make it out what, but he assumed it was about boys. 'What were their ages,' he wondered, 'they must be close to what Crystal would had been. No, Crystal would be older. Closer to the age of Hope, and Nelson would be about Ruben's age.' He tried to picture what she would have looked like as a teenager, but he couldn't. Nor could he picture what his son would have looked like. Was time beginning to effect his memory? It was getting harder for him to hold on to those moments he had cherished with his family. He tried to remember the good times, the times he cherished with them, but those memories would always be replaced by the memory of the crash and their dead bodies. They were gone and someday his memory of them would start fading. Then all that he will have left is their ghosts to haunt him.

He was contemplating stopping at the neighborhood bar or buying some beer and going home and getting drunk. Then he noticed a young Latin woman sitting by herself at a nearby table. She did not have the same facial features as Angela, but her skin tone was the same. He assumed that she also might be from the Caribbean. He wondered if she might be also be from the Dominican Republic. The four young ladies at the other table looked pale against her rich complexion. It couldn't be the color of her skin that attracted him to Angela; was it her looks? Or her mannerism? Whatever it was he knew that he wanted to see her again. Maybe Father Rafael was right. It was time for him to move on with his life. He removed his wallet and took out a napkin and unfolded it to reveal the name of Angela Perez and her phone number.

A small light complexioned boy with big dark eyes, opened the door. It was not what Seth was expecting. He wondered if he was at the right place. "Hello." The child stared back at the man as he stood half hidden behind the door. "What is your name?" Seth held out his hand. But the boy backed away.

"Jason, say, 'Hi' to Mr. Proctor. He is a good friend of ours. Shake his hand."

As the two shook hands Jason said. "Hi…" He looked to his mother for help.

"Mr. Proctor."

"Mr…… Pop."

Seth smiled and said, "Why don't you call me Seth, and we will forget about the formalities."

The boy smiled back, as if he knew the meaning of the word formalities.

"I'm glad to make your acquaintance Jason Perez."

"Go and play," Angela told her son. "Dinner will be ready in a little bit."

As Jason left the room Seth said, "I thought that I was going to take you out for dinner."

"And spend all of your money?"

"You don't know how much money that I have, do you? I might be rich."

"Sure, you are a millionaire, and you're working for tips just for fun." She became serious. "I don't know what you want. If you just want a piece of ass or what, but if that is all you're after, then there is the door. If you want more, well, then I think that you should know what you are getting in for. I'm talking about the whole package. So, do you want to stay for dinner? Or do I tell Jason that you had to go home to your wife?"

"I'm not married."

"I know."

"How do you know?"

"Oh, I have my ways."

"I see. Giving good tips to the waitress pays off."

""So, are you staying and having dinner with me and my son? Or are you going to spend the evening with someone that isn't burdened down with a kid?" she asked.

"It's been a long time since someone has called me a jerk; usually because I did something to deserve it, but not this time."

"What are you saying? Are you staying or not?"

"I'm saying that you should at least read the first chapter before you throw away the book," commented Seth.

"So, you staying?"

"I'll be delighted to."

"I hope that you like my food. It will be ready soon." She walked across the small apartment to the stove. "Do you like rice and beans? If you don't then I can make something else."

"I'm sure that your rice and beans will be delicious." He put his arms around her waist and looked over her shoulder at what she was cooking. She turned and they kissed. It was a long kiss. A kiss like one that he had known only in the distant past. One always remembers that first kiss, especially with the one that you are falling in love with.

The meal was chicken with rice that was seasoned with garlic, herbs and pimento olives. It was accompanied with beans in tomato sauce and fried plantains. Towards the end of the meal she give him another beer and told him, "Have more chicken and rice."

"No thanks. I don't think that I can eat any more," he said as he patted his stomach.

"Here. Have some more," she said as she put another scoop on his plate.

"Mommy, can I have some flam? Asked Jason.

"If I eat this, I won't have any room for flam." Seth said, not knowing for sure what flam was.

He watched her serving her son the custard. "Do you want some coffee?" she asked.

"Isn't he a little young for coffee," Seth asked, jokingly.

"Not for me. For you," the child said with a smile. He looked at his mother and said, "He is silly." Then back at Seth and said, ""You are silly."

He smiled back. He wondered what his family and friends would think of him, being with someone who was not white. Should he care? Should he be concerned of what others might think? These were the thoughts that were racing through his head. He knew that if he could not be able to put aside his fear of prejudices that others might have, then it could not be fair to Angela. Yes, he may be able to take advantage of her, but could his own self-gratification be worth more to him then the price that Angela might have to pay. These questions he had asked himself before, but only in the abstract. Now he was facing the reality. The desire to go beyond a kiss was dominating his thinking. This was a person that he wanted to be close to-closer than anyone since the passing of his wife, so many years ago.

After Jason was put to bed, Angela dished out the flam and poured the coffee. "How much sugar do you want," she asked.

"I'll pass."

"None? No sugar?"

"None, I drink it black."

"No sugar. No milk," she said as she carried the flam and coffee to the table.

When Seth took the first mouth full of coffee, he made a face. He tried to hide his displeasure, but it caught him by surprise. He tried to conceal his disapproval, but it was too late. "You don't like it?" she asked with a disappointed look on her face.

"It's a little strong," he replied as he carried the coffee cup to the sink. After he had diluted it with hot water down to one-eighth of the original strength, he tasted it. "You make a good cup of coffee. It might be a little on the cold side, but, never the less, it's a great cup of coffee." He laughed.

"I'm sorry. I'll make another pot."

"Don't worry. This is fine. I'll nuke it."

Angela laughed. "You Yankees sure do like weak coffee."

"What can I say?" She smiled as he came back to the table. "You said that you wanted to lay your cards on the table?" She nodded. "If I'm out of line tell me."

"What do you want to know?"

"Well, you are Catholic, aren't you?"

"I guess you can say that. If I'm anything I would be Catholic. I might not be a good one, but I guess I am."

"Well, Jason isn't a Christian name, is it?"

"Do you think that would piss the Pope off?"

"You are mad at the church?"

"Might be."

Seth studied her face. "Is it something to do with Jason?"

"You want me to put my cards on the table? Yes, it does. Jason….Jason's father was, or I should say still is, a priest. Yes, Jason is the bastard son of a priest. A man who chose the church over us. Oh, yes, they know. They knew alright. All of them know that one of their fair haired priests got one of the flock knocked up. I was an embarrassment to all of them. Whose fault was it? Not the priest. No, not their fair hair priest, he couldn't do anything wrong, could he. No, it must been the young know nothing girl who must have taken advantage of their innocent man of the cloth.

Seth watched the tears fill her eyes. "Man of God," he heard her say. "He was nothing but a coward. A damn coward that hides in the church. Sure, he claimed that he had to be true to his vow to God. What a bunch of bull shit. So, they shipped me up here, out of the way, up here so I won't be an embarrassment to the Church. They aren't nothing but a bunch of hypocrites."

"And that's why you named him Jason?"

"Yeah, I knew that would piss him off. That serves him right. He has never seen his son and he never will."

"I do understand how you feel. I don't blame you one bit, but you can't condemn the whole Church because of one priest, can you?"

"Why in the hell not? I can do any damn thing that I want to do. And I want to condemn him and all of his kind. They all can go to Hell far as I'm concerned. I don't give a damn. Who in the Hell needs the Church anyway? I sure in the hell don't."

"In a way I can go along with you on that, but still maybe not the whole Church."

"Why in the hell not." Angela challenged Seth.

"Because we do need the Church."

"Why?"

"Because we all need guidance sometimes, don't we? Without that we would be like a ship without a rudder."

"Without a rudder? What in the hell are you talking about? You say that we need the Church, what for? To let those hypocrites tell us what is right and what is wrong? No thanks, I'm capable if thinking for myself. Do you?"

"No, I'm capable of thinking for myself, but still I feel that there are times when I might need little guidance."

Angela walked to the door and opened it. "You can use your rudder to steer your ass out of here."

CHAPTER 15 ━━━━━━━━━━━━━━━━

Seth was leaning against his car as he waited by a large printing and mailing service company. He was imaging what was going to happen when Angela sees him. Will she turn and walk away? Or will she tell him to get lost? Those were real possibilities, but he felt that she might come over to him and ask, 'What are you doing here? And he would say, "I just happen to be in the neighborhood, and I thought that you might need a ride to pick up Jason.' After a while she might give in and the relationship would be renewed.

The door that was marked 'Employee Only', opened up and the workers began to file out. The color and the workers were mixed, but most of them were tan like Angela. He saw her talking with her co-workers. To his surprise, when she noticed him, she hurried to him and throw her arms around him and give him a long passionate kiss. Then she whispered in his ear, "Are they watching?"

"Yes, they are."

"Good. Let's go."

"Sure," he said as he opened the car door for. When he got in behind the wheel he saw her waving to the other women. "Where to you want to go??"

"I don't care. Just go." As they pulled out onto the street she said, "This will give them something to talk about."

"Should we pick up Jason?"

"He doesn't get out of school for over a good hour. So, what do you want to do? Go back to my place and have a quickie?"

"What?" He did not know how to respond. She had a big smile. He wondered if she was laughing at him. Was she serious or was this a test? They had just kissed for the first time since she kicked him out of her home. And that kiss was to show him off in front of her co-workers. He felt that he was in a catch twenty two situation. If he said yes and he was lying. "I can't win, can I?"

She let out with a loud laugh, which caught him off guard. He was the brunt of her joke. Was he someone that she was serious about or not? She seemed to him to be the kind of person that could go from a state of delight to being hurt in a moment. She kissed him on the cheek before she said, "I do want to go home. I need to take a shower. I'm all sweaty and dirty. You don't mind, do you?"

"Yes, I do. I like my women on the sweaty and dirty side." The two smiled at each other. "I feel a little dirty myself, maybe I'll join you."

"So, you want a quickie?"

Later the two of them and her little son, Jason, entered Seth's home. It was a brick bungalow that Berwyn was well known for. Unlike Angela's home, where everything was scattered around, here everything was in their proper place. There was not even dust on the pictures of his family nor on the rosary that draped over them. It make her feel as if she was an intruder. He was a warm man and he was trying to make them feel comfortable in his house, but she still felt that his house was a shrine to his late family, a place that she did not belong.

""Welcome to my home."

""It's nice," she said as she walked over to the pictures that were hanging on the wall.

"Those are….Those were my family. They are deceased."

"I know. The waitresses told me that they were killed in a car crash."

"Thank you. This was my wife, Grace," he said as they looked at his wedding picture.

"She was very pretty."

"Yes, she was that. She was very pretty indeed, and she was a good wife and mother. I wish that I had appreciated her more than I did while she was alive."

"We all wish that we appreciated the ones that we lost more then what we did, but I'm sure that she knew that you loved her."

"I hope so, because sometimes I was a real bastard, especially when things weren't going good."

"We all have times that we aren't on our best behavior," she said as she squeezed his hand.

"And this is a picture of my son, Nelson." It was a picture of a boy holding a baseball bat. ""He wanted to be a ball player like his old man was. The truth is that he probably would have been better then what I was. He probably would have made it to the majors. He was a natural-one in a thousand, maybe one in a million. I had to work at it to be good, but he didn't have to. He was a natural."

There was a moment of silence before he moved to the next picture, which was of a little girl holding a bouquet of flowers. "This is a picture of my daughter, Crystal. She was a flower girl. She was a pretty flower girl. She would been a," he choked-up, "a beautiful bride if I hadn't...."

"I'm getting hungry," she said, stopping him from condemning himself.

Seth give Angela a little smile, approving of what she had done. "You cooked for me. Now it's my turn. What would you like?" he said, going along with the change of subject.

"Pastelon," she laughed.

"Pastelon? I don't know what that is.

"It's meat between two layers of mashed plantains."

"Like a pie?"

"You could say it's something like a pie, but it's doesn't have a hard crust, more like lasagna."

"It sounds good, but, I hate to tell you this, it's not in my repertoire. And I'm fresh out of plantains," he said as he was looking in the refrigerator. He pulled out two pounds of ground beef, "I do make one hell of a meat loaf, if I do say so myself. But it will take a good hour."

"That will be okay, only if it is worth waiting for."

"I make it like my mother used to do."

"Used to? Is she dead?"

"Yes, so is my father. I'm a thirty-five year old orphan."

"Welcome to the club," said Angela.

"Both of your parent past away?"

"My mother and as far my father goes he might as well be dead."

Jason entered the kitchen, carrying a model car. "Miria Mami. Un carro." He held it up to show his mother.

Angela looked at Seth. His face was a blank. She could not tell what he was feeling. "That's not yours. Put it back."

"Mami, yo quiero."

"No lo puedes tener, no es tuyo." She took the car and handed it Seth.

He looked at the child with wanting eyes. "It was my son, Nelson's, but he is gone. He has no use for it now," he said as he handed the car back to Jason.

"Gracias," said the boy.

"In English," his mother demanded.

"Thank you," he said as he turned and started to leave the kitchen. Then he stopped and asked, "Where did he go?"

"He went to Heaven with his mother and sister," answered Seth.

"Oh." The boy tried to comprehend what he heard, but it was too confusing. Did they die or did they just go to Heaven? Or did they do both? And why didn't he go with them if Heaven is a good place? Life and death were confusing to him, much like why do some children have both a mother and a father and he doesn't.

"That was nice," Angela said after Jason had left the room.

"Maybe the Priest was right. I've been clinging on too much to the past and it's time to move on with my life."

"We always have to move on, but the question is do we look for something new or do we look for a replacement?"

"Right now I'm looking forward to having dinner with a pretty lady and her nice son."

She smiled.

CHAPTER 16 ———————————

Hope hesitated before pushing the button on the office building that read Coldman Studio.

"Who is it?" the voice over the intercom inquired.

"It is I." Soon as the words came out of her mouth she realized that they might not recognize her voice. "I'm Hope Adamsen."

"You are right on time. We are on the six floor." The voice was followed by the buzzer.

On the way to the studio she could not help from feeling that she was going to do something wrong. But now, without the financial support from her family, she felt that she had no other choice. The money that she will make for posing for a painting might make up the difference, anyway, a part of it.

Dick greeted her at the door with a smile. He was larger than she remembered. That made her feel somewhat intimidated? She looked past him where she saw Max and Lenny standing here. There was no easel. But there were the tools and props for a photographer. Among the props was a bed. "I thought that you were going to paint me," she said as she looked at Lenny.

"No. No. I'm sorry that you misunderstood," Dick said. "We are shooting today. We'll see how thing go. If everything goes okay, and I'm sure that it will, then we'll do the contract. Have you ever done any modeling or acting before?"

"Only in school plays."

"Well, we are all starting off together today. Today we are doing our first project. You are getting in on the ground floor. I'm confident that we all will do well."

BEYOND THE GARDEN | 67

"I hope that you are right," she replied, not quite knowing what he was talking about.

He could sense that she was a little uncomfortable. "I think that a relaxer is in order.

Max, get the lady a drink," he said, giving him a wink. "What is your poison?"

"What's my poison? I don't know. Maybe a wine cooler."

"We don't have any wine coolers. Will a beer do?"

"Yes. That will be fine." She never drank that early in the day before, but she wanted to fit in.

Max brought her the open bottle of beer. As she was drinking it she noticed that she was the only one that was drinking.

"Tell me, how are you fixed on money?" Dick inquired. "If you need couple hundred bucks, we can give you a little advance now."

"That would be terrific."

"Do you want it in cash or check?"

"Cash," she said slowly.

Dick took out two hundred dollar bills and laid them on the desk. He typed, 'I received two hundred dollars against my first pay check.' Then typed Hope Adamsen. She signed her name and dated it. Then she put the money in her purse.

"Here," Dick said as he tossed her a negligee.

"You can change behind the screen," Lenny said.

She felt strange but she removed her outer clothes and put on the gown on. When she stepped out from behind the screen the men laughed at her.

"Very funny," said Dick. "Now, get those damn underwear off."

She went back behind the screen and removed the gown and laid it across the top of the screen. She stood there, unable to bring herself to finish disrobing. "What in the hell is taking you so damn long?" she heard Dick demanding. She removed her brassiere and also laid it on the top of the screen. Then she took a deep breath before she slid off her panties and heard the men snicker. She quickly put the gown back on, looking down at her body and seeing that all of her privacy had been revealed. 'What would my parents think,' she thought. 'Why should I be concerned? They don't really care about me anyway. What difference will a few pictures make?'

After she justified her action to herself she stepped out from behind the screen.

"Shouldn't she shave first?" Lenny asked.

"No. let's see how it goes first," Dick said. Then he told Hope to get on the bed.

"Relax," Lenny said as he turned the camera on. "Let's have some fun. Remember that you are the star. You the one that all the guys will be fantasizing about."

Max began to disrobe. A fear of horror came over her. This was not going be a photo shoot. It was going to be an X-rated movie. He embraced her and when he followed it with a passionate kiss, his hand cupped her breast. She pushed him away.

"Don't play so hard to get," Lenny said.

"No! I'm out of here," she cried as she headed for her clothes. Dick grabbed her arm and threw her back onto the bed.

"Where in the hell do you think you're going? I've invested way too much time and money on you. And I'm not going to let you run out on me. What in the hell is your game. What are you trying to do? Extort more money? Or what?"

Hope again tried to escape, but she was thrown back onto the bed. "I'm not a whore!" she cried as she climbed back on her feet.

Dick threw her into Max's grasp. Then he ripped the negligee off of her, leaving her naked among the three men, leaving her exposed to three strangers that she had little defense against. With all of her might she twisted her arms and kicked her feet trying to escape from Max's grip, but he was too strong. She kicked at Dick, but fell short, but Dick's hand did not. His large open palm hit her face with an impact that she had never felt before. Then all of the fight went out of her. Max kept her from collapsing to the floor. Half unconscious, she watched Dick remove his clothes. He threw the naked young woman back on the bed. She tried to fight him but it was futile.

Lenny was overwhelmed with the feeling of sympathy for the young woman that was being raped before his own eyes. He turned and started for the door. Max grabbed his arm.

"Where in the hell do you think you're going?"

"No place. Just checking my equipment."

"You aren't trying to run out on the party, are you?" Dick said with an intimidating voice.

As he finished, Dick was replaced by Max. "Come on. Get undressed. You're next."

"I'm not in the mood."

"Not in the mood?" Dick laughed. "What in the hell you do mean? You don't want a piece of ass from this pretty little filly?"

Lenny looked at the helpless child-like woman that had curled up into a ball after Max had finished. With his eyes, he pleaded to Dick.

"Max is right," Dick laughed. "You are nothing but a God damn fag. It takes a real man to teach a girl how to be a woman. That leaves you out, doesn't it?"

Feeling sick at his stomach, Lenny stared at the young woman whose innocence had been ripped away from her; a person without any refuge. She yielded to her vulnerability. She lay there with her naked body exposed, crying. He was torn between trying to comfort her by holding her or running fast as he could through the door. But he realized that he could do neither. He watched as Dick pulled her off the bed and dragged her into the shower. He heard Dick telling her that she smelled. Max joined them. As soon as he was alone Lenny removed the memory clip from the camera and sneaked out.

CHAPTER 17 ────────────

Hope was oblivious to the sound of the car horn. With the covers wrapped around her, she stared into space. The rain that was plowing against the window was in sync with the rhyme of her heart beat-fast and hard, then the pounding would ease for a moment, but that moment would be short lived. Soon, another wave of anxiety would grip her again and hold her until she gasped for air. Again the horn sounded. And again she did not respond. Soon there was knocking at her door. At first it was a gentle rapping, then it grew louder.

"Hope!" the muffled voice of Nicole came through the door. "Are you in there?" There was no answer. She pounded on the door as she hollered, "Hope! Hope! Are you in there? Open the damn door." She must not be home Nicole thought. She waited for a few moments before she started to leave. Then the door slowly opened. In front of her stood a person that looked in a way that she had never seen her look before, with her hair messed up and a red mark on her face, where Dick had slapped her. "What in the hell happened to you?"

"I'm fine."

"You sure as hell don't look fine to me."

"I didn't sleep good last night. That's all."

"And you was sleepwalking and you ran into the wall? Don't shit me, tell me what happened."

"Nothing happened."

"Girl, you can lie to lots of people but I'm not one of them." Nicole took both of her hands.

Hope's lips began to quiver and her eyes began fill up with tears. She broke away from Nicole and retreated to her bed. There the two young women sat on the edge of the bed with Nicole's arm around her. "You know

70

that I'm your friend, don't you?" Hope nodded her head in agreement. "You can tell me what's wrong."

After a moment of silence, Hope said, "I was … raped." It was the first time she said that word out loud, that awful word. The word echoed over and over in her head like a bad nightmare that would not end.

"Raped?" Nicole said so softly that Hope barely could distinguish her friend's word from her own thought. "Who did it to you?"

With her hands covering her face, she mumbled, "I can't tell you. They will hurt me. They might even kill me."

"They? There were more than one?"

Hope nodded.

"Two?"

"Three."

"Three men raped you?"

"No. Only two of them. The other one was just there."

"He didn't try to help you?"

"He was too scared to."

"He was a damn coward."

A part of her wanted to agree with Nicole, and a part of her wanted to defend Lenny.

"Did you go to the police?" Before the words got out of her mouth, Nicole knew the answer. "Did you go to the hospital? Of course you didn't. A trained nurse that won't go to the hospital. Have you told Ruben?"

"No! No! Please don't tell him. You have to promise me that you won't tell him."

"But he needs to know."

"No! He does not need to know. He will go after them. They might hurt him. They might even kill him. Please, please don't tell him. I beg you. Please, don't tell him."

"Okay, okay. But he still needs to know. He is your boyfriend, after all. You shouldn't keep secrets from your boyfriend."

"Like you don't keep secrets from Austin?"

"That's different. He is an ass. Anyway, sometimes. Well, most of the time. But Ruben isn't like Austin. Is he?"

"Please promise that you won't tell him."

"Don't worry. I won't tell him. If you don't want me to, I won't."

Hope looked like a hurt child. "Are you going to stay here or go to The Garden?" Nicole asked.

"I should. I need the money. But I can't. I just can't. Will you call them and tell them that I'm sick?"

"Sure. Anything for you, girlfriend. Are you going to work at the store tomorrow?"

"I don't know," Hope said.

"I have to go. But don't hesitate to call me if you need anything. Don't forget that I'm your friend." Hope nodded her head. "Will you be alright? Can I get you anything before I go?"

Hope did not say anything, only shook her head 'No'. Nicole give her a hug before leaving. Then she watched her walking out of the bedroom and listened to her friend's footsteps crossing the living room floor, followed by the sound of the front door closing. Again she was all alone. No one there to comfort her. She felt like a little child that had been an abandoned. She felt that she was both a victim and the perpetrator.

In the curtain drawn bedroom it was impossible to tell what time of day it was-only that it was light outside. But in the room it was dark and still as it had been for the past two days when the phone began to ring. One ring of the phone was followed by another then another. Hope slowly rolled over stared at it as it rung for the fourth and then the fifth time before she answered it. "Hello," she said softly.

"Is this Hope Adamsen?"

"Yes."

"This is Mrs. Olson from Human Resources. Our records show that you have missed three days in a row without an excused absence. Do you have a reason for your absence?"

"I'm sick."

"Have you been to see a doctor?"

"No."

"Why not? You are aware that if you miss three days in a row without an excused absence it is grounds for dismissal?"

"Yes, but I am sick."

"Then why didn't you notify us, and why didn't you go to the doctor? It is required if you miss more than two days in a row to have a note from your doctor."

"I don't know. I couldn't make myself get out of bed."

"You couldn't get out of bed? That is your excuse? I'm going to have to check with your supervisor. I'll call you back." There was no sympathy in her voice. Not even a 'good bye'.

'They will understand,' thought Hope. 'They won't fire me for not calling in sick. No, I am too good of an employee. I am very good with the customers. Anyone can see that. No, they won't fire me. And when I go back to work I will show them just how good of an employee that I am. I will out sell everyone. Yes, I will be the best employee that the store has.'

The silence was broken by the ringing of the phone. Hope answered it with a soft, "Hello."

"Miss Adamsen, I have spoken with your supervisor, and he feels that it would be in the company's best interest to terminate your employment. I regret that it is the store policy to respect our supervisor's wishes. Your dismissal is going in effect immediately. You can come in on next Friday for your settlement. Are there any questions?"

"I'm fired!"

"I'm afraid that you have been terminated. I'm sorry, but it is out of my hands. The decision has been made. There is nothing that I can do. If you don't have any questions I will have to go now. Do you have any questions?"

"No. I guess not."

"Then, good bye."

"Good bye," Hope whispered in the phone before it went silent.

For a long time she lay in bed. She felt that she was trapped under an enormous weight, a weight that paralyzed her. For a long time she lay there, crying, not knowing what she could do. She was hoping that she could go back to sleep and then when she awakened she would find that the last twenty-four hours were only a bad dream, a nightmare. But she knew what had happened to her was real, and nothing was going to change that. Finally she forced herself to get out of the bed and went into the kitchen and got a glass of water from the sink. Her hand began to shake, splashing the water on herself. She threw the glass against the wall. Then she cried out, "That damn Nazi." She began to cry uncontrollably.

Chapter 18

"Can I help you, Venice?" Grant asked the elderly man who was wearing a plaid shirt.

"No thanks. I can climb upon the stool by myself."

Grant smiled and said, "That's a funny line. Can I use it in my Great American Novel?"

"You writing a book? What in the hell is it about? How to over charge for watered down drinks?"

"It's about this grumpy old man who is the last man in Chicago whose favorite football team is the Cardinals."

"Ah. You must be one of those damn Bears' fans. I knew that there was something about you that I didn't like, other than that you always water down the drinks."

"What do you want? A watered down vodka and tonic?"

"Nah. You might try to poison me. Better gave me a bottle of beer. Make it a cold one, this time. The one you gave me last week was so warm that it made me sick."

Grant removed a bottle of beer from the cooler, acting as if it was freezing his hands. He opened it and handed it to him with a glass.

"Is this my birthday drink?" Venice asked the smiling bartender.

"Wasn't last week your birthday?"

"Yes, that right. You owe me two drinks. For my birthday last week and the one for this week" he said as gave Grant the money.

Grant nodded to Ruben as he rung up the beer. "Venice is a famous man. He was the first man to put sawdust in a crankcase." The two bartenders laughed at the joke.

"So, you're going to be a writer when you grow up," Venice said. "Dreams are nice, as long as reality doesn't screw them up. I always thought that I was a handsome man until the other day when I looked in the mirror. That damn reality thing, it will screw things up every time."

Through the opening to the dining room Ruben saw Hope approaching a table of a middle age couple and a younger man. Ruben saw the younger man, who was wearing a suit and tie, stand up and smile at Hope. He shook her hand, but he did not let go of it right away. The hand shake was more like holding hands. They were too far away to make out what they were saying, but it was obvious that they not only knew each other, but they were more than just friends.

"Do you know who those people sitting there are?" Ruben asked Grant.

"That's Doctor....Something. I thank its Doctor Price or Pears. Something like that. That's his wife. The young guy, I don't know."

When Hope came to the bar to get the wine for the table Ruben asked, "Who is your friend?"

"Oh, that's Doctor Carmichael. He worked at the hospital with me, when I was a nurse. He's very nice."

"I'm sure he is," he mumbled as he signed off the ticket.

Throughout the dinner Ruben observed the interaction between the two. Looking to see if he could detect what their relationship was. Could there be something there or not? He kept asking himself. And if there was, how could he compete against a doctor?

That night, after Ruben took Hope to her apartment, he started to hold her. But she twisted out of his arms. "Not tonight," she said.

"Not tonight!" She could hear the hurt in his voice. But she knew that she must not tell him that she was raped only four days before. And she was not ready for a sexual relationship. She did not want to hurt his feelings, but she knew that she must keep her secret from him for his own sake. She emotionally needed him more that night than ever before.

"Is it because I'm not a doctor. No, I'm not a doctor and I will never be."

"I'm sorry." she said, grabbing his arm as he started for the door. "Please don't go."

He turned and stared at her. "Do you want to make love or not?" She stared back at him with a blank face. "That's my answer. I'm out of here."

"Please, don't go. I need you."

"To keep you company until someone better comes along. No thanks."

The slamming of the door made the room vibrate before it went silent, a deafening silence. In the stillness of the room she was all alone and isolated. All that she was left with was the horrible secret that she could not share with him. The secret that made her felt guilty and ashamed.

CHAPTER 19 ━━━━━━━━━━━━━

"What's the matter with her?" Seth asked Yvette as he watched Hope carry away a tray of cocktails that he had just made, towards the dining room.

"Why? She looked like something is wrong?" she asked as she set some dirty glasses on the counter.

"I don't know. She looked to me like she was on the verge of tears."

"And with my woman's intuition, I'm supposed to know why?"

"I just thought that maybe…." He never finished.

"I know, I know, Mother Yvette will take care if everything," she said with a sigh. "I'll talk to her later, but now I have orders." She read off her list of drunks for him to fill. She watched Hope moving slowly among the tables, not with her usual lightheartedness, but as a person that was carrying a great burden.

Towards the end of the night, just before last call, Hope was sitting alone at a table in the back of the room, waiting for Nicole. The D.J. was playing soft music for the last few couples that still had not called it a night. At the bar Seth was the solo bartender that night. The kitchen staff had already had gone home. That's when Yvette joined Hope at a cocktail table. Yvette looked at her tips that were in a rock glass on her tray. "Mondays isn't hardly worth coming in for. I could have spent the night home with my family, watching TV. With the children or fighting with George. You know what I mean?"

Hope did not answer until Yvette looked at her squarely in the face. "I could be home, sleeping," Hope answered.

"By yourself?"

"Yes. By myself."

"Not with Ruben?"

"We….He broke-up with me."

"Why?"

"I don't know. He just broke-up." Hope saw that Yvette knew that there was more. "I wouldn't have sex with him."

"You had sex before, didn't you?"

"Yes. But I couldn't. Not last night. Might not ever."

"Why not? What happened? If you don't mind me asking?"

Hope choked up and then she begin to cry. "I was raped."

Yvette moved her chair next to Hope's to hold her. "I'm sorry." She could hear and feel her young friend sobbing. "Do you want to talk about it? It might help."

Nicole joined them. The three women sat at the table, waiting for someone else to speak. "They…" Hope started to say. "They hurt me. They hurt me so bad." She buried her face on Yvette's shoulder.

"Who hurt you?" Yvette asked.

"I can't tell you."

"Why?"

When Hope did not answer Nicole spoke for her. "She's afraid that if Ruben found out, he would go after them. And he might get hurt."

"So, you knew about this?"

"She made me promise her that I wouldn't tell anyone." Nicole said in her own defense.

"So, you never went to the hospital or called the police or anything, did you?"

Hope slowly shook her head no.

"We need to report this to the police," Yvette said. "Also, we have to get you to the hospital."

"Isn't it too late for her to go to the hospital?" Nicole asked.

"I don't know," Yvette said. "The police will know. Maybe they will send Joan. I'll ask for her. She is someone you know."

"Please, please don't let Ruben know," Hope begged.

"But he needs to know," said Yvette.

"He will go after them. I know, and you know it too. Won't he? They are too big and too many. They will hurt him bad, real bad. They might even kill him. You have to promise me that you won't let him know what they did to me."

Yvette looked at Nicole then back to Hope and said, "We promise."

When the two officers, Joan Fisher and Jack Walker, arrived the last of the customers were leaving. The owners were in the office and Seth was closing down the bar, and the three women were sitting at the table in the back of the room. As the two officers approached Yvette and Nicole got up from the table and moved away. But they stood close enough to hear. Joan sat down across the table from Hope. "You were attacked?" Joan asked.

Hope nodded.

"Raped?"

Again she nodded.

"Was there more than one?"

Hope nodded and held up two fingers, "Two."

"Two men raped you?"

"There were three, but only two of them raped me."

"Did the other one help them? Did he hold you down or anything like that?"

"No, he didn't. They wanted him to join them, but he wouldn't"

"Do you know them?" asked the policewoman.

"Dick and Max raped me. The other one's is name is Lenny."

"Do you know what their last names are?"

"Lenny last name is Chopin. I think that one of them, probably Dick, is named Coldman, the other one I have no idea."

"When did the attack occur?" the Officer asked.

"Five days ago."

"Five days ago? Have you washed the clothes that you were wearing?"

"I wasn't wearing my clothes."

"You weren't wearing your clothes? You were naked?" Officer Walker spoke for the first time.

"No. Yes." Hope said as she looked up at him, then she turned back to the female officer. "I had on a negligee, but they ripped it off of me."

"Where did this take place?" she asked.

Hope reached in her purse and pulled out a business card that she handed to the officer. "Coldman Studio? Is this where it took place?"

Hope nodded her head. "I...I thought that I was going to pose for a painting. But they wanted me to be in an X-rated movie. They wanted me to have sex with them. And they were going to film me having sex and then they were going to sell it. Everyone in the world would see me having sex. Everyone would think that I am a whore. That would have killed my parents. I wouldn't do it. No way. I wouldn't do it. Have sex with them? In front of a camera? What kind of a person did they think I was, anyway? A whore? No. I wouldn't." She broke down and cried uncontrollably. Yvette and Nicole put their arms around Hope. After a while she continued, "I tried to fight then off, but it just made them madder and they raped me."

"Did you have any contact with them before that encounter?"

"Yes, but I had no idea what they were up to."

"How did you meet them?" Officer Fisher asked.

"Here. They were customers."

"And they asked you if you would pose for them?"

"No. Not like that. They said that Lenny was an artist. And I told him that I would like to have my picture painted. And he said that he would. He said that he would pay me to pose for him. I thought that I was going to have my portrait painted, not to be in a sex movie."

"By any chance did they pay you?" Jack asked.

"They give me two hundred before we started. They said that it was an advancement."

"That shouldn't matter," Yvette butted-in.

"It might make it harder to prosecute," he replied.

"You were told that this Lenny was an artist here at The Garden?" Fisher asked.

"Yes. Here. They were customers."

"Do either of you two remember those men," the lady officer asked the two waitresses.

They looked at each other and shook their heads. "I don't recall them," Yvette said. "But that doesn't mean anything. People come in all the time. We can't remember all of them, but if Hope said that she met them here then she met them here."

Jack took the business card and walked across the room, to the bar. "Does this mean anything to you?" he asked Seth as he handed him the card.

Seth studied the card then said, "Get-a-Way. Yes. Get-a-Way is the name of their boat. The big guy's boat. They were there on the night of Ruben's birthday." His eyes were fixed on Hope. "What did they do?"

"I can't say."

"What did they do? Did they hurt Hope?"

"Yes." Nicole said as she walked up to the bar. "They raped her."

"Raped?"

"Yes."

"That's the allegation she made," Officer Walker asserted. "She claimed that they attacked her."

"Just what in the hell do you mean she claimed!" Nicole growled. "If she said that those God damn bastards raped her, then they raped her. I saw the red mark on her face where they hit her. There is no doubt about it, those rat-ass-bastards raped her. Do your damn job. Go out and arrest those sons of bitches."

"It doesn't work that way," Officer Fisher said as she joined them. "Something like this we will have to get a warrant before we can arrest someone. That's why we first have to take her to the hospital."

"Hasn't it been too long for there to being any evidence left?" Yvette asked.

"I'm not a doctor, but it is necessary for the report."

After the officers and Hope left, Nicole said, "They won't arrest them. No, they will get a way, scot-free. That is something that you sure in hell can count on."

In the examining room Hope felt that it was surreal. Again her body felt as if it did not belong to her. It was only an extension of herself, and it was something that she no longer had any control over. As she waited for the doctor to return. She was reliving over and over the steps that brought her there. She questioned every decision that led her to the cold and impersonal examining room. Not only did she question her decision concerning the involvement with Coldman Studio, but questioned her actions that led to the separation from her family.

The doctor returned with a forced smile. She motioned for Hope to sit down. She took a deep breath and said, "We have the result of the test. It was positive. You're pregnant."

"Pregnant?"

"Yes. The result was positive."

"No. I can't be."

"I'm afraid so."

"How long?"

"When was you're last menstrual period?"

"About three weeks ago."

"Then you are less than three weeks."

"There aren't any ways to know who the father is now, are there?"

"Not now. It's too early, and it is too late for the morning after pill. You will have to have an abortion to terminate the pregnancy. You have two months. If you like, we can do it now."

"No. No. It would be wrong. I can't have an abortion."

"Do you realize that the father could be one of the rapists?"

"I know. God, I know."

When Hope and the doctor entered the waiting room they were greeted by Yvette, Nicole and the two officers. Hope was given a hug by the two women that she worked with, as the police officers were consulting with the doctor.

"What did they say?" asked Yvette.

"They..." Hope looked at the doctor. "She said that I am pregnant."

"Did they give you the Morning After pill?" Yvette asked.

"She said it was too late. I am pregnant and they cannot give a pregnant woman that pill."

"So, get an abortion." Nicole said.

"No. I'm not going do that."

"What? Why not?"

"Think about it. It could be the rapist. Do you want a child of a rapist? That will be your child forever." Yvette commented.

"It might be Ruben's."

"It might not be."

"You said that he broke-up with you. Isn't that what you said?" Nicole questioned her.

"Is that it? You want to have Ruben's baby? You think that if you are carrying his baby that he will come back to you?" Yvette said. "It doesn't work that way."

"That's for sure," Nicole added. "I know lots of girls that try that. And I can tell you it's not a good idea. They either won't marry them or if they do, it don't last long. Anyway, you will be stuck with the baby by your little old self. And that isn't anything you want, to be a single mom."

"That's true. Most men don't want an already made family. And you don't know who the father is."

"It is wrong," Hope said, defending her position. "My father always said that the greatest sin is to kill someone. And that is what abortion is, murder."

"But you said that you were done with him, didn't you?" asked Nicole. "What do you care what he thinks. He's not having your baby. You are."

"The Bible said it's wrong. And that is the word of God is it not? How the baby was conceived is irrelevant."

Yvette and Nicole looked at each other. They knew that they could not change her mind. "I think it is time for us to go, don't you?" Hope asked before they left the hospital in silence.

CHAPTER 20 ━━━━━━━━━━━━━━

"So, this is it?" the big Lieutenant said as he looked up from his desk, after reading the report. "Let's get this right. This young lady, what's her name? Hope? She had sex with two guys after they had paid her to make a porno film. Is that right, Officer Fisher?"

"She wasn't aware that it was for a porno," Officer Fisher replied, defending Hope, with Officer Walker by her side "She thought that she was going to pose for a painting. She is young and naïve, but that did not give them the right to rape her, did it, Sir?"

"No. It didn't. But we are going to have one hell of a hard time to get the District Attorney to prosecute them. There isn't any physical evidence, right? It is their word against hers, and they have those two bills on their side we need more. We need physical evidence. And we don't have any. And without any evidence the charges would probably be dropped at the arraignment."

"There might be," Officer Walker spoke up. "If it happened the way that she claimed, and I assume it did, then it might be on film."

"That's a possibility," the Lieutenant replied, "but don't count on it. If it was me, I would have gotten rid of it as soon as it happened. I wouldn't let something like that bite me in the ass."

"I don't think we are dealing with rocket scientists," said Officer Fisher.

"They might or might not be. They did make her wash away all of the evidence. Like I said it probably will boil down to her word against theirs, and I doubt that it will be good enough."

"I'm not aiming on letting Hope's rapists get away with it."

"Is this Hope Adamsen a friend of yours?"

"No, I wouldn't say a friend. An acquaintance would be a better word, not a friend. But I'm still aiming on making those scumbags pay for what they did to her."

"Officer Fisher, you have done your part in this case. It is time to turn it over to the detectives. We'll let them handle it."

"But…"

"You are not a detective. You are a patrol officer. Let's leave the investigation to the detectives. You're going to have to wait until you make detective, O.K.? Until then we are going to have to let the detectives handle it."

She look at the Lieutenant with contempt. "Yes Sir," she said as she started to leave without being excused.

"Officer Fisher, I do appreciate your feelings, but we have protocol which dictates that investigations are done by detectives. Do you understand?"

"Yes Sir," she said again before the two uniforms left the office. Once outside she told Jack, "They're going to get away with it. I know it. Those scumbags are going to get away with it."

A couple of hours later the lieutenant recalled the two assigned detectives back into his office. The senior one was Detective Long. He was a big man, both in height and in bulk. He was the only one in the precinct that always wore a red tie. It brought out the red in the hair, the little that was left, most of which had already turned gray. Under his wing they gave him Detective Newman. She was his quite the opposite from him. She was much shorter; she did not come close to reaching his shoulder. She always wore dark suits and no jewelry nor make-up. Her dark hair was cut in a boyish style.

"What did you find out so far?" the lieutenant asked them.

"The Coldman Studio is licensed under a Richard Coldman," Long said. "He has no criminal record. He is clean, and he is a member of the Coldman Foods family, the super market chain."

"So, we are dealing with money?"

"Yes Sir. Big time."

"Wealthy and properly well educated? It might be tough."

"I don't know Sir," Newman spoke up. "I don't think that we are dealing with Rhodes scholars."

"Don't underestimate them," warned the Lieutenant. "She left there with no evidence that she had been raped. It seems to me that they knew what they were doing. They might even be serial rapists, but I doubt it. This Dick Coldman guy might be a control freak. And that's why he did it. This Max guy just went along for the ride. But Lenny didn't. He is the one that I would go after. He might roll over on the other two. But without a film or Lenny's testimony there is not much of a case. But don't count too heavily on him testifying against his friends. You can bet that they have already got to him. That is why I'm telling you not to allocate too much of your time on this."

CHAPTER 21 ━━━━━━━━━━━

The mirror reflected the face of a woman that had undergone a transformation from an innocent young lady to someone whose image of reality had been shattered, overnight. Her hair was haggard and her face was drawn. Her youth had been stolen from her. She returned to her bed and for a long time she stared at the ceiling. Eventually her solitude was interrupted by a phone call. "Hello," she answered slowly.

"Hope, this is Yvette. I have just dropped the kids off at the school. So, what do you say? Want to get something to eat? It's my treat."

"I don't know. I don't feel like…."

"You are by Pulaski, right? Near Midway? I'll be there in about thirty, forty minutes."

"I…" The phone went silent before Hope could come up with an excuse for not going.

In a restaurant, some distance from Hope's apartment, she and Yvette were seated in a booth at the far end from the entrance. "What is good?" she asked the waitress, to see her response.

"Have you had breakfast yet?"

"Not yet."

"You might want to try the Eggs Benedict. The Hollandaise sauce is quite good. It's home made."

Hope scanned the menu for the Eggs Benedict to find the price. "I don't know. I never had that before." After she found the cost, she added, "It's expensive."

"I said that it is my treat," Yvette told her. "We both will have the Eggs Benedict."

"Would you like anything else?"

"Yea," Yvette answered. "I think that I will have some wine. Yes. I think that I will have some bubbly. Do you have any champagne split?"

"Yes, we do," the waitress answered.

"Do you want to join me?"

"I don't know. I am pregnant. It might hurt the baby."

"Do you think that one is going to matter that much?"

"I guess not. One shouldn't hurt. But, isn't it a little early to drink?" Hope replied.

"It's never too early. Besides, you're supposed to have champagne with Eggs Benedict." Yvette turned back to the waitress and said, "Gave us both a splits."

After the waitress left, Yvette smiled at Hope, trying put her at ease. "They say that one of the best ways to judge a restaurant is by their Hollandaise sauce. So, I guess we will find out how good this place really is."

"I guess so. But I have never had it before."

"Never?" Yvette questioned her as if she was her child.

"Never."

"Well, first time for everything."

"Everything?"

The way that Hope said 'Everything' took Yvette by surprise. "Look, Honey, it's just a saying. It don't mean that all bad things are going to happen. It just means that everything that happens, happens for the first time. Sure, lots of bad things are going to happen. I can assure you of that, but I can also assure you that there are going to be lots of good things to come your way too."

"Like what?"

"You have lots going for you."

"Sure, I got a car that is broken down, an apartment that I can't afford, and the only income I have is a part time waitress job. And the worst thing of all is that I am carrying a baby that I don't know who in the hell is the father." Tears ran down her cheeks. "I'm sorry, but I cannot feel that everything is going to be hunky-dory. I don't know if the father of the baby is a man who won't have anything to do with me or is a rapist."

"Don't you have a family that can help you out?"

"My family? My loving and understanding family? The ones who told me to get lost? Is that the ones that I should look to for help?"

"I know you are going through a rough time, but we all do. You have to hang in there." Yvette could tell that she was not having any influence on her. "I was once in a similar situation as you. No, I wasn't raped, but I was pregnant and single. So, I do know something about what you are going through. I know the feeling of isolation and guilt. Specially guilt. I'm Catholic. And no one is taught guilt like the Catholics. I once asked if Jesus was illegitimate. Sister Mary Beth did not find that funny at all." Yvette laughed which brought a smile to Hope.

The waitress returned with the wine. She poured the champagne into flute glasses. "Your order will be out soon."

As the waitress walked away Yvette raised her glass and tapped it against Hope's. "To better times."

"To better times," Hope said, half-heartily.

"I know that men can be bastards and life never is what we want it to be. You're never sure what's behind the next door. But that's life. Sure there are going to be some bad times, but you can count on the fact that good things lie ahead too."

"I know, but I feel like I'm trapped. I feel like running away. Running as far as I can, and never looking back, if only there was a place to run to. But there aren't any, are there? That is how you say it, 'that's life'."

The waitress brought out the Eggs Benedict. "More champagne?" she asked.

Yvette looked at Hope's empty glass and said, "Sure."

After the waitress left Hope asked, "So, what happened?"

"What happened?"

"Yes. What happened with the baby?"

"Well, that was Scott. Don't tell him that he was conceived out of wedlock."

"How old is he?"

"Sixteen."

"Sixteen? I think that he probably has already figured it out."

"Damn it. I always said that they shouldn't teach math in school," Yvette said. Then she smiled.

"So, you kept the baby?"

"Yes, I did. And Mike married me, and we are living happily ever after." She smiled as took a sip of the wine. "Oh, he says that he loves me and he would have married me anyway, but…sometimes I wonder. Would he have? Would I have? I don't know, and I will never know. But, we both felt like it was the right thing to do at the time. So, we got married. What is done is done. We have two more kids. We don't love them any more or less then we love Scott."

"Is that possible?"

"What do you mean?"

"I don't know. It's just that I don't see how you can love the one that forced you into a marriage the same as the others. That's all."

"That's all?"

"Well…..Yes."

"So, you think that you won't be able to love your baby? Is that it?"

"I always felt that the best thing that a woman can be is a good and loving mother, and the worst thing is a mother that does not love her children."

CHAPTER 22 ━━━━━━━━━━━━

When Hope got home there were the two detectives waiting for her. The older one asked her, "Are you Hope Adamsen?"

"Yes," she replied cautiously.

"I'm Detective Long. This is Detective Newman," he said as he held out his badge. "We are here to follow up on the charges that you made. Can we go inside to do this?"

Hope led the two detectives into her unkempt apartment. She felt embarrassed about the condition of it. "Excuse the mess. I haven't been feeling well lately. Usually it's not this bad."

"We're not here to inspect your home, but to follow up on your complaint," said Detective Long. "You stated that you were under the impression that you were going to have your portrait painted?"

"Yes sir that was what I thought."

"Was there any painting equipment there-any easel or canvas?"

"They said that they weren't painting that day. They were shooting a movie. They told me that they wanted to see what I would look like on film."

"You're been drinking, haven't you?" Detective Newman asked.

"I don't see what that has to do with anything."

"I agree," said Detective Long.

"If she's been drinking this early in the day, how reliable will her testimony be?"

"She is the victim, not the perpetrator."

"But, if she has a drinking problem…."

"Had you been drinking before you went to the studio?"

"No, but they did give me a beer."

"Was there anything strange about that?"

"Well, I was the only one that had a drink. They said that it would relax me."

"Did it?"

"I guess so. Come to think of it, it did. I don't drink much, but it seemed to have an effect on me."

"How?"

"I don't know. It made me feel like all of my cares went away."

"Ecstasy," Detective Newman proclaimed.

"Date Rape?" Hope asked. "Do you think that those damn bastards used Ecstasy on me?"

"It's a possibility," Detective Long replied.

"So, you think that is the reason why I was so willing to go along with them?"

"It could had been. The combination of alcohol and Ecstasy, especially with someone who doesn't drink much can make people to do things that they wouldn't normally do," Detective Long said. "Let's take it from the top. Tell us what happened, step by step. Be as precise as you can. You might find it to be embarrassing, but I can assure you that it isn't our intention. It is important that we have the facts. We don't want anything to come back and bite us. Do you understand?"

"But I already told the other officers everything."

"We know. But we need to hear it for ourselves. Do you understand?"

"Well, I don't really know where to start. I met them at The Garden. That is where I'm a waitress. This Lenny said he was an artist and would pay me to pose. I needed the money. So, I decided to take him up on it. I didn't know that they were making X-rated movies. I thought that he was going to paint my picture. I had no idea what they were up to. When I got there I didn't see any painting stuff. There wasn't any easel or canvas or anything like that, but there were cameras." For a few moments Hope was in deep thought. They let her mind dwell on the events that led to the assault. "He gave me money."

"Who did" Detective Long asked.

"Dick. He give me two hundred dollars. I didn't ask him for it. He just gave it to me. He asked me if I needed money and I said yes. And he gave me two hundred dollars."

"When was this?"

"When they gave me the beer."

"Before they had you to change?"

"Yes, Dick gave me the money and had me sign for it. He told me that it would be taken from my first pay check."

"Do you still have it?"

"No. I spent it."

"You should have kept it," Detective Newman told her.

"I brought food with it. What was I supposed to do? Go hungry?"

"You should have kept it. It was evidence," stated the female officer.

"I'm sorry. But I didn't have any food in the apartment. Was I supposed to go hungry?"

"Of course not," said Detective Long. "This Dick probably uses money as a tool. He manipulates people to do what they normally wouldn't. That way you would be more likely want to please him."

"They gave me a negligee. A small see through one. I left my underwear on, but they made me take them off."

"Couldn't you have said no, and just left?" inquired Detective Newman.

"No. I couldn't."

"Why not?"

"Because they had given her money. And there was no way that she could give it back," Detective Long said, coming to Hope's defense.

"I lost my job. I needed the money, and I still do. I didn't have any choice." She began to cry.

Detective Long started to put his arms around Hope, but he pulled back. "I know that this is hard, but it is necessary. Please continue."

"Well, I put on the negligee. And when I came out from behind the screen, they laughed at me. They told me to take off my under clothes, and I did. I had to. I had no choice. You understand, don't you?"

Before Detective Newman could speak, Detective Long said, "Of course. Please go on."

"They told me to get on the bed, and I did. When I turned around, this Max guy was standing there, naked. I knew then that it was supposed to be an X-rated movie. I wasn't going to be any part of it. I'm not a whore. I tried to get away, but they wouldn't let me. He held me, and Dick slapped me. He hit me hard-real hard. I thought that I was going to pass out. Then he ripped the negligee off of me. I was naked." She began to cry. "Max threw me on the bed and Dick raped me. When he was finished, Max did the same. Then they made me take a shower."

"Did Lenny rape you too?" Detective Long asked.

"No. He refused. When I got out of the shower he was gone."

"You shouldn't have taken a shower," Detective Newman said. "You washed away all of the evidence."

"I had to. They made me. They stood there and watched. They made me wash my privates for a long time. Dick said that I stunk, so I had to wash myself until it hurt."

"Was that it?" Detective Long asked. "Was there anything else that you can remember?"

"Yes, there was one thing that I thought was strange. He made me to drink lots of water. Dick said that it was for my own good. Like he really gave a damn about my wellbeing. He said they were teaching me how to be a woman, and if I tried to cause any trouble they would 'take care of me'."

"They were trying to remove any trace of the Ecstasy," Detective Long said.

"Can water wash-a-way the Ecstasy?" Detective Newman asked.

"Well, somewhat. It doesn't remain in the system very long-only a couple of days. And water will dilute it."

"They knew that water will dilute it?" Hoped asked.

"Probably."

"So you're saying that they were aiming on giving me Ecstasy all along."

"Yes. They could have," he said. "But it's hard to say for sure. Are there any other things they did?"

"No. That was it. I got dressed and left."

"Isn't there anything else that you can add?" Detective Newman asked.

Hope shook her head, no.

"You didn't give us much to go on," Detective Newman commented. "What we need to know is why you…."

"Thank you for you information. I can assure you that we will do our best to make them pay for what they did to you." Detective Long handed her his card and told her, "Don't hesitate to give us a call. We are on your side."

When the two detectives were outside Detective Long asked in an angry voice, "What in the hell were you trying to do? Make her think that we didn't believe her? She doesn't need that shit."

"I think that…"

"No! You don't think. There is no reason to make her feel that it was her fault that she was raped."

CHAPTER 23 ━━━━━━━━━━━━

"Where are you going?" Yvette demanded to know as her son was going out the door.

"Over to Jay's," Scott replied.

"Have you done your homework?"

"Yeah, Mom. It's all finished."

"Don't forget that this is a school night," she called after him from the front door.

"Don't worry, I'll be back before daybreak," he yelled back as he waved to her.

She smiled at his joke as she returned the wave. She watched him until he was out of sight. She remembered telling Hope that she loved all of her children the same, but she knew that it wasn't true. She loved them all, but Scott was special. He was the one true love of her life. Not her husband nor her other two children, but Scott. As she turned back to the living room, which doubled as a family room in the small house, her husband Mike was watching the baseball game on the T.V. in his work clothes while her youngest daughter Anna was at the computer. "Do you want dessert?"

"I'll have a beer," Mike replied.

"What are we having?" Anna asked.

"I don't know. How about a Sundae? Does that sound good?"

"With chocolate syrup and whip cream?"

"Yes."

"And cherries?"

"I think we are out of cherries." She turned to her husband and asked, "Hon, you're sure you don't want a Sundae?"

"How about combining the two and make me a beer float?"

"What do you want?"

"A beer will do."

"Go and get your sister," Yvette told Anna as she went into the kitchen for the beer. When she returned Anna was still playing on the computer. "I thought that I told you to get your sister."

"GAIL!" Anna hollered.

"Gee, thanks. I could have done that myself. Now go upstairs and get your sister."

Gail came to the head of the stairs, holding her cell phone. "What?"

"Do you want a Sundae?"

"I have to go. I'll talk to you later," Gail said to her friend on her cell phone as she bounced down the stairs.

As the three females of the house sat down to their ice cream dessert. Yvette could not help from noticing how much her oldest daughter had begun to develop. Soon, if not already, Gail would be the object of the boys' fancies. And the question was would she come to the same fate that Hope did? Would little Anna also being facing problems with boys and even men? Yes, it is a possibility that they might be facing the same anguish that Hope was going through. "You, both of you, are getting to that age when boys might try to take advantage of you."

"Mom," Gail laughed, "Is this the bird and bees talk?"

Feeling a little embarrassed, Yvette glanced at Anna. She was also laughing. "I'm not talking about sex. I'm talking about rape. It is something that might happen to you, both of you."

"What brought this on?" asked Gail.

"Nothing. It just that a girl can't be too careful, that's all."

"That's all?"

"Someone that I know got raped."

"Who?" asked Anna?

"You don't know her. She is a dining room waitress at work."

"Did she know him?" Gail asked

"Them. Yes, she knew them, well, anyway she thought she knew them."

"Are they in jail?"

"Not yet, but they soon will be. They know who they are, it just a matter of time. I just don't want anything like that happening to you two, that's all. Be careful and don't get yourselves in a situation that the same thing might happen to you. Even if you think that you can trust them, you still have to be on your guard."

"So, you're saying that I can't ever go out with a boy, because he might rape me?" Gail protested.

"Well, you're too young to date anyway. But what I'm saying is when you are old enough you still have to be careful. Not only when you're dating, but any time you might be in danger."

"If someone tries to rape me I would kick him between the legs," Anna boasted. "And then I will run away. That's what I would do."

"Sometimes it's not that easy," Yvette informed her daughter. "But if it does happen to you don't feel ashamed, and tell someone, tell me, tell Daddy, tell the police, your teacher or anyone. It doesn't matter who. Just tell someone of authority. O. K.?" Both of her daughters nodded their heads in agreement. But still she wondered if she got through to them.

CHAPTER 24 ───────────────

Without warning, the door to the Coldman Studio swung open. "Freeze!" Detective Newman yelled, standing next to her was Detective Long. They were accompanied by two uniform officers.

They were met with, "What the hell's going on?" the big man said as he stepped between the authorities and the couple on the bed, that were in a compromising position that was being filmed by a bearded man.

"Are you Richard Coldmann?" Detective Long said as he held up his badge.

The couple on the bed got up methodically and started putting on their clothes. The uniform officers stared at the naked couple. They gave each other a quick smile, while the young bearded man's eyes darted around the room, in bewilderment.

"Are you called Coldman?" Detective Long asked Dick. After the man nodded yes, he handed him a document. "This is a search warrant."

"A search warrant for what? We aren't doing anything illegal. We are licensed."

"Read the warrant. We are here to collect evidence on a possible crime that occurred here."

"What crime?"

"Rape," Detective Newman said quickly.

"Rape? Here? Max, did you rape anyone?"

"No. I don't need to rape anyone to get my rocks off," he replied as he was putting on his shoes.

"Tommy, how about you? Did you rape anyone?" The photographer did not answer. "Roxy?"

The young woman smiled as she was zipping up her blue jeans. She shook her naked breast towards the officers. "Do I look like a rapist? But if one of these good looking officers want to rape me it will be okay with me."

"Roxy is just a generous young lady. Always wanting to do her civil duty," Dick laughed. "You see, there isn't any crime happening here. We are all good law abiding citizens."

"Then you won't mind if we take a few things, will you?" Detective Long said.

"Be my guest, but I do want our films back."

"As soon as we are done with them."

"What's the matter?" Max snickered at Detective Newman "You need help to figure out how it is done?"

"You want to figure out how you're going to get your ass out of jail?" Detective Newman recoiled. "Then you better keep your damn mouth shut."

Detective Long smiled at her and said, "I don't think that I could have said it better myself." It was the first time he ever heard her using any profanity. He thought, 'Maybe there is hope for her after all.'

As the officers started to bag possible evidence Detective Long asked the bearded man, "So your name is Tommy?" He nervously nodded yes. "Lenny doesn't work here anymore?" he asked Dick.

"No. I had to get rid of him. I couldn't trust him. You couldn't believe a word that came out of his mouth."

"Why?" Detective Newman commanded. "You couldn't trust him to lie?"

"Now, that's not a nice thing for a pretty young lady like you to say?"

"You won't think that I'm so pretty when you're behind bars, will you?"

"First you will have to convict us of a crime," Dick said with a smile of confidence. "We never did anything wrong, and you won't be able to prove otherwise."

"We only started our investigation," replied Detective Long."

"So, you're going to try to railroad us. If you think that we are going to roll over and play dead then you are badly mistaken. You have no evidence on us, because there isn't any. All you have is the word of a whore who feels remorse or is trying to extort money from us. There are many real criminals out there, go after them. Don't waste your time with us."

"Thanks for the advice. We always hear what the ones that we are investigating have to say. I think we have everything," said Detective Long as they started to leave with two small bags.

"You will find that all of those drugs are over the counter," said Dick.

"Have a good day," Detective Newman said as they were departing.

"What in the hell was that all about?" asked Tommy after the officers had left.

"A little case of buyer's remorse," Dick explained. "Sometime it happens. After they make a movie they feel a little guilty. They don't want people see them as whores. So, they try to undo what they have already done. In this case, the little bitch hollered rape. Don't worry. It's no big thing."

"No big thing? I'm sorry. But, I'm on probation," Tommy said. "Guy has to watch his ass. I'm not going to go back in. I'm out of here.

CHAPTER 25 ━━━━━━━━━━━

"Someone at the door," Lenny said into the phone as the knocking grew to loud banging.

"Police! Open up!"

"You sure in the hell better keep your God damn mouth shut, if you know what in the hell is good for you." With that Dick hung-up.

As he opened the door he was faced with four officers, two plain clothes and two uniformed policemen. "Are you Lenny Chopin?" asked Detective Long.

"Yes," he replied, trying to hide his nervousness.

"We are investigating a rape of Hope Adamsen. We understand that you were present when it took place. Is that right?"

"No, no. I wasn't there."

"You weren't there? So you do know about it?" the Detective asked with an inquisitive tone to his voice.

"I don't know anything about a rape."

"But you said that you weren't there when the rape took place. It sounds like you know about it. How do you know? Were you there or not."

"I wasn't there."

"But you know about it, don't you? How do you know about it if you weren't there? Did they tell you about it?"

"I know nothing about any rape."

"Lying to the police is a crime," inserted Detective Newman.

Detective Long give her a butt-outlook. "What she said is true. It is a felony to lie to a police officer. Miss Adamsen stated that you were there when it took place. Where you there or not?"

"I think that I want a lawyer."

"A lawyer? You haven't been charged with anything as of yet."

"If you going to keep hounding me I want a lawyer."

"You aren't under arrest."

"Then leave."

"We have a search warrant. We are looking for a film that you made of the rape. If you want to cooperate then you won't have to worry about being charged with lying to the officer of the law."

"Go ahead and look all you want. You won't find a damn thing," Lenny said defiantly.

The police were just finishing the search of Lenny's home when Dick and Max arrived. "Sorry, but this is off limits. We are in the middle of an investigation," a uniform officer said.

"Well, well, look who we got here. If it's not the choirboys," Detective Long said. "Why are you here? Are you afraid that something might turn up? Something that a judge might find interesting?"

"We just stopped in to see how our old friend, Lenny, was doing. Can't a guy just stop by to say 'hi' to an old buddy?" Dick said with a smile and a hint of sarcasm.

"So, Lenny, my old friend, how in the hell are you doing?"

"I'm doing fine." the little man with a goatee said nervously.

"I see that these fine officers of the law are rearranging your place. I'm sure they will put everything back the way that they found it. Say, talking about finding things, did they find anything interesting?"

"And what would that be? A little movie?" Detective Long said as he stepped between Dick and Lenny. "Let me put it this way. You are getting awfully close to being arrested for interfering with an investigation, which happens to be a felony. Also the same goes with tampering with a witness. Do I have to spell it out to you?"

"Hey, we just stopped by to see how our old friend is doing. And now we are leaving," Dick said as he and Max departed.

On the other side of the street, the two waited for the police to leave. "Do you think that they found the memory clip?" Max asked.

"I don't know. I hope that he wasn't dumb enough to keep it in his apartment."

"Do you think that he might have?"

"Well, if he did hide it there, then you sure in hell can count on the cops finding it. You can bet your bottom dollar on that. That's for damn sure."

"Will that be it? I mean, if they find the clip are we facing hard time? We're going to have to do time because that bastard took that damn clip home."

"Don't go into a panic mode. Even if they do find the clip, it would still be our word against hers. Don't you remember that I gave her two hundred dollars, and she signed for it? We can say that that little bitch knew what she was getting into."

"No clip, no case?"

"That's about the size of it."

"You still here?" Detective Long said coldly as the officers were leaving. "Don't forget what I told you two, about interfering with our investigation."

"We wouldn't think if it," Dick answered.

As soon as the police were out of sight, the two men returned to the apartment. Lenny was at first reluctant to answer the door until he heard hard pounding. He knew what waited for him on the other side. He opened the door and was faced with two men that were bigger then he was. He did not say a word. He stood holding the door partway open.

"Aren't you going to invite your old friends in?" Dick said as he pushed the door open and they stepped inside. "My, my, they sure forgot to straighten-up before they left, didn't them? Don't worry, we are here now. See, you always can count on your friends. The police are never around when you need them, but we are, aren't we?"

"Yes, we are," Max agreed.

"You left without saying good bye. That did hurt my feelings."

"I know that you are the sensitive kind."

Dick laughed, "That's right, my little friend. I was afraid that you might have gotten sick or something. You know that I'm always concerned about your welfare. That reminds me, whatever happened with that little clip that you were shooting? You know, the one that you were shooting when we were having a little fun?"

"Don't worry. It's in a safe place, where it will stay, unless something happens to me. In that case it will automatically be turned over to the authorities."

"Now, it sounds like you don't trust us," Dick smiled as if he was playing poker. "Do you think we would do you any harm? Forget about that. You are fighting against wind mills. You have nothing to fear from us."

"I'm sure. But I think that I will hang on to the clip a little bit longer, if it's alright with you."

"Of course. And to show you that my heart is in the right place, I will offer your old job back. I'm assuming that you are a member of the vast army of the unemployed."

"That's right."

"Good. Then I will see you tomorrow."

Lenny watched the two men leave. He knew that Dick could not be trusted. He would be playing with fire. But he was faced with the monetary reality of that time, and that sometimes dictates one's decisions.

CHAPTER 26 ━━━━━━━━━━━━━━━━

On the stage in the lounge an old singer with his raspy voice was singing old ballads of forlorn loves. Songs that held special meaning for some of the ones that had come to listen to his performance. For he told of the sadness that they all harbored in their hearts. Each were unique, for each of them were individuals with their own stories, but at the same time they held the remembrances of the same heart breaks that bound them together. A few danced to the music, but most sat and listened as they nursed their drinks.

Seth watched as Hope approached Ruben, who was on the service station, with a drink order for the dining room. She smiled at him and made small talk, trying to win back his affection for her, but to no avail. Yvette also was observing. After Hope went back into the dining room, Yvette said to him, "Why don't you give her a break? It's obvious that she still likes you, only God knows why, and I would guess that you feel the same about her."

He gave her a disapproving glance as he took her order ticket. "I don't remember asking for your advice."

"That's right. You didn't. You don't ask for any one's advice, do you? Because you think that you know everything. But I can assure you that you don't. There's things, you don't know. Things about Hope that you don't know."

"What in the hell you mean? What things that I don't know?"

"That's not for me to say," she abruptly broke off the conversation as she took her drinks and headed towards the cocktails tables.

"What in the hell was she talking about?" Ruben halfway asked himself and halfway asking Seth. "What things I don't know?"

"She's just one of those people that always have to be right. Always have to have the upper hand. I wouldn't pay much attention to her. It's none of her business what goes on between you two. But maybe she is right about one thing. Maybe you should give Hope a second chance. She is a nice girl that does care about you."

Before Ruben could tell him that he did not know if he could trust her or not, Seth went to the other end of the bar to refill a customer's drink. Ruben looked towards the dining room and wondered if he might have been too hard on her. But still he had feelings of insecurity in their relationship, as he did in all of his relationships. His feelings for her had gone far beyond sexual desire, to the level that had left him in a state of vulnerability, a state in which he would no longer have a defense against being hurt if she ever would reject him. And what might that lead to? Back to that child whose father they took away to prison. Back to that emotional time that he had spent so much effort to leave in his past. The question was would he, could he, let Hope once again bring back that feeling of abandonment? Could this man with the tough exterior let himself be exposed to that kind of hurt again?

When the bar had a slowdown, Ruben told Seth, "Yvette always likes telling people what they should do-like her life is so damn good."

"Yeah, that's for sure."

"She thinks that she knows what I should and shouldn't do. Shit, I am not going to put up with that crap. I'm capable of thinking for myself. Only cowards let other people do their thinking for them. And I'm no damn coward. That's for damn sure. And I don't give a God damn who they are. Isn't that the way you see it?"

"That's the way I see it," Seth agreed with him. But at the same time he felt as if he was somewhat of a hypocrite. For deep down in his heart he knew that in his whole life he always had someone to tell him what he should do, or should not do; his parents, his teachers, his coaches and his church. There was always someone that determined what was right and what was wrong, for him. He had never been faced with that question before. Was he a coward that let others decide for him what was right or wrong? Did he or didn't he have the guts to determine on his own what was morally right or not? That was a question that he did not know what the answer was.

Seth watched his co-worker mixing drunks. This long hair, tattooed, younger man, who would be a better match for a bikers' bar than The

Garden. This uneducated man, sometimes even rude, this man who never finished high school, who often used poor English, this man who Seth always felt was inferior to himself, asked him a question that he did not have the guts to answer truthfully. Why? Maybe he was a coward. Maybe he did not have the guts to determine for himself what is morally right or not, and always relied on others, than on himself.

Chapter 27 ━━━━━━━━━━━━

In the Lieutenant's office, he was with the two detectives and an assistant district attorney. "This is Detective Long, and Detective Newman," the Lieutenant introduced them, "and this is Jacob Black from the D. A. office." When they shook hands he noticed that Detective Long's handshake was firm but not too firm, whereas when he shook Detective Newman's hand she was trying to over compensate for how she might be seen.

"I reviewed your report," Black said. "You stated that you were convinced that she is telling the truth, but there isn't any evidence. Is that the way you sum-it-up?"

"I'm afraid that's that it in a nut shell," Detective Long confirmed. "Hope Adamsen was naïve and she was desperate. She thought that she had an opportunity to make some money by posing for a painting, but what they wanted was for her to make porno. She had no idea what she was getting into. When she realized what was going on it was too late. She told them that she wanted out, but they felt that they had the right to do anything with her that they wanted to do, including raping her."

"You said that she received compensation."

"Yeah, she took two-hundred in advancement."

"That she kept it and did not give it back?"

"That's right, she needed the money for food stuff. But I am convinced that she is telling the truth."

"I'm sorry, but that doesn't sound like will be enough."

"But she is telling the truth," Detective Newman stated.

"I know, and my heart bleeds for her, but again, that isn't enough."

"You can try."

"Sure, we can try, but we will probably lose. And what will that get us? Nothing! It will only make us look bad."

Detective Newman came back with, "If you don't try then you will look bad."

"Look, the harsh reality is that we don't have the manpower to go after everyone that commits a crime. We would if we could, but we can't. Every time we lose a case it makes us look bad and they think that they can get away with anything. In this case there isn't enough evidence to bring charges against them. Look, this Richard Coldman is a member of the Coldman family, the ones that own the Coldman Supermarkets, right? They have the money for the best lawyers. Innocent as she may be, they will tear her apart. They will make her out to be a common whore who was trying to distort them out of more money."

"So, that's it?" Newman demanded to know.

"I am afraid so. Unless you can come up with some evidence, and I would say, at this late in the game, it's not likely."

"So, what do we do now? Go and tell her that her word doesn't mean a damn thing? That the men who raped her are going free, nothing is going to happen to them?"

"Sorry, Newman," the Lieutenant said. "The reality is that we cannot put all of the scumbags away, but sooner or later they will screw-up again. And when they do we will get them, but now we have to move on."

"So, who's going to have the job of telling her that she's not going to have her day in court?"

"I hate to inform you, Newman, but that is part of your job description."

Then the two Detectives got into the car, Detective Newman asked angrily, "What a bunch of bull? What are we supposed to tell her? That the D.A. thinks that she isn't worth the time and money to give those scumbags what they have coming to them? That sucks."

"Don't you think that I don't feel the same?" replied Detective Long as he pulled the car out. "But there aren't a damn thing that we can do about it. They realize that if they bring them to trial that they might lose, and that couldn't look good. Best thing to do is to let it go."

"We're sorry Miss Adamsen, but we don't really give a damn about you. We care more about how we look than about you."

"Look, we can't torture Chopin into telling where he's keeping the film, can we? Far as that goes, we don't even know for sure that there is a film, do we?"

"I think there is," said Detective Newman. "You could tell that he was lying. He just was too damn scared to say anything, right? Maybe we should have applied more pressure on him."

"Like a rubber hose," with that Detective Long ended the conversation.

Chapter 28 ━━━━━━━━━━

Detective Long looked at the young woman that stood in front of him. "Hope; we presented your case to the District Attorney, and they feel that at this time there is an insufficient amount of evidence to go forth with the case. I'm sorry"

"Is that it? They raped me and nothing is going to happen to them? They're going to get away with it? If it was her," she indicated Detective Newman, "they wouldn't get a pass, would they?"

"I'm sorry. I know how you must feel, but there isn't anything that we can do. Our hands are tied. They said that it would be your word against theirs. The jury might believe you, but that would not be enough for a conviction. There's just no evidence. And with the fact that you were paid will work against you."

"Nothing is going to happen to them?"

"Only if other victims come forth. I'm sorry."

"I'm very sorry, too," Detective Newman added.

Hope felt that she should thank them for their effort, but she could not. She held the door for the two officers and watched them descend down the stairs. She went to the window and observed them getting into their car and driving out of sight. Once again some one that she felt cared about her had been removed from her life, probably to never return. In their eyes, the eyes of the law, she was not a victim but only the accuser.

Again, Hope was alone, all alone; isolated from the world. The world that had no knowledge of her agony, she was suffering. How one dream after another had finished. Her dream of being a doctor, then being a nurse. The latter one was not only emotionally devastating to her but it placed her with a financial burden that was beyond her means. She felt that she did not have the support of her family nor the man that she loved. Now they had rejected her claim of being violated. She was the one who was guilty of lying, not the men that had raped her. She was the one that who must wear the scarlet letter for everyone to see. She was not only trapped in her apartment, but she was trapped by her feelings of vulnerability and guilt. And there was no way to escape, no place to run to, no place to be free from the chains of her burdens. She was filled with dispirit and guilt. She felt that she would be forever in a state of depression.

For a long time she sat all alone. She felt like crying, but no tears came. She was going to have a can of soup, but she did not have any appetite. She was tired, but she knew that she would not be able to go to sleep. She went into the bathroom to get an aspirin for her persistent headache. She poured an aspirin into her hand. Then she thought that one might not be enough. So she poured out another one. Then the ubiquitous thought of suicide crossed her mind again. No, it was not the first time. But she had always held out hope that things would be better. Now the possibility seemed to be too remote. She put the two aspirins back in the bottle. She then took a bottle of sleeping pills and poured them into her hand. 'Yes, these can make everything go away. No more being depressed, no more feeling shame and disgrace. Nothing will ever be able to hurt me again.' The thought of not being a part of the world gave her a sense of euphoria. And she never wanted those bad feeling to ever return again.

She put the sleeping pills back into the bottle. She surveyed her apartment then in a mechanical manner she began to put everything in order. First she took the dirty clothes to the laundry, then she washed the pile of dishes that were covering the sink and counter. After all of the dishes were put in their proper place she swept and mopped the floors and cleaned the windows. Then she retrieved the clothes and put them away.

On a plain envelope she addressed it, 'To My Family'. On a plain sheet of typing paper she began to write in long hand.

> Dear Mommy, Daddy, Chuck, Desiree and Andy:
>   I want you to know that I love you all so very much. I don't want you to feel bad, nor think that my passing was you fault. It is mine. I am sorry that I am weak, but no longer can I endure the pain that I've been suffering.

I have to make the pain go away. I hope that you will understand and forgive me. It is not your fault. It is mine.

Love through Eternity

Hope

On another envelope she wrote 'Nicole'.

Again she wrote a letter.

Dear Nicole;

I am sorry to burden you, but I know that I can count on you to notify the necessary people when you find my body. I want you to know that you are my only true friend. I want you to know that I do appreciate our friendship. Please be a friend to Ruben, for he will need someone to care for him.

Love,

Hope

At last, with sadness, she wrote on the third envelope the name of Ruben.

Dear Ruben;

You are the only man that I had ever loved. I want you to know that I was faithful to you. And I would always have been. I will love you through eternity.

Good bye my love, good bye

Hope

She took a shower then she put on a white night gown and bushed her hair. She removed the outer shower curtain and laid it over the bed, then she covered it with two sheets. She went back into the bathroom and took all of the aspirin and the sleeping pills. She unlocked the front door so Nicole would find her the next evening.

She lay down on the bed, between the white sheets. She heard the sounds of the city and it made her feel far removed from her childhood home on the farm in Wisconsin, the place and time that she wanted to return to. But she knew that it was impossible. As she approached her fate she wished that Ruben was here, holding her before she slipped into unconsciousness. In the distance there was a baby crying.

CHAPTER 29

The lower level of The Garden was divided into two parts. On the right side of the stairs was the Mediterranean Room. The employees nicknamed it 'The Hole.' It was decorated in the mold of a Greek garden, with a mural and replicas of statues of the Greek gods. On the other side were the maintenance room and the liquor room, along with a dumb waiter and the back stairs that led up to the kitchen.

Ruben had just finished vacuuming the Mediterranean Room and was wrapping the cord up when he heard someone coming down the stairs. It was Nicole. When they saw each other she began to cry as she ran and threw her arms around him. They had never been that close, even though he had once defended her. And now she was holding him tightly and crying. Instinctively, he put his arms around her.

"She….she. I'm sorry. She…I'm so sorry."

"Sorry about what?" Soon as the words came out a cold chill ran down his spine.

"Hope."

"What about Hope?" he asked slowly.

"She dead."

He let go of her and turned and walked away. She started to follow him, but stopped when he asked, "What happened?"

"Suicide."

"Suicide?"

"She took sleeping pills and aspirins. I'm sorry. I should have been able to see this coming, but I didn't. I could have done more for her. I know, I should have."

"Me too," he whispered.

"I found her. She was laying on the bed, like she was sleeping. She was just lying there. She left the door unlocked, so I would find her."

"Why? Did she leave a note or anything?"

"She left three. One to her family, one for me and one for you," she said as she removed his letter from her purse.

The reality of Hope's death began to set in as he read the letter. "It was my fault, wasn't it?"

"No. It is not your fault. That I know."

"How?"

"We talked. She told me everything. She told me about why you broke up with her. She wasn't cheating on you. She loved you. She loved you with all of her heart. That is the reason that she could not tell you that she was raped."

"Raped! She was raped? Who in the hell raped her?" Ruben said as he gripped Nicole's arm.

She twitched lose. "She didn't want you to know. And I'm not going to tell you now."

"Why?"

"Because, because she was afraid that you would go after them. And they would hurt or even kill you. That is the reason that I'm not going to tell you who they are. I lost one friend and I don't want to lose another one."

"More than one?"

"Yes. Two. That's all I'm going to tell you. Please don't ask me to tell anymore."

Ruben looked at the young black woman who just got through calling him a friend. That was something that he had never imagined would ever happen. But it must be true. She came to him to share her grief with him. He knew that that was what friends do-share their grief. But it was something that he had never known before, not even when his father left. Now, for the first time in his life he was sharing his grief with someone, and she was black. "Thanks for coming and telling me. You didn't have to."

"Yes. I did."

They wrapped their arms around each other and held tight for a long time, feeling the other one releasing their emotions. The first time they hugged Ruben felt uncomfortable, but the awkwardness had been replaced with a feeling of closeness. For a long time the two sat at a banquette table.

Both were studying each other's face, trying to find comfort, but little was to be found.

"I think that she fell in love with you on the first night that she worked here, but you were too blind to see."

"Fell in love with a mug like mine? That's hard to believe."

"Don't be silly, you're a good looking man. Besides looks have very little to do with it."

"That's why you had me take her home, so she could give me a birthday present." He watched her smile. "You know that you wasn't fooling anyone, don't you?"

"She was too scared to ask you, so I had to give her a little push."

"Did she ever thank you?"

"Every time she smiled when she mentioned your name."

"You were a good friend to her."

"And I'm a good friend of yours too."

They gave each other a long hug before Nicole departed. After he watched her walk back up the stairs, he read and reread the letter, over and over. And each time he read it his guilt grew greater. Was his jealousy the cause of Hope's death? Or was it the dirty bastards that raped her? Or both? The feeling of anger and guilt overwhelmed him.

CHAPTER 30 ———————

Two days later Ruben was called into the office for him a phone call. It was unusual for him to receive calls at his work. He answered by saying, "Hello. Can I help you?"

"Ruben?"

"Yes."

"This is Evelyn Adamsen, Hope's mother. I'm calling to let you know that her funeral will be Monday morning, at ten o'clock. It will be held at the church by the house. You will be there, won't you? I know that we departed on not the most pleasant circumstances. But it's very important that you come. Pleases come, won't you?"

There was a long silence, then he said, "I'll be there."

"Thank you. I'll be looking forward to seeing you again. I wish that it would be under more pleasant circumstances."

"Me to," Ruben said just before he hung up the phone.

"You are going to Hope's funeral?" June asked her employee.

"Yes, it is Monday. I hope that it won't be any problem with me taking off Monday. I can clean up Sunday night."

"Don't worry, we will be fine. You need to go, I wish that we could go with you, but we can't. You'll probably be the only one going from here. So give her family our condolences. We will send flowers."

"Of course," he replied, but he knew that facing the Adamsens would not be easy.

The question that he wondered about was why they wanted him to come, the one that led their daughter, in their minds, to a life of sin, which eventually caused her death.

That evening The Garden had the usual activity for a Saturday night. Throughout most of the evening the dining room was filled, and in the lounge a local blues band played. The employees displayed their usual professional manners towards their guests, but the death of Hope had taken the life out of servers. Her name was hardly spoken until they were sitting down for a night cap, when Ruben confronted Davy. "You do know that Hope was raped?'

"Of course."

"Who were they?"

"Davy!" Yvette yelled.

"Who were they Davy?"

"Davy!" Yvette repeated.

"Who were they?"

Davy glanced back and forth between Ruben and the others. "H-He's going t-to find out s-sooner or later."

"It was those three men that were in here on you birthday," Grant said. "The ones that were doing shots when Hope brought you the birthday cake. The ones you wouldn't have one with them? Remember? Well it was the two bigger ones. Now that you know, does that make you feel better? What are you going to do? Are you going to go out and beat them up? Or maybe even kill them? I'm sure that would be what Hope would have wanted."

"It's not your job to seek out justice. That wouldn't be justice, it would be revenge," Seth said. "Let the police handle it. It's not yours or anyone else's place-only the authorities."

Grant put his arm around Ruben's shoulder. "Look, we all feel bad. Maybe not as bad as you do. But we all do feel bad. I was told that you are going to her funeral. That's good. It will gave you closure. That is something that you do need."

"Are you going to the funeral?" Nicole asked.

"Her mother asked me to."

"Can I go with you?"

"Sure. Why not?"

"Where will we meet?"

"I don't know. I guess that I'll pick you up. Where do you live?"

"In Summit," she said as she wrote down her phone number and address on a napkin.

"I'll pick you up about six. It's a long drive."

"So, you going to go to a li-lily white little town?" Davy joked.

"Are you going to be an ass again?" Yvette asked.

"Again?" Grant inserted. "Has he ever stopped being an ass?"

"What is wrong with a small lily white town?" Nicole asked.

"Nothing," Yvette replied. "Not a damn thing."

"Xenophobia," Grant said. "The fear of strangers. People sometimes don't feel comfortable around strangers, especially if they are different than themselves."

"You saying because I'm black they will fear me? What in the hell are they scared of, that I will seduce their kids and give them black grandbabies?"

"They might," Grant responded. "Although I would say that you might be taking it a little bit to the extreme. But you might represent a change. There are all kinds of things that people are afraid of, and change is just one of them. You will represent something different. People are apprehensive about things that are different. Religion, politics and the changing of the status quo or anything else that might take them out of their comfort zone, including race. I can ensure you that it won't be like it was in the old South. You won't have anything to worry about."

"You're saying that I should go?"

"By all means, go. You can't let your fear of what people that you have never met before, might think dictate your action. If you do, then you would be exhibiting a form of xenophobia yourself," Grant smiled at Nicole. "She was your close friend. You need to go. You also need closure."

CHAPTER 31 ━━━━━━━━━━━━━━━━

In the open casket lay the lifeless body of Hope. It was all that remained of her. Gone were all of her hopes and dreams; the dream of marrying the one that she loved, and having children and watching them grow and also having children of their own. She was a person whose whole life had lay in front of her. And now it had all been taken away from her. Her soul had been removed from her body, leaving behind only her empty cold corpse. The world will have to continue without her.

In front in the first pew was her mother, Evelyn, who was watching friends and family entering into the church. They smiled in acknowledgment to each other, usually followed by a hand shake, before they took their places in silence. These were the people who had been part of her life. There were ones that not only knew Hope as a child, but some also had known her parents when they were children too. Others were her classmates and friends, all come to mourn the passing of Evelyn's daughter.

She saw Ruben entering the church, with him was a young black lady. She left her family and headed towards the back of the church. Each person seemed to feel obligated to stop and give her their condolences. She gave them an appreciative smile as she continued hurrying towards the couple.

She gave Ruben an unexpected hug. Then she told him, "I'm glad that you were able to make it."

"I told you that I would come."

"I know you did. And who is your friend?"

"Mrs. Adamsen, this is Nicole. She was a close friend of Hope's."

"Nicole." Evelyn took her out reached arms and pulled her into a hug. "You were the one that found Hope's body?" Nicole nodded. "She spoke highly of you. I got the impression that you were her only real close friend."

"We were best friends. I'm sorry that I didn't do more for her, Mrs. Adamsen."

"We all feel the same as you do. We will talk later. But for now come with me," she said as she took their hands and led them to the front of the church.

Ruben went to the open casket. His hands clinched the cold box that enclosed Hope's corpse, the box that would forever separate the two. He knew that soon the casket would be closed and she would be only a memory, and again he would be alone. Nicole joined him. For a few moments, together, they looked down at their friend. Then she took him by the hand and turned him towards the pews.

Next to the aisle sat Hope's father, Gene. He stared ahead with a blank expression. Beside him was his wife, Hope's mother, Evelyn. Then sat Chuck, who nodded at them. Desiree got up from between her two brothers and moved past Andy and stood on the outside. She motioned for Ruben to sit next to her. She gave him a hug and shook hands with Nicole.

The church became quiet when the minister started the service. He led the congregation in prayer. Nicole opened her eyes to see if Ruben was praying. He was staring at Hope's casket. She wondered what he was thinking. She could see his eyes tearing up. She squeezed his hand long and hard, but there was not any response. She wondered if her action was out if place. A moment later he returned the squeeze.

After the prayer every one stood and sang 'Amazing Grace'. Nicole saw the irony in the fact that her ancestors were slaves and the song that they were singing was written by a man who was a former slave trader. And she was standing next to the only one that was not singing. Was it because he did not know the song or was it because he did not share its sentiments? She remembered what he had said about religion-what seemed so long ago. Her feelings towards him had always been somewhat complex. But now she saw him in a different light-a man with deep feelings. A man who was not religious but still was highly moral in his own way, which in itself was a contradiction to her conception that all morals come from religion. She wondered if it was possible that she was falling in love with her best friend's boyfriend at her funeral, and would that not make her unmoral?

The minister started the eulogy. "We are gathered in the house of our Lord to acknowledge the passing of one of our own. Our beloved Hope

Marie Adamsen, who was taken from our midst much too early. For this we feel great sorrow. The deeper the love the greater the hurt."

After all the sandwiches and the cakes had been consumed and the last of the condolences were given, one family at a time, the mourners were leaving the Adamsen's home. Each of them were thanked for coming, the only two that were left were Nicole and Ruben. "I'm glad that you were able to find it in your heart to come," Evelyn said as she motioned them to the dining room table.

"Andy, don't you have something to do outside?" she said to her youngest son.

"Why?"

"Because we have something that we need to discuss with Ruben that doesn't concern you."

"Is it about Hope? Then it concern me. She is my sister."

After a moment of silence Gene said, "He is right. He does belong here."

"But he's too young," she answered back.

"He has the right to know."

"Very well," she conceded, giving her husband a disapproving look. "Ruben….I don't know how to put this delicately, but we do know that you had relations with her, in a marital matter. Were you the only one?"

"What! What kind of question is that? He responded.

"I'm sorry, but we need to know."

"He was the only one," Nicole jumped in before Ruben could speak. "If there was anyone else then I would have known. He was the only one."

"That is true. I was the only one before she was raped."

"Raped!" Andy said loudly. "Hope was raped and no one thought that I had the right to know."

"Andy! Please don't interrupt. We are discussing something else now," Evelyn told him.

"Why do you ask?" Ruben replied.

"Because we believe that you have the right to know that she was carrying your child." A silence fell over the house as they looked at Ruben's stone face. "I'm sorry," Evelyn said with tears in her eyes. "I wish that I didn't have to tell you this, but you have the right to know."

Ruben took a deep breath then he said, "Thank you for telling me."

"Who did it?" Chuck demanded to know as he stood up from the table.

"Why? So, you can go and beat them up? Or kill them?" Evelyn said. "Or be killed. I lost a daughter. I don't want to lose a son too."

"Them?" Andy asked. "There were more than one?"

"There were two." Nicole answered.

"Do they know who they are?" Chuck asked.

"Yes."

"Are they in jail?" Andy wanted to know.

"No," Evelyn told her youngest son. "There wasn't any evidence. Only her word against theirs. They said that they felt that the judge would say there wasn't enough evidence."

"You mean that those scumbags are going to get away with it! They raped her and drove her to suicide and nothing is going to happen to them?" Chuck demanded to know, as he stood up, although he already knew the answer. "I won't let that happen. I'll break their God damn necks. When I get done with them, there won't be enough left of them to throw into jail."

"No you won't!" Ruben said as he stood up and faced Chuck. "I will."

"She was my sister."

"She was the woman that I loved. And she was carrying my child. I think that that trumps you."

"No! No!" Evelyn nearly yelled. "I won't hear of it. There won't be any revenge in Hope's name. Not now, not ever." She looked at Chuck then at Ruben and said, "I want you two to promise me that you won't go after them."

"I'm sorry, but I have to do what I have to do. I've got to make it right by Hope." Ruben spoke as a man of resolve.

Out of frustration Evelyn turned to Gene, "Don't just set there. Say something."

"What do you want me to say? Let their transgression go unpunished. No. It is wrong to let criminals get away with their crimes. If the law of man won't be just, then it is necessary to take other measures to bring about justice."

"That's what I say," Chuck agreed. "I will go with you. We will teach them a lesson, one that they won't forget."

"I'll go with you too," Andy said with both anger and with enthusiasm. "We will beat them up. Yes, we will. We will beat the snot of out them. Yea, that's what we will do, beat the snot out of them."

"Andy!" Evelyn scolded her son. "You aren't going to beat up anyone." She looked at the others and said coldly, "None of you are going to take the law in your own hands. That's not how we do things. That's not who we are. I don't want to hear any more of this talk of revenge. Is that clear?"

Chuck and Andy reluctantly sat back down in submission. But Ruben removed himself from the table and started walking towards the door, with Nicole following. He stopped and turned back when he heard Evelyn ask, "Have you put this foolish talk about revenge out of your head?"

"Call it whatever you want, but I can assure you that Hope will get justice."

"Promise me that you won't kill them," Evelyn demanded.

"I promise that I won't kill them," Ruben replied.

"Or hurt them."

"I don't make promises that I might not keep."

CHAPTER 32 ━━━━━━━━━━━━━━━

Ruben waited outside of an office building in the cold rain, because the door had a buzzer, he had to wait until someone opened it. When a woman was exiting he yelled, "Hold the door!" She responded by obeying, holding the door open for him. They exchanged smiles as they passed in the doorway. He found Coldman Studio on the directory. He took the elevator to the fifth floor where he knocked on the door.

Max opened the door and looked at the man who now had crew cut hair. He looked familiar, but with the short haircut he could not place Ruben. "Yes? Can I help you?"

"I'm here to let you know that Hope Adamsen is dead."

"Hope Adamsen?"

"Yes. Hope Adamsen, the girl that you raped. Because of that she committed suicide. You bastards killed her."

"I'm sorry about your friend, but we didn't rape anyone," Dick said as he approached the two men.

"If she is dead then the police will leave us alone," Max said with smile of relief.

Max smile was interpreted as being mocking. It magnified all of the anger that had been raging inside of Ruben. He released all of his fury in one mighty blow to the face of Max. The blood spattered as Max fell backwards onto the floor. Dick charged the intruder, but Ruben side kicked him in the gut, bending him over. Ruben grabbed his head and pulled it down at the same time he brought his knee up, smashing the bigger man in the face with great violence breaking his nose, and falling to the floor. Max stumbled to his feet and rushed Ruben with head down. Ruben side stepped him and threw him against the wall. Dick got back to his feet and charged and was again stopped by a massive amount of blows to the head, sending him back to the floor. Again Max rushed Ruben. This time he was stopped by being kicked in the head, sending him to the floor, next to Dick. As Ruben was facing the two bloody men, he was not aware that Lenny had entered the room. He picked up a chair and slammed it across Rubens' back. The blow knocked him to the floor. Before he could recover the two bloody men began to viciously kick and stomp him with brutal revenge. Long after he had become unconscious they continued kicking him.

"Stop it! Stop it!" Lenny yelled as he tried to pull them away from Ruben. "If you don't stop you will kill him. We will be facing murder charges. And I don't want to go back to prison. You might not give a damn, but I sure in the hell do."

"No damn bastard comes in here and attacks me without getting his ass killed," Dick said as he kept kicking Ruben.

Lenny grabbed Dick and spun him around. "Stop and think. What in the hell is going to happen? If he dies, what in the hell's going to happen? They're going to charge us with murder. They probably will get a conviction." he said as he tried to stop Max from kicking Ruben.

"A guy has a right to defend himself."

"Not to be beaten a man to death, he doesn't."

"I don't give a God damn if he dies," Max said as he continually tried to kick the lifeless body.

"You're a damn idiot."

"He's right," Dick said. "They would love to have the chance to pin a murder rap on us."

"We going to let him get away with attacking us?" Max scorned.

"Yes. That's right," Dick said. "It's over. He won't bother us anymore."

"What in the hell are you doing!" Max yelled at Lenny.

"Calling 911."

"You're calling the cops?"

"I'm calling an ambulance."

"You damn fool!" Max cried out as he lunged for Lenny's phone. "They will call the cops."

Guarding his phone, Lenny told him, "The cops will find out sooner or later."

"He's right," Dick stepped in. "Let him make the call. It might put us in a better light. We might need all the help that we can get."

CHAPTER 33 ━━━━━━━━━━━━

In a panic, Lucy rushed into the emergency room. "Where is my son?" She demanded to know from the nurse at the reception desk.

"What is his name?"

"Ruben, Ruben Garcia. I was told that he was here."

"Are you related to him?"

"I'm his mother. Are you going to tell me where my son is?"

"He is in the operating room."

"Is he going to be alright?"

"The doctors are doing their best. I can assure you of that."

"Can I see him?"

"When they take him to the recovery room. Have a seat. We will you let know his status as soon as we know."

"What happened to him?"

"I don't know. Maybe the policeman can help you."

Until then Lucy was not aware of the officer. She asked him, "Do you know what happened to my son?"

"All that I can tell you is that he was in a fight."

"A fight?"

"That is all that I know. I'm sorry."

"We will need you to fill out some papers. Does he have any insurance?" the receptionist asked.

Lucy shook her head 'no' as she took the forms and a pen and she took a seat. She was in the company of others who were also waiting; waiting to be seen by a doctor or waiting for someone to return. For her the wait was long and atrocious. The minutes became hours. The faces around her kept changing-still they were all the same-faces of agony and stress-agony because of the pain, and stress because of what might lay ahead. She became hungry, but she was afraid to leave the room for there might be news of her son and she would not be there to receive it. Her fear alternated between concern for her son and concern for herself. Without Ruben she might not be able to afford the apartment. Even the bare necessities would be hard to come by.

"Mrs. Garcia," A nurse called out.

"Yes. That's me."

"Will you came with me?"

"How is he?"

"That is something that you will have to discuss with the doctor, but I can tell you that he is out of the operating room. He is in intensive care." Lucy was led to a small waiting room, where the nurse told her, "The doctor will be with you soon," before she departed.

A doctor, wearing scrubs, entered the room. "Are you Mrs. Garcia?" She nodded. "I'm Doctor Morris. I'm head of the E.R. and I was the principal surgeon for you son. I regret to tell you that he suffered severe injuries. He had five broken or cracked ribs. One of them punched his right lung. He also has a broken left hand and a broken nose. His right fibula was also broken. He had lesions to his face. Our plastic surgeon, the one who did the facial work, feel that his scars in time won't be that noticeable."

"He will eventually be alright?"

"I would like very much to tell you yes, but he has sustained severe head injuries. He took several blows to the head; mainly to the frontal lobe, the front part of the brain. As of now we have no way of knowing the extent of the damage. It might be minor or it might not. You must prepare for the worst and hope for the best. He also has suffered internal injury. Mrs. Garcia, I must inform you that your son did not came out of the anesthesia." He saw the horrified look on Lucy's face. "But as of now he is in a coma."

"A coma?"

"It's not unusual for a patient with a frontal lobe injury to go into a coma. It gives the brain time to heal."

"How long?"

"No way of knowing. He might wake up tomorrow and then it might be a long time."

"Never?"

"That is a possibility, yes. But more than likely he will recover. He did suffer severe trauma to his head. It might take some time before he will recover. But there aren't any reasons to think that he won't. We have to have faith that he will recover."

'Is he saying that he will be okay or is he saying that he won't,' she wondered. "Can I see him?"

"Sure, but only a few minutes as long as he is in the I.C." She nodded. "I must warn you that right now he will not be pleasant to look at, but in a few days the swelling will go down and he will turn back to his normal color."

As Lucy entered the room she saw a nurse standing in front of the bed, blocking her view of her son. She walked next to nurse to see Ruben lying on the bed. He was covered with bandages with an I.V. attached to him. The doctor tried to prepare her for what she was going to see, but nothing could have prepared her for the horror of seeing her son under that condition. Under the bandages she could only see a small part of his disfigured face. "Oh my God! What did they do to you!" she cried. She began hyperventilating. "Why would someone do this?" she asked the nurse. "What kind of monsters are they? I hope to God that they will spend eternity in Hell for this."

CHAPTER 34 ────────────

In a cool sterile room that was filled with the lingering smell of disinfectant was where Ruben lay. He was unaware of his surroundings. He was unaware of the I.V. or the monitors registering his heart beat and other vital signs. Nor was he aware of the medical staff that were caring for him. Nor was he aware of the visitors that came every day, talked to him or read to him, in the hope that he might respond. His mother, Lucy, came and sat by his side. There was another one that came nearly every day. She was Nicole. She would spend long hours by his side reading to him. She did not know what kind of books he preferred but she was told that it did not matter. It was the sound of her voice that counted. So, the selections were romantic novels. Sometimes, when no one was around, she would rub his hand and talk to him about everyday things. But there were other times she would share her most intimate feelings. The feelings that she could never be able to express to him if he was conscious.

The hours became days and the days drifted into weeks. Then one day it was over. He awakened from the coma. The bright light hit Ruben's eyes. As soon as he had opened them he closed them again. He was engulfed in pain. When he inhaled a sharp pain penetrated both of his sides. He felt the bandages that covered his body. He slowly reopened his eyes again. As he looked around he saw a room that was filled with medical equipment. Among them were an I.V. that was attached to his arm. He wondered how long he been there? And what had happened to him to put him in the hospital? Then he spotted Nicole sitting and reading a book out loud. It seemed strange for her to be here, especially reading out loud. But then everything seemed strange. "Good Morning?" he said to her, not knowing the time of the day.

Nicole jumped up with her mouth open, dropping the book onto the floor. "Oh, my God! Thank you Lord Jesus, thank you," she said as she took his hand and held it against herself. He could see the tears running down her smiling face. "I'm so glad that you are awake. They said that you might not ever wake up. But I prayed. I prayed to Lord Jesus. I prayed all of the time. And Jesus answered my prayers." She kissed his forehead and she looked at his lips, but she did not kiss them.

The questions that were foremost on his mind were replaced with does Nicole really care for him that much? Was there a relationship between them that he could not remember? He ran his tongue over his rough lips. He discovered that he was missing some teeth. 'Am I too hideous to be kissed?' he wondered. "How long have I been here?" he asked with a slur.

"Three weeks."

"Three weeks?"

"Yes. Three weeks and one day. That's a long time. But you're awake now. And that is what counts, isn't it?"

"Have you been here all of the time?"

"Not all the time," she smiled. "But someone needed to be here."

"They do have nurses here, don't they?"

"They have other things to do. They can't watch you all of the time."

"In the last three weeks, how many days didn't you come?" he smiled.

"Maybe four."

"Thank you."

"You're welcome. I didn't have anything better to do."

"How did I get here?"

"In an ambulance," Nicole replied as she pushed the nurse call button.

"No." A sharp pain pierced his side when he laughed. "No. I mean, what happened? Why am I here?"

"You don't remember?"

"No. The last thing that I recall was having coffee and toast."

"When was that?"

"The morning after we got back from Wisconsin."

"That was three days before it happened."

"What happened?"

"We can talk about that later. Now, what is important is to get you well."

"Don't I have the right to know what happened to me?"

"That's what got you here in the first place. Sometimes it's better to let things slide."

"Honey, go ahead and tell him. He's going to find out, sooner or later," said a nurse who had just entered the room. She studied the monitors. "You look like you're out of the woods, but you're going to have to be more selective in who you fight."

"Is that what happened? I got my ass kicked?"

"It was those guys that raped Hope." Nicole watched Ruben's face turn to stone. "You have to let it go. Promise me that you will let it go."

"I don't make promises that I might not keep."

"That is the same thing you told Hope's mother, and look where it got you. Do you want that to happen again?"

"You friend is right," the nurse added. "The next time they won't bring you here. They will take you straight to the morgue."

After the nurse left the room for a long time the two did not speak. But they remained holding hands. "In those days that I cannot remember, did something happen?"

"What do you mean?"

"You know. Between us. Did we?"

"Did we do what?" she teased.

"You're not going to let me know if we did anything or not."

"Do I look like that I'm the type of girl to kiss and tell?"

Detectives Long and Newman entered the hospital room. "Well look here. The police show up before my dear old mom."

"Yes. We hear that you woke up from your little nap. So, we hurried over fast as we could," said Detective Long.

"That was sure nice of you. You can put the flowers on the table."

"I'm sorry, but the flowers slipped our minds. Maybe next time. But for now, we need you to tell us what happened."

"I would love to, but I can't."

"You can't or you won't?" demanded Detective Newman.

"I can't. I don't remember a damn thing. The last thing that I recall I was having coffee and toast three days before the little mishap. So, if you want me to tell you about how I made my coffee and toast, that I can do, because that was the last thing that I do remember."

"Your friends said that you were in a bad mood. You broke their noses," said Detective Long.

"So, I got in a lick or two," he said with a slight smile.

"That you did, but it looks like you forgot about the third guy. He must have hit you with a chair. There was a bent one at the scene."

"I'm sorry that I only broke their noses, but I think that they might have done a little more than that to me."

"So you admitted that you attacked those men," Detective Newman demanded to know.

"I don't admit to a damn thing. Look Lady, I said that I don't remember a damn thing that happened. So, how in the hell can I confess to something that I cannot remember? You can't be that God damn dumb, can you?" He turned to Detective Long and said. "I want a lawyer. I want a good lawyer. Not one of those damn rookies that just got out of law school. I want someone that has been around the block a time or two."

"We can't get you a lawyer because you aren't under arrest, and we aren't the ones that pick the lawyers," said the senior detective.

"We're still getting the pieces together to get a clearer picture of what happened. When we do, we'll…." Detective Newman was interrupted by Detective Long.

"Look Kid, we are just trying to sort things out. That's all. We aren't out to get you. I don't know if I wouldn't have done the same as you. So, with that note, we will wish you a speedy recovery."

""I hope that you don't mind if I don't walk you to the door."

"Are you related to Russell Garcia?" he asked.

"Why?"

"Are you?"

"He's my father. Why?"

"No reason. I just remember him, that's all."

As the two officers started to leave Lucy entered the room. The two detectives watched as she went to her son's side. "My poor son, I'm so glad that you are awake. How do you feel?"

"Not too bad," he said as he tried to hide his pains.

"Is he going to be alright?" she asked the two officers.

"Sorry, but we aren't doctors," Long replied.

"No, Mom. They're old friends of mine. They just stopped in to see how I'm doing. Isn't that nice of them?"

"Yes, it is. If you say so." She turned to them and said, "I am Ruben's mother."

"Glad to meet you. I'm ….Dan Long. And this is my friend, Emily. I'm sorry, but we have to check on a couple of his old friends."

"You look familiar. Have we met before?"

"Yes, I believe that we might have, a long time ago. And I would love to stay here and try to remember when we met, Lucy. But, as I said, we have some old friends to see. So, good day."

After the two officers left the hospital room, Lucy asked, "How did he knew my name?"

When the two got back to the car Detective Newman confronted her partner, "Why did you interrupt me? He needed to know that we meant business."

"I think that he already knew that. He was ready to lawyer up. In the South they have an old saying, 'you can catch more flies with honey then you can with vinegar'."

"He assaulted two men, and you want to play nicey nice with him? He's a criminal."

"Those men that he assaulted that we are talking about are not what I would call innocent. What they got was only a fraction of what they had coming to them."

"That's not the point."

"That is the point. Let's face it. They got what they deserved. When the jury finds out why he did what he did they will recommend him for a Purple Heart?"

CHAPTER 35 ━━━━━━━━━━

Much to Ruben's surprise, the next day Evelyn and Desiree came to the hospital. "How do you feel?" Evelyn asked as she set a bouquet on the table.

"I'm going to live. Nice of you to stop by."

"We were in the neighborhood," Desiree said with a smile.

"Mom, this is Mrs. Adamsen. She is…was Hope's mother and her little sister, Desiree."

"I'm sorry about Hope. She was just a lovely girl. She was so young too. What a shame. A beautiful little thing like that."

"Thank you for your concern," Evelyn said to Lucy. She turned to Ruben and said, "I can't help but feeling that I am somewhat responsible for the awful thing that happened to you. I shouldn't have told you that she was with child."

"She was pregnant?" Lucy said as if she was surprised.

"You were right. I had the right to know. It's not your fault that what happened. It's mine."

"I still feel bad."

"Don't. I'll be out of here soon, I'll be good as new."

"They're going to send him home in a day or two," said Lucy. "I don't know what I'll do. I have to work."

"I'm a big boy. I'll be able to take care of myself."

"I don't see how. You can barely move. They are kicking him out because we don't have any insurance. If we had insurance then they would keep him until he is well. That's how they are."

"I will take care of him." With those words everyone looked at Desiree. "Why not. School is out now and Daddy is selling the farm. I have no reason not to. After all, he got hurt on Hope's behalf. We owe him."

"We will have to see what your father has to say."

"Mom, it's my decision. I don't know if you have noticed, but I am a big girl now. I can take care of myself."

"Where would you stay?"

"With them."

The next day a man in a pin striped suit entered Ruben's room. "Excuse me, but are you Ruben Garcia?"

"Who's asking?"

"If you are, then I'm here to represent you. I'm Ire Greenfield, Attorney at Law."

"You a public defender?"

"No. I'm a criminal and civil lawyer. You have a friend that sent me."

"A friend? What friend?"

"He wishes to remain anonymous."

"Well, I'm glad that I have at least one friend. How much do you charge?"

"My rate is five hundred per hour."

"Five hundred? Nice meeting you, but here is the door. Don't let it hit you in the ass on your way out."

The lawyer laughed. "I'm taking your case pro bono."

"What's that?"

"Sometimes we take on a case for no charge."

"You're shitting me, aren't you? Nothing?"

"Nothing?"

"How do we know which side you are really on?" asked Nicole.

"Sometimes it is best to look a gift horse in the mouth," added Lucy.

"That's a fair question. But I can assure you that I would never be that big of a fool. I would be risking everything. Not only would I lose my license, I would be sentenced to jail for obstruction of justice. I owe a favor. This is the pay back."

"To who?" Ruben asked.

"That's not important. Let's just say that we have a mutual friend and leave it at that, okay?"

CHAPTER 36 ━━━━━━━━━━━━━━━

"My father didn't love me," Lucy mumbled as the man brought another round back to the table, which was covered with beer bottles and glasses with the remains of gin and tonics. "That's right," she said with a slur. "He really didn't, you know?"

"I know what?" the man asked with a puzzled look on his unshaven face.

"That he didn't love me."

"Who in the hell are you talking about?"

"My dad, Daddy, Daddy O, Pops, what in the hell you want to call him. What you call your dad?"

"Nothing. I never knew him."

"He didn't love me."

"Do you still live with him?"

"Hell no. He's dead. Been dead a long time. I'm not going to live in a grave yard," she laughed.

"Then what in the hell does it matter?"

"You don't know a God damn thing, do you? You keep buying me drinks, but you don't even know my name, do you?"

"Lucy."

"Who told you?"

"You did."

"I did, did I? I don't know your name, but then it doesn't really matter, does it? You're the just the nice man who's buying me drinks. I'll call you Drink Buyer. Say Mr. Drink Buyer, why are you buying me drinks? Are you trying to get laid?"

"Are you?"

"That is not something you ask a lady, but it is a damn good question. A damn good one. You know, I would like to get laid. Yes, I would. I haven't got laid in a long time-years. My husband's been in prison for the past eight years. That's a hell of a long time." She studied the man's face, trying to figure what he must been thinking. Was he disappointed in the fact that she had a husband and he might not have sex with her? "I'm sorry, but I can't have sex with you. I'm married."

"He's in prison, He won't know." He put his arm around her.

"That is true, but I will know. And that is a God damn shame. I must go home and take care of my son. He just got out of the hospital."

"Why was he in the hospital?"

"Got beaten up, real bad. He was in a coma for a long time-three weeks. That is a long time. But he's home now. I have to take care of him. And that, Mr. Drink Buyer, is why I can't have a one night stand with you, although it would have been nice." Lucy finished her drink, got up and patted the man on his shoulder. "I have to go now. Thank you. You're a real gentleman," she said before she staggered out the door.

The bright sun blinded Lucy. She tried to get her bearings. Nothing seemed familiar to her. When she was going home the bus came to her stop, but she just stayed on it. She knew that she should have gone straight home to Ruben, but that day, at that time she felt a need to put off her obligation. The bus drove on, passing one block after another. Soon she was out of her neighborhood. She was still on a street that was familiar, but one that she never paid any attention to. On that day she looked out of the bus window at the shops that lined the street. With the passing of each of the storefronts she felt that they represented something that she could not have, something that was beyond her reach. She felt that she was trapped in a life that offered very little. When the bus stopped in front of a tavern with neon lights that announced the beers that were being offered. The signs beckoned to her, and she answered the call. Now she was faced with the reality of not knowing where she was or how she was going to get home, for she did not have any cash left. Standing on the side of the street, the intoxicated woman was not even sure which direction was her home.

"Are you lost?" came a voice from behind her.

She nearly fell down as she was turning around. "Well, Mr. Round Buyer." She wanted to say something more but what it was had escaped her. "I think that I might have had a teeny-weeny bit too much to drink." She held her hand up to illustrate the excess that she might have drunk.

"Can I take you home?"

"Whose home? Yours or mine?"

"I think yours."

"But I don't want any funny business. I'm a lady. A married lady."

"I can assure you that I'll be a gentleman."

"As long as you give me your word as gentleman, an officer and a gentleman," she laughed. "You may take me home."

When they reached the address that Lucy gave the man he drove onto the driveway. "Don't park here," she told him, which he obeyed.

"Do you live here?"

"I used to. Long time ago, in another life. It was so nice. I didn't think so back then, but it was nice." She looked at the gentleman to see if he was listening. "I was living here with my husband, Russ, and our son, Ruben. He was such a good boy. He never got into any trouble or anything. He was a good boy. That's what he was - a good boy, until they took his father away. Then things changed. We had to sell the house and move away. Away from all of our friends and everything. I didn't want to, but I had to. We had to leave our house, our friends, our life behind. If I had one wish it would be that we were still living here, the three of us. Do you think that will ever happen again? Sometimes I don't think so, but maybe."

CHAPTER 37 ────────────

"Gentlemen, I'm Ira Greenfield and this is Jan, my paralegal," he said as he looked at the four men setting across the conference table "I assume that you are Arthur Banks?"

"You assumed correct," the short and plump man in a three piece suit said as he reached across the table to shake hands. "These are my clients; Richard Coldman, Max Springer and Lenny Chopin."

"I'm representing Ruben Garcia. He isn't here because he's convalescing from nearly being beaten to death by your clients."

"We were just defending ourselves."

"Mr. Springer!" Banks scolded Max. "I'm here to represent you. Let me do my job, okay?"

"But he was the one who attacked us."

"Yes, I know, but let me be the spokesman. That's what I'm paid for." Banks looked across the table and said, "I find it most unusual to have to bring my clients in before we have negotiated a settlement."

"I find that the situation is somewhat cut and dry. Both parties will drop assault charges. That leaves only compensation." Ruben's lawyer said.

Banks made a pyramid with his fingers as he tried to hide his delight. "So, you're proposing that they drop the charges and your client will pay compensation to them?"

"Not quite."

"Not quite?"

"We will drop the charges if you will do the same. That's what we agreed to, but only on the stipulation that your clients will pay all of Garcia's medical bills and any future therapy that he might have to have; plus compensate him for any lost wages."

"What?"

"I think that I have made our position quite clear," Greenfield said nonchalantly.

"What in the hell is he saying?" Dick demanded to know. "He's saying that we have to pay that little bastard? No God damn way I'm giving him a God damn thing."

"That's fine with us. We will go to court and let a jury of his peers settle it. If that's something that you prefer. Of course, we will have to amend the complaint to include punitive damages." Greenfield handed them the agreement. "It is time for lunch, so Jan and I are going to grab a bite. When we return, if you have not decided to agree on it, well, my wife wants me to pick-up some milk, so I'll have to go by Coldman Supermarket and get some." He smiled at the men that were sitting across the table before he and Jan left.

"What is this shit he is trying to pull?" Dick demand to know. "It sure in the hell sounds like blackmail to me."

"You could call it that," Arthur Banks said nonchalantly.

"I will," Dick reverberated angrily.

"Yes. You're right. It is blackmail, but I'm afraid that what he is doing is legal. It is called negotiating. That girl who charged you with rape never made it to the news, but if he takes this to court, it will. Needless to say that the bad publicity will hurt Coldman's Foods, probably more than what they are asking for. And if it makes it to court, there is a strong likelihood that the court will rule in their favor on everything, including punitive damages."

Dick looked at his two associates who were sitting beside him. They looked away. "You saying that I should take this deal?"

"I'm afraid so."

"Just throw in the towel? Just give up without a fight? That's not going to happen. No damn bastard is going to come into my place of business and attack me and get away with it. And now, you're saying, I have to pay him? Out of my own pocket? Because I doubt if my insurance will cover this. I say the hell with him."

"Dick, I'm sorry, but you are in a no win situation. Even if you do win, which is unlikely, the amount that you'll save will not be enough to offset the cost that Coldman's Food will suffer. The best thing that you can do is to hold your nose and sign the settlement."

A silence came over the room that was broken when Lenny said, "It's that damn restaurant. Those are the ones that are giving us all of our problems."

"That's for damn sure," Max agreed. "Those bastards think that they can get away with any God damn thing that they want. Someone should kick their dirty little asses, and teach them that they can't mess with the bulls."

"Yea," Dick agreed. "Maybe I should buy that damn greasy spoon and fire their damn asses. Better yet, I should buy it and burn the damn place down. That way I might be able to recoup my loses."

"Hell," Max added, "cut out the middle man, and just burn the damn thing down."

Chapter 38 ━━━━━━━━━━━━━━

The apartment had been rearranged. Ruben's bed was moved to the living room and the couch was moved into his bedroom for Desiree. And the ambiance of the apartment also had been transformed from a place to sleep to a place where people gathered, were everyday someone would show up with a pizza or something comparable.

One day when Lucy was off working, the occupants of the small apartment were visited by Nicole, Grant, Seth, and Davy. The combination of pizza and beer were the menu of the day along with off color jokes.

The room became somber when Davy said, "To bad that you d-didn't k-kill those b-bastards."

"That's for sure," said Desiree.

"I will the next time," said Ruben.

"What in the hell do you mean? The next time?" demanded Nicole.

"I'm not going to let them get away with murder. Someone kills one of mine, they are going to pay for it."

"That's the law of the jungle. Kill or be killed?" Grant said.

"It's my duty. If I don't then they will just do it again. To who? I don't know. But they will, you can bet your ass on it, that's for damn sure. They will do the same damn thing over and over until someone stops them. I had to come to a mutual agreement with those bastards, saying that we would not press charges against each other. And without Hope's testimony, the law is not going to do a damn thing to them. They won the first round, but they sure in the hell won't win the next time."

"You crazy ass, there isn't going to be a next time," Nicole said firmly.

"Nicole is right. If you do anything to them, they will lock you up and throw away the key," Grant added.

"Just let them get away with it?" Ruben demanded to know.

"You fought a good fight, but the battle is over," Grant answered him.

"How about Hope?" When Desiree spoke them all saw the dark side of her for the first time. "Is it over for her? Is it? I look around the room and I don't see her, why? Because she isn't here, that's why. She is six feet underground in the graveyard, that's where she is, laying there in her prom dress, decomposing. Yes, she is still dead and those assholes are still running around, like what they did was nothing wrong. You say that we should forget about it. But I say that they should pay for what they did to my sister. Don't you agree?" When she finished she looked each of them in the eyes.

"So, what are you doing? Are you saying that we should kill them?" asked Seth.

"Maybe. Why not?" Desiree said nonchalantly.

"If everyone takes out revenge on his own then we would have chaos," stated Grant. "That is why we have law and order."

"L-laws are made b-by the ones in power," Davy argued. "Law and order? Th-they are m-made by the haves to keep th-the have nots in th-their place. Th-they are the ones th-that call the shots. Th-there is a reason that th-they call it 'law and order', not 'law and justice'."

"But you are advocating for anarchy," said Grant.

"You w-were in the army, t-tell me, did it matter who was right? No, only who had th-the authority. Am I not right?"

"You are talking about the military."

"Military, the government. It's all th-the same damn thing, isn't it? Th-they are th-the ones who make th-the rules, not us. So why in th-the hell should we go b-by them?"

"Revenge is mine said the Lord," quoted Seth.

"You don't know what it's like to kill someone, do you?" Grant questioned everyone in the room. "I do. When I was in Vietnam I was faced with a situation. One that I pray to God that you won't ever have to find yourself in. I had to kill a man. A Viet Cong; a soldier like me, maybe a little younger than me. A boy. A boy that no doubt had a family and many years ahead of him. But I stole all of that from him. I killed him. I took his life away. I shot him in the chest and watched him gurgle his last breath. Did I have that right?" For a long time the room was still before he continued. "Every day I wonder if there wasn't a way that I did not have to kill him, or anyone else. As long as I was a soldier I knew that I would be faced with that reality. 'Kill or be killed.' So, I quit being a soldier. They court-martialed me and sent me to Leavenworth and I got a dishonorable discharge. There is always a price to pay for whatever you do, regardless how noble you feel your actions are."

"So, let them off scot-free?" Ruben asked.

"No, that's not what I said."

"It's sure in the hell sounded like it."

"What I'm saying is that there are other ways that you can make them pay for what they've done other than killing them."

"How?" Nicole asked.

"Well, there is an old saying, 'To kill a man's dream is like killing him'."

"Kill their dreams? What in the hell are you talking about? Killing their dream is not like killing them," Ruben said.

"Every person has something that they want, a dream. Something that they feel like they have to have to make them complete. The thing that they live for, the thing that they conceived that will bring them happiness, real or not. You can call it the love of their life. The thing that if it is taken away will destroy them."

"That's a dangerous game, is it not?" Seth interjected. He looked at Grant and continued, "You once told me that hatred is something that someone sees that is standing between them and happiness, their love. You said that is the reason why some men will go berserk and kill their wives or ex-girlfriends, because to them they see their ex-lovers as being evil, because they are preventing them from being happy or being fulfilled or whatever in the hell you want to call it. So they hate them because they are preventing them from what they think will bring them happiness. The ex-lovers are standing in the way of them finding love. So that's the reason that they kill them, because in their minds they are eliminating the evil that stands between them and there would be happiness, even though in their minds they are trying to limit the one that they are in love with so they will be able to find love. I know that that sounds crazy, but isn't that what you said? So stop and think about it. If that's true and you are going to destroy somebody's dream, the thing that they think is going to make them happy, and you don't think that there won't be any repercussion? Face reality. There will be repercussions, you can count on that."

"Oh, they m-might get p-pissed off. And w-we surely don't want them to be mad at us?" Davy ridiculed Seth. "That would be too b-bad. M-maybe you should g-go and go s-sailing or something. The only thing t-that you will p-piss off will be the fishes."

Seth stood up and glared at Davy. And then he looked at each one of them, making eye contact. "Do whatever you want, but remember what I say. You can't declare war on someone and don't expect them to fight back."

"Sure, there's going to be some risk," said Grant. "I know what you are saying, we will have to watch our asses, that's all."

"That's all? You will watch your asses? You make it sound so simple, like they are going to roll over and play dead. The harder you hit them the harder that they will strike back. You can count on that. I don't want to be any part of it."

"Then leave," Davy demanded.

"It's not just myself I'm concerned about. You will be putting everyone in jeopardy. Every one of you will be at risk, which includes Nicole and Desiree."

Nicole said, "We are not asking you to be a part of this. You are free to go."

Seth went to the door, before he left he told them, "Do what you want, but don't get yourselves into something that you can't get out of."

After Seth had left Grant said, "You know that he is right. We will be putting ourselves at risk."

"Everything has r-risk. I'm not a damn coward l-like Seth," Davy said.

"If anyone here isn't sure that you want to go through with this feel free to leave." said Grant. "We won't think any less of you if you do, but in for a penny in for a pound."

"I think that we have decided, we all are in," Nicole replied as she looked at the others to confirm her statement.

"Even Desiree?" asked Grant.

"Hope was her sister. She has as much right as any of us to be in on this. So shut up, and tell us how we are going to find out what their dreams are?" demanded Nicole.

"They had already told us that," Grant answered.

"When?" Ruben asked.

"The night of your birthday. Remember? Hope gave you a birthday cake and you made a wish. Well, they all told us what they wanted. What they would have wished for. Don't you remember?" Grant asked.

"That was a long time ago," Ruben said.

"Not that long ago," Grant replied.

"I do remember something about the trilogy of man."

"Yes, the trilogy of man's desires. Fortune, fame and love. Those are the things that drive men. Dick, the big guy, the leader, said that he wanted money, more money. He is the type of a person that never has enough. That's his identity. It is based on his wealth, it's his power. He uses money to dominate others, making him to be the top dog. Remove wealth, take away his money then he is nothing, a man without any power. That, my friends, is how you'll destroy him."

"So how are we going to take away his money? How we going to do that?" Ruben wanted to know.

"I'm not saying it's going to be easy, or risky. He didn't strike me as being a dumb man, and like Seth said, you can count on him not going to roll over and play dead either. No doubt about it, Seth was right, we are going to be playing with fire."

"So, do you have a plan?" asked Nicole.

"Off the top of my head, no, I don't. We can't destroy his property because he more than likely would have it all insured. Besides it is a felony. And I for one don't have any desire to be thrown into the can."

"Couldn't we just tell everyone what he did?" asked Desiree. "We could run an ad in the paper or on TV. Then everyone will know how bad he is, and they won't have anything to do with him."

"I don't think that that is the answer." said Grant.

"Why not?"

"Well, for one reason the papers and the television stations wouldn't run it. It is an unproven allegation. He could sue us for slander. Another thing is that it might not do any good. If someone is making money by doing business with someone that they know is immoral they will dismiss the charges, saying it's irrelevant or unsubstantiated, and will continue doing business with him. So, that's not the way to go."

The room went silence, each of them were trying to come up with a scheme to separate Dick from his wealth, but none could think of a way. Then Nicole asked, "How about this Max guy? What was his dream?"

"The lover boy?" Grant replied. "Strange enough the lover boy's wish was to be loved. That's probably why he's a porn star, trying to over compensate for his lack of feeling that no one really loves him."

"So he just wants someone to love him?" Nicole asked Grant.

"That's the way that I see it."

"There isn't a man that I can't destroy," Desiree said in a factual manner.

"N-Nothing like having a little con-confidence in oneself," Davy remarked.

Desiree gave Davy a sexual smile.

"I still think that she is too young to get involved in something like this," Grant stated. "It could be too dangerous."

"You sound like my father. I'm a big girl. I can take care of myself. Don't you think that you will be better off with me? Especially with the lover boy?" Desiree looked at everyone, even Grant, in the eye. Not one showed any indication of disagreeing.

"So, she is in," Grant conceded. "Even though I'm not for it."

"So, let's get down to business," Ruben said. "Who are we going after first?"

"I say the o-one with the money. That's their strength," Davy reasoned. "If he falls, then the other w-will be easier."

"He was the first one to rape her," Nicole said. "I think that he should be the first one we get."

"People with money feel like it's their moral obligation to protect it, regardless how they got it. It's like a religion," Ruben said. "He will be the hardest one."

"He's right," Grant agreed. "Money is much more then wealth and security. It's their social status. It's who they are. Without it, they have a fear of falling from their social level, and that scares the hell out of them."

"W-What I still don't understand is this Max guy," Davy said. "He's paid to have sex with beautiful women, and he still w-wants love."

"You're a typical man," Nicole said. "You think that love and sex are the same thing." Nicole scolded him.

"Aren't they?" he laughed.

"You're a pig."

"Why did he rape my sister?" Desiree wanted to know.

"It's hard to say," Grant answered. "Maybe he has a deep seated hatred for women. Lots of men like him do. Or he was just going along with his boss. Who knows? He probably doesn't even know himself."

"Are we going after the artist?" Nicole asked.

"Why not? He was there, wasn't he? He could have done something more than running off, like a damn coward," Desiree stated.

"She is talking about the dirty bastard that hit me in the back with a chair," Ruben said. "If we go after one then we should go after them all."

"I'd like to see these men, so I'll know what we're up against," Desiree said.

"It-it sounds like you w-want to take them on by yourself," Davy commented.

"If I need to."

"Okay, I'll take you to their place of business. More than likely they won't recognize me. 'All of us blacks looks the same'."

"You might be right," Ruben said. "You weren't at the bar when they came in. Were you?"

"I don't remember them, so they might not remember me."

"Maybe you should check them out before we decide on what we going to do," Grant said. "After all they say that revenge is best served cold."

Chapter 39

"Is that them?" Desiree asked Nicole as they watched from inside of Nicole's car. There were five people approaching the office building. The three that were involved in Hope's rape, Dick and Lenny, were walking in front. Behind was Max with two young woman one on each arm. They wore revealing clothes and heavy make-up. Both of them were attractive, but not as attractive as Desiree nor her late sister.

"I think so. I don't know for sure, but they must be."

"I don't think that they are all that pretty. Do you?"

"I guess not." replied Nicole.

"I think that they would rather have me."

Nicole look at Desiree, "What are you saying?"

"I'm saying that they will prefer me over either of those two. That's all. Matter-of-fact, I think that they could prefer you too."

"I thought that you… What are you saying?"

"Nothing."

"Nothing? Girl, don't lie to me. You have something on your mind. What is it?"

Desiree turned her head and smiled as she looked at Nicole and said, "Statutory rape."

"You're crazy. You're crazier than hell."

"Why not. You want them pay for what they've done to Hope, don't you? I won't be eighteen for another couple of months. And look at that Max. You have to admit that he is pretty hot."

"You're sick."

"Tell me that you wouldn't do him?" Desiree questioned Nicole.

"That bastard?"

"Forget about what he's done for a minute. He is a good looking guy. And Coldman paid Hope two hundred up front, and she didn't ask for it. I'll bet you that we could easily get a thousand a piece."

"A piece? Girl, what in the hell are you talking about?"

"What do you think I'm talking about? It's simple. We go and make a movie. And then we have the police break in and arrest them for statutory rape. Simple as that. And the best part is that we will keep the money."

"You're crazy. No way."

"Why not."

"There are so many things that could go wrong. I don't even want to think about it.'

"Like what?"

"First thing, I'm not a nymphomaniac. I don't want to get laid by someone just because he's good looking, or for money. I'm not a whore. You might be, but I'm sure in hell not," stated Nicole.

"I think that you're scared. That's it. You are scared. Am I not right? Sure, there will be some risk, but nothing that we won't be able to handle."

"If they arrest them, then what happens to us? We will be in a sex scandal."

"So?"

"So? I don't want to be in a sex scandal. You might not care. But I do," said Nicole.

"Maybe it will be just me. Maybe you could leave before the cops come in. That's it. You can tell them that you remembered something and you have to go. And when you leave the cops will come in and arrest them. That's a good plan. Nothing will go wrong," Desiree tried to insure her friend.

"I still think it is awful risky."

"Are you in?"

"I don't know. I should have my head examined."

"So, let's do it." Desiree said with enthusiasm.

"First thing, we need to know if they are the right ones," Desiree said. "And if they will recognize you or not."

After thinking for a moment, Nicole said, "I used to be a bike messenger. I can pretend that I still am a messenger that happened to mistakenly gone to the wrong office."

"You were a cowgirl?"

"Cowgirl? What are you talking about?"

"Grant said that bike messengers are like the modern day cowboys."

"Well, lots of them drink like the old cowboys did."

Desiree smiled and said with a western drawl, "Well, partner, let's go and round-up those bad guys."

CHAPTER 40 ─────────────────

With a bicycle helmet and a messenger handbag, Nicole in a skin tight spandex suit, waited with Desiree outside of the office building. When a man was leaving, Nicole grabbed the open door and gave Desiree a nervous smile before she went in. She looked at the directory and noted a name of a company that was on a floor above Coldman Studio and wrote the name on a brown envelope. When she got to the Coldman Studio she unzipped her top, showing all of her cleavage. Taking a deep breath she rang the doorbell.

Max, the young blond headed man opened the door and saw the pretty shapely young black woman. His eyes fell from her face to her cleavage. With a grin he said "Well, well, what we got here?"

She glanced around the room. She saw Lenny, a small man with a goatee sitting in front of a computer. Through an open door she was able to see the two women that she saw outside the day before. They were getting undressed without a hint of modesty. Dick, a big man with the air of an executive about him, entered the front room, closing the door behind him. Max took the envelope from her, without looking at the address, and handed it to Dick. She feared that he might open the empty the envelope which would put her in a precarious situation, for there were nothing inside, and what that would lead to she did not know. He read the address on the envelope and told her, "You are on the wrong floor. It's the office above this one."

"I'm so embarrassed," she said with a shy girlish smile. "How silly of me." When she received the envelope she moved in a way that showed off her breasts.

"What is your name?"

She never thought of what name she should use. "Why?" she asked, trying to give her more time to decide what name to use.

"You do have a name, don't you?"

"Nicole."

"Nicole, do you mind if I asked how much you make as a messenger?"

"Enough."

"Never enough." He paused before he told her, "Come back after you make your delivery. Okay?"

"Why?"

"We might be able to do some business. I can assure you that you will make more than what you will being a messenger."

After she left the younger man said, "She's going to be one of our actresses?"

"That might be a good idea," Lenny commented. "The contrast in skin color could be a plus."

"I guess," Dick said. "But I was thinking more in the line of marketing. Lots of people fantasize about what it would be like to have sex with someone from another race, for one reason or another."

"Probably in their minds they are destroying the social order, allowing them to be free, without any social restraints, or they just want to fantasize what it would be like to get their rocks off with a strange piece of ass," Lenny joked. "Yes, it is nice to be living in the days of enlightenment."

"I never had a piece of black ass before," Max said. "But, what the hell, first time for everything."

"Words spoken by a guy who is a real connoisseur of women, "Lenny said sarcastically.

"Hey, that's me."

"I rest my case."

"Connoisseur of women?" Dick laughed. "That is what's going make us succeed, all of those men that see themselves as connoisseurs of fine women."

The doorbell rang and they let Nicole back in. "So, did I peak your interest?"

"Maybe."

"I'm Dick," he said as he shook her hand. "This fine young man is Max. He is a good actor." They shook hands. "And this is Lenny. He's the photographer."

"You make movies?"

"Yes. Adult movies."

"Adult movies?"

"Exotic."

"Exotic movies?" She looked it Max and then the other two. She wondered what she should say. If she said yes, would they want to start making the movie right then?

"It's not nothing that you haven't done before, is it? A pretty girl like you must have done lots of boyfriends, and what we do is very natural. It is something that everyone does, but you will get paid for it." He waited for her to respond but she did not. He handed her his business card and said, "Think it over and give me a call, but the offer won't last forever."

She started to leave when she turned and said, "I have a good friend. She's a beautiful natural blond. Would you be interested in her too?"

"A beautiful blond? Sounds good. Bring her in with you tomorrow. Say about ten?"

"Ten o'clock," she confirmed it before she closed the door.

When she was outside she told Desiree, "We have a ten o'clock appointment."

"Both of us?"

"Yes, the both of yes. At ten o'clock."

"Now what?"

"What do you mean? 'Now what'?" Nicole asked.

"I will need an I.D., won't I?"

"Yea. I guess so. Where are you going to get an I.D.?"

"I don't know. I've got a Wisconsin driver's license, but I can't use it. It has my name on it and it says that I'm a minor. Also they will know that my last name is Adamsen."

"We might need someone to help us, but I don't know anyone in the business of making false I.Ds."

"You think that someone at The Garden might help us?" asked Desiree. "Who?"

"I don't know. Someone who won't think that we are crazy."

"You kiddy me? Everyone there think that will are crazy already," Nicole said with a smile. Then she said soberly, "And I'm afraid that they might be right."

CHAPTER 41 ━━━━━━━━━━

To Grant's surprise, when he answered his door bell he found Nicole and Desiree. "Well, what do I owe this pleasure to?" he said as he let the two in.

"We went to The Garden and June told us where you're living," said Nicole.

"We need a big favor. Will you help us?" begged Desiree.

"Usually when someone asks you to do a favor before they tell you what it is it's because it is something that they know that they won't want to do."

"Desiree needs an I.D."

"An I.D.?"

"Yes, I need an I.D. by ten o'clock tomorrow morning."

"I'm not in the I.D. business. And doesn't she already have a driver license?"

"Yes, but it won't do. She needs one with another name."

"Should I ask why?"

"She got a job. And they might ask for an I.D."

"Far as I know, people from Wisconsin don't need a green card to work in Illinois, so tell me what this is about?"

"It's about avenging my sister."

"So, let me guess. You're going to make an X-rated movie at the Coldman Studio, so they will get them on statutory rape?"

"You said that you didn't want them to get away with murdering Hope?" Desiree was trying to put him on the spot. "This is a way we can make them pay. Were you serious or were you just blowing wind out of your ass?"

"Do you two have any idea what you're getting into? First thing you will have to have sex with this Max guy or someone else."

"If it will mean getting justice for Hope then I will," said Desiree.

157

"I will too," Nicole echoed her.

"You realize that you also might be charged with statutory rape."

"Me?" Nicole reacted as if someone had thrown a bucket of cold water on her.

"Yes, you too. You taking her there to have sex, knowing that she is under age. You could be charged as a conspiracy to commit statutory rape."

"I'll just leave before the police come in, that's all."

"Or maybe I'll go by myself," said Desiree

"We will work something out," said Nicole. "You don't have to worry about that,

I'm not aiming to get my ass thrown in jail."

"Well, I guess I won't be able to talk you two out of this. But for the record, I think that this will put you two in great danger." Grant looked at the two young women as he debated if he should help them or not. He took a deep breath and said, "So, you need an I.D.? I assume that you were going to tell them that you lost your driver license or got a speeding ticket. So, you need a school or work I.D. or something. One that has your picture and your age on it. I guess that a work I.D. wouldn't have your age on it, would it? So, that leaves us with school, college. They would have your age on it, in case they catch you drinking. So, what college will it be?"

"What college?"

"Whatever one you want. I guess that it might be better to have one that has dorms."

He took a picture of Desiree and typed in University of Illinois at Chicago above it. "What name do you want to use?"

"I don't know. What do you think?"

"Maybe it would be best if your first name sound lots like the name that you already have. That way if someone calls you then you will be more likely to answer them."

"When I was young they called me Dee Dee. Maybe a name like Dianne or Denise. I will tell them that they can call me Dee Dee."

"Good thinking. Which one?"

"Dianne."

"After the Greek goddess of the hunt."

"Yea," Desiree said with a sinister smile. "That is what I'm going to do. I'm going to hunt down those bastards and make them pay for what they've done to my sister."

"You putting it that way, I guess that Dianne is an appropriate name. Now that is settled, what about your last name?"

"I don't know, what you think."

"Maybe something simple like Johnson?"

"Yea. I know some Johnsons."

"How about Dianne Lynn Johnson?"

"Yea, that will do."

"When is your birthday?"

"August the 29th."

"How about May the 29th? We will make you just turn twenty-one. I don't know what age you have to be to make porno in Illinois, so to play it safe we will make you twenty-one. Also there might be booze involved."

Grant finished the wording on the I.D. on his computer and printed out a copy. "Here you are Dee Dee. You will have to get it laminated. That I can't do for you."

She looked at the I.D. It looked perfect. It had the University of Illinois at Chicago logo on it. "Hey, not bad," Nicole said, looking over Desiree's shoulder."

"Yes, not bad."

"So that is what their I.D. looks like?" asked Nicole.

"I don't know what they look like, but more than likely they won't either. I doubt that they will ever try to pay anything into Social Security, but they might ask your number, just tell them that you had your purse stolen. So, you lost your Social Security card and your driver's license, and that is the only thing that you have."

"Thanks." Desiree said as she give the older man a hug and a kiss on the cheek.

As the two young women were leaving Grant asked, "How are you going to catch them?"

"We will figure something out," Nicole answered as she waved to him.

"Be careful. And good luck. You will need it."

"Joan," Nicole said as she and Desiree walked up to the booth where Officers Joan Fisher and Jack Walker were sitting in their blue uniforms.

It took a moment for Officer Fisher to recognize her. "You're a waitress that works at The Garden, aren't you?"

"Yes, I'm Nicole, and this is Desiree. Hope was her sister."

"I'm sorry about your sister. It was too damn bad. I liked her. She always seemed to be so nice."

"Thank you. But can I ask you why you think that she took her own life?"

"Well….That's a hard question to answer."

"Is it?"

"No. I guess not. But you already know the answer, don't you?"

"Because she was raped and not a damn thing was done about it? You think that that was the reason? That justice wasn't done?"

"What are you two up to?" Officer Fisher's eyes looked back and forth between them. "Are you planning on being her avenging angels? And you need help?"

"Maybe," Desiree said as she looked at Officer Walker.

"Oh, this is my partner, Jack Walker," she said as she slid over to make room for Nicole to set down. Jack shook hands with Desiree then made a place for her next to himself. "You can feel free to talk in front of him." Officer Fisher said as the waitress approached the booth, but was waved off. "So, what do you have on your minds? Or should I be afraid to ask?"

"I have a ten o'clock appointment with them. And they want me to bring along Desiree."

"I'm not eighteen."

"I see. And they don't know that you work at The Garden?" asked Officer Fisher.

"You're crazies. You want to get them on statutory rape?" Officer Walker looked at Nicole and told her, "You could also be charged with statutory rape, because you are the one that is taking her there."

"He's right. That is a serious charge. It's a sex crime. You probably would do time. Even if you get probation you will be a sex offender for life. And that is something you don't even want."

"Maybe I'll go by myself. And after I'm there, for say an hour or so, you can come in and arrest those ass holes."

"That's not going to work. First thing is that the place is not in our precinct, we won't be able to justify why we will be there. In the second place, we won't be on duty, we work nights. And also we will have to catch them in the act. How will we know when they are having sex with you?" asked Officer Walker.

"Maybe she could wear a tape or something," answered Nicole.

"She will be naked," he commented.

"Maybe not on herself, but on her cloths or in her purse or something." said Nicole.

"To do that we would have to get a court order, and there aren't any judges that will go along with that," said Officer Fisher.

After a long period of time, Nicole broke the silence, "What can we do?"

"Let it go," said Officer Walker. "Look, sometimes you have to let things ride. If they figure out what you're up to they will be pissed off, to say for the least. You are dealing with some dangerous men. They raped Hope. What will they do to you? Only God knows."

"I'm afraid he is right. You have to have faith that they will eventually get their due,"

"When? If ever," Desiree said. "I'm not going to let those bastards get away with what they did to my sister, with or without your help."

"We would love to help you, but I, for one, am not going to get kicked off the force and spend time for conspiracy to commit rape," he tried to defend himself.

"We thought that you would help us, but I guess that we were wrong." Desiree got up from the booth and headed towards the door. When Nicole caught up to her, she heard her say, "We will bring those assholes down ourselves. One way or another."

As the two ladies were leaving he asked, "You think that we should run them in for their own good?"

"I would like to," she shook her head, "but I doubt it would do any good."

"Where are your friends?" asked Lucy to her son, as she draped her wet rain coat over the back of a dining room chair.

"They went out," Ruben answered.

"I can see that. I thought that Desiree was supposed to watch you. I guess that I was wrong."

"She went out with Nicole. She can't stay locked-up here all the time. I can't blame her for wanting to take a break. I think that I would have thrown in the towel before now if I was her."

"Well, they could have waited until I got home before they went gallivanting around. Sometimes she acts like she's on vacation, and she is using this place as her private hotel."

"Sure she is," Ruben said sarcastically. "When I go to a hotel, I always give the employees a sponge bath."

"I never liked the idea of Desiree giving you sponge a bath. It's just not decent."

"Well, Mom, you don't have to worry about that anymore. Now that they got most of the casts off."

"Why she always waited until I wasn't here before she gave you your bath. I'm sure that is the high light of her days."

"Mom!"

"And Nicole? Does she also give you baths to? I bet that you really enjoyed that, didn't you? Having that black girl rubbing all over your body. Yeah, I bet you liked that; having an orgy with those two."

"She's black? Is that it? Is that is what you're afraid of? That you might end up with a black grandkid?"

"No! No, it's not like that. I'm only concerned for you. Do you have any idea what it would be like to have a black wife? Look, Honey, I don't have anything against the blacks. But…"

"But what? You're scared to hell that I'll marry one, isn't that it?"

"What about Desiree? Why is she here?"

"Because I got hurt going after those damn bastards that raped her sister. That's why. Simple as that."

"Simple as that? I bet."

"What in the hell is the matter with you. She just happens to be a good person who wants to help out. That's all."

"But what I can't figure out is why you went after those guys."

"I told you."

"But you two had already broke-up."

"She was carrying my baby"

"Your baby?" she whispered as she backed away.

The strong wind had subsided, although it was still raining hard, when Nicole and Desiree returned to the apartment. As promised, they brought with them a bucket of fried chicken. "I don't have anything against this," Lucy said as she looked up from the table at Desiree. "But a home cooked meal would be nice."

"I'm not a very good cook. My mom did all the cooking at home," Desiree replied. "I can bake chicken. Would that be okay?"

"Don't forget that we have an appointment tomorrow," Nicole reminded her.

"What kind of appointment?"

"A job," Desiree quickly answered.

"What kind of a job?"

"Well, actually I have two job interviews. One with a retailer and one with The Garden." Desiree turned to Ruben and said, "I'm sorry, but I'll more than likely be gone most of the day."

"Well, good luck," he said.

"Maybe you can help out a little financially."

"Mom!"

"What? Needless to say that things are a little tight around here. You can't work and we have more mouths to feed and all. Little money would really help out. That is all that I'm saying."

"We will manage."

"Your mom is right. Long as I'm here, I should try to help out."

"Maybe it would be better if Nicole moved in too," he gave her a wink. "But first we would have to get married," he was teasing his mother.

"Better yet, we could become Mormons and you could marry me too," Desiree joined in on the fun.

CHAPTER 42 ━━━━━━━━━━━━━━━━

The streets were still wet from the earlier rain when a funeral procession passed by the two young women who were standing outside the office building. "Do you think that we should go through with this?" asked Nicole.

"I thought that we already decided on that," said Desiree. "Why? Are you chickening out?"

"No. It's just that we should think this over before we jump in."

"You want us to talk ourselves out of this. Right? If you don't have the guts then say so, but I'm not going to back out. You do what you want, but I'm going to go through with it, with or without you."

"Okay, okay, we'll do it. We will make those poor bastards pay," Nicole replied as she rang the buzzer and glanced at Grant waiting in his car.

"Who is it?" a male voice asked.

"Nicole and I'm with my friend D-Dee Dee."

The two young women, one who had not yet reached eighteen, were buzzed in. When they got off the elevator they found Max waiting at the door. "Well, I see that you came back and you brought your friend."

"I said that I would, didn't I?"

"I'm Max. And you are?"

"Dee Dee."

"Dee Dee," he said with a smile as his head nodded up and down. "She wasn't lying about having a hot friend. I think that you'll work out just fine."

With her head cocked to one side and a big smile Desiree said, "You were right, he is a cutie."

Nicole remembered her saying that she could make any man fall for her. Now, she was going to prove it.

Dick came out from the back room. "So, I see that you did decided to join us. Welcome aboard. And this lovely lady is the one that you spoke about?"

"Yes, this is Dee Dee. And this is Mr. Coldman."

"Mr. Coldman was my father. Call me Dick."

"Dick."

"I see that you have already met Max." he turned and called to the other room, "Lenny, come and say hi to our newest members of our little family."

The small man with a goatee came to the door and paused before he said, "Ladies. You were right. Your friend is very lovely." He shook their hands as he studied them before he motioned the two to follow him into the other room. There were the two other women and another man, who were sitting among furniture and other props. There was a bed that had three cameras aimed at it. Dick and Max took a seat on the bed. Nicole and Desiree were the center of attention. The conversation in the room had ceased and all of the eyes were turned on the newcomers. Both were there on false pretenses. The fear of being exposed did not elude them. They heard Lenny tell them, "Please disrobe."

'This is getting too damn real,' Nicole thought. She glanced around the room, looking for a place that she could hide behind to get undressed. Then she noticed that Desiree was smiling at Max as she was disrobing in a provocative manner. 'She must not have any modesty about her or she was a damn good actress. She sure is playing the part of someone who did not have any sense of modesty about her. Maybe that is what I should do, pretend that I am taking off my clothes to take a bath. No, they want more. I will imagine that I am going to make love with Ruben, and I am going to turn him on, and if he was watching he would not be able to control himself.' That state of mind allowed her to lose her self-consciousness. She half-heartedly flirted with her audience, but it was obvious that most of their attention was on Desiree.

When both of them were standing naked in the middle of the room, in front of a camera, Lenny motioned for them to turn around. Wearing only a false smile, she felt the same as her ancestors must have so many years ago, when they were standing on the slaves' auction blocks. All of her dignity had been stripped away. And next to her was Desiree dancing around naked like a nymph.

"Thank you," Lenny said. "You can put your clothes back on." He turned to Dick and said, "They will be fine." He looked towards Desiree and reiterated, "They will be real good."

Dick led the two back into the office and sat down at the desk and motioned for them to sit across from him. He pulled out two applications and gave one to each of them.

"I'll need your drive licenses and social security cards."

"I don't have any," Desiree said as she handed him her false I.D. "I had my purse stolen. They took everything. My driver's license, my social security, my cell phone and all of my money. The college gave me this school I.D. I'm sorry, but this is it."

"Well, when you get them replaced, bring them in, okay?" He said as he took the application from her. "You didn't put in your address."

"Oh…It's the same as Nicole. We are roommates."

"I see," he said with a smile. "This is the way we work. You will be independent contractors. You will be paid on commission. It will be based on how much we sell the movies for and how many performers are in the movie."

"I don't have any money. When that jerk that stole my purse it had all of my money that I had. Now I don't have any money. I wonder if I could have an advance."

"Advance? How much we talking about?"

"How long before we can expect getting paid?"

"Maybe a month or a little longer?"

"Twelve hundred?"

"Twelve hundred? That's lots of money."

"That's only four hundred a week. Better make it sixteen hundred."

"Sixteen hundred?"

"You don't think that I'll make enough to pay you back? Didn't you say that we would make big bucks? Sixteen hundred isn't that much, is it? Unless you can't afford it."

Dick laughed, "Dee Dee, you are something else. Not only are you sexy as hell, but you are a natural salesman. I think that things are going to work out just fine. You have to be checked out by our doctor before we can make your first movie. That will take a few days. Don't go around having unprotected sex with anyone. No, don't have sex with anyone, period. We have a loose atmosphere here, but, never the less, this is a business. And we cannot afford to have a bout of S.T.D. Do you understand? It will knock everyone out of work." Dick said as he cut her a check. "Here's a thousand. After the first shooting I make out another check."

"How about me?" Nicole asked. "I sure in hell could use an advancement too."

"How much?"

"A thousand?"

"A thousand? How about eight hundred?" he said as he cut another check. "If for some reason or another, if things don't work out here, you have to pay me back, but I'm sure that won't be the case."

"Hey, Max, run these young ladies to the doctor's office." Dick tossed him the keys for his Lincoln. "I'll see you ladies in a few days." With a surge of adrenaline Max lead the two young ladies out of the office.

"I'm sorry," Desiree whispered to Max as she held his biceps. "We're going to have to wait."

After the three hurried out Lenny commented, "Two thousand dollars? That's a lot of money."

"That's a small investment for a star. And that little blond sex pot is going to make it big."

The big Lincoln pulled back into the office building parking lot and the three climbed out of the car. "I got Dick's phone number, but I don't have yours'," Desiree said in a flirting manor.

"You want my number?"

"Maybe we could get together."

"Maybe," he replied as he removed a Coldman Studio business card from his wallet. On the back of it, he jotted down his name and number.

"But remember no sex until we get the results back." She took the card and gave him a tight hug, making sure that he felt her breasts against his chest. Then she gave him a long and passionate kiss.

"I hate to have to break up you two love birds, but we have to go," Nicole said as she started walking toward her car. Desiree followed her, with Max watching.

Once they were in the car Desiree waved to Max and threw him a kiss as they pulled away. "Now what?" Nicole asked.

"Let's cash the checks."

"That might be a problem. Your check is made out to Dianne Johnson, right?"

"Yes. But don't you have a banking account? I just endorse it over to you. The problem is gone."

"That one might be, but we might have another one. They think that we live together. What happens if they find out that we don't?"

"Yea, that would blow our cover. And they could be pissed off, wouldn't they?"

"To say the least." Nicole agreed.

"Maybe I should move in with you. Yea. Why not. We can go halves on the rent, as soon as I get a real job. Yea, that will be fun."

"Fun? My place is barely enough room for me."

"Well, then we can move into a larger place." Desiree said with enthusiasm.

"I know, 'The problem is gone'."

"So. Are we roommates?"

"I guess that I don't have any choice. Do I?" replied Nicole.

"Guess what?" the smiling young blond asked Ruben.

"I don't know, Desiree. But I'm sure that you're going to tell me."

"I'm moving in with Nicole."

He looked over at the less enthusiastic Nicole. "So, am I being banned?" he teased.

"I will nev… I will still come over. Don't worry. You will be well taken care of." Nicole really wanted to say, 'I will never abandon you,' but she did not.

"When are you moving out?" Lucy wanted to know.

"Tonight." Desiree quickly replied.

"Tonight?"

"Is that a problem, Mrs. Garcia," asked Nicole.

"No, no, I guess not. It just that he has come to depend on you two. That's all."

"She won't say it, but she has learned to like you being around here," he said about his mother.

"They have been helpful, I admit that, especially Desiree when I'm not here."

"Don't worry Lucy, I will spend my days with him."

"I can take care of myself," Ruben stated. "In a couple of days I'll be back at work. Thank you two for all that you did for me, but I think that I'm capable of taking care of myself."

"It sounds like you're running us off." Nicole teased.

"No, Nicole," he took hold of her hand. "You two will always be welcome, especially when it comes to cooking."

"Very funny," Lucy shook her head. "He never appreciated my cooking."

"I do avoid restaurants that claim to cook like your mother."

"Very funny."

"Your cooking isn't that bad," Desiree said in the defense of Lucy.

"See? Someone appreciates my cooking."

Ruben turned to their guest and said, "She is a real good cook. You should try one of her T.V. dinners. She has them down pat."

"See what I have to put up with. No respect."

"No respect? I respect you like you're my mother."

"My one and only son is full of shit." After everyone stopped laughing she asked, "You going to sleep over there tonight?"

"I'm going to sleep on her couch."

He watched Nicole roll her eyes.

After the furniture had been relocated back to its original place and with the departure of Ruben's two female companions, he sat at the kitchen table with his mother, as they ate T.V. dinners. - One for her and two for him. His appetite had returned as he was regaining his health. With the help of a cane he had the ability to move around the apartment. In the past when they shared a meal together they usually watched a situation comedy on television' but not that night. They sat in silence; both buried in their own thoughts until Lucy said, "its sure quiet with them being gone."

"You saying that you're going to miss them?"

"No, not really. I did get used to having them around. It was nice to have other women to talk to." Ruben was surprised to hear his mother say, "Nicole is a good cook."

CHAPTER 43 ━━━━━━━━━━━━

From the back yard, Seth entered his kitchen with Jason. He and the little boy both had baseball gloves. Jason had inherited his from Seth's deceased son, Nelson. It was too big for the child, but never the less he held it with great pride. With a hand on the boy's head the man in paint splattered clothes said, "I think that we might have a big league pitcher there. As soon as he learns to throw a spit ball."

"So, he's going to play for the Cubs?" Angela joked.

"Your mother is trying to be funny."

The boy had a big smile on his face, even though he did not understand the joke. To him it was still funny, because they felt that it was funny. It was the first time in the young boy's life that he felt that a grown man really cared about him. This must be what it's like to have a father. Could this white man become his father? Could he have both, a mother and a father?

From the back Seth held Angela around her waist and rested his head on her shoulder as she was cooking. The unique aroma of the Caribbean species filled his kitchen as it had her home. She turned around in his arms and gave him a kiss. It was not a hard passionate kiss that expressed a strong desire to have sex, nor was it a little peck just to acknowledge his presence, but it was a long and soft kiss that told him that she had fallen in love with him. And he was feeling the same, but neither had the courage to say it. In her mind she had always told herself that she was in love with him as a way to justify having sex with him, but now it was no longer a lie.

Smells always play a role in if one feels at ease at a place or not, especially with young children. At first Jason felt uncomfortable in Seth's house, not only a feeling of resentment against Seth for the competition for his mother's attention. He felt that he did not belong in the white man's world, a world that spoke with a different language and ate different foods.

But now the abnormalities seemed to have diminished. Now he looked forward to spending nights at Seth's home, but he remembered the other men that had entered into their lives and then departed. Sometimes there would be a fight before they would leave. And there was hardly anything more terrifying to a child then two adults fighting, especially if one of them was his mother. But this man seemed that he would never hurt his mother. He would not make her cry. Could he possibly become his father? Could they be a family like he sees on TV? Having both a mother and a father?

Each of the three brought something to their relationships. And each took something from their relationships. Seth brought material things; his house, his boat and his car. But he also brought more, the role of a father, someone that Jason could emulate. Of course he provided companionship for Angela, someone that she learned she could count on. First time since the demise of his family did Seth start doing the things that fathers did; playing catch with Jason, reading stories to him, telling stories, and most of all just being there. When the Anaheim Angels came to town he would take Jason to the game where he would introduce him to his former teammates.

What Angela brought to the relationship was a different perspective, more of a realistic view, not so idealistic. She lived more for the day, not dwelling on the past. She was in love with him, but she knew that he wasn't without his faults. There were times he was depressed and wanted to be by himself, and she knew it, even though he tried to hide it. Every day she would see the pictures of the family that he had lost and she knew that she was not the only woman in his life, for he still cling to the memory of his first wife. Yes, Grace was the dragon in the garden.

Jason was what all children were meant to be, a delight to his parents. He had an unending curiosity, he was always asking them questions about everything. But one was why Seth would sometime call him David.

Chapter 44 ━━━━━━━━━

The sound of the rock music and the flashing lights permeated throughout the large night club, from the crowded mezzanine to the main floor, where the young adults, held drinks in their hands, as they were tried to talk over the loud music, to their companions, making comments about the appearance of the other ones who were doing the same about them. They were all wondering how they were matching-up with the competition. For the most part they were searching for a mate, some for life long relationships, while others were looking for one for only that night. In either case they were participating in the ritual that some believe goes back to the time when Eve enticed Adam with the apple.

In the midst of the dancers under the disco ball was one who was there under false pretenses, for not only was she under age but her motive was to deceive. For the beautiful blond had no intention of giving her heart to the man who brought her there. Her goal was not to bond with him, but to destroy him. Ever since Max picked-up Desiree at Nicole's place, she deceived him with her flirtatious manner. Now, on the dance floor, she turned on all of her charms. The two of them danced to the siren song that promised him of the love that he always was yearning for. With the grace of a ballet dancer and with the sex appeal of a goddess, she would twirl around him as she encircled her victim, smiling a smile of false love. He felt a rush of excitement that he had never known before. Yes, an excitement that only one feels when they are falling deeply in love. His heart pounded with the rhythm of the music. She danced close to him, giving him a mock kiss, then she would fade away from him, in a teasing manner, exciting all of his passion that was buried deep inside of the young man. This was the person that would not only be his sex partner, but his soul mate, the one that would be his one and only true love. She was the one that the believers of true love had promised him. Yes, he had fallen in love.

Throughout the night and into the early morning hours she incapacitated him with her charms, as Delilah did to Samson, as Cleopatra did to Caesar. She assured him that her love for him was even greater then his for her, that true love at first sight is real. By the time that they returned to Nicole's place he had hopelessly fallen in love with her. The spider had caught the fly.

Nicole stared at the intoxicated young black man. He weaved as he gave her a big smile, "How you going Babe? I was having a beer or two with some buds when I thought of you. So you not working at that honky place tonight, are you? Good, we can get down." He pushed his way past her. She tried to stop him, but he was too big and too strong. When she put her small hands on his chest, he only saw it as on attempt to embrace him. He pulled her to him and kissed her. "I think this calls for a drink." He went to the refrigerator, knocking over a chair along the way. He started pushing things over as he was looking for the beer. "Where in the hell is my beer?"

"In the store," she said firmly as she grasped his shirt and yanked him away.

"Woman! I had a six-pack in there. What in the hell happened to it?"

"What in the hell do you think? I haven't seen you in two weeks. You think that you can take off for two weeks and everything will be the same. You're crazier then I thought. Things have changed. I don't have any beer and you can't spend the night."

"Honey, don't talk like that. Let's go into the bedroom and make-up."

"You're crazy if you think that I'm going to have sex with you. Listen to me, Austin. We are through, we are done."

"What? What in the hell are you talking about woman."

"I'm telling you it is over between us. And you have to get out."

"What you're talking about woman? It's over?"

"I'm moving on. That's what I'm talking about. It's time for you to go." She walked over to the door and held it open.

"How about one more night? It won't hurt anything. Just one more night? You aren't going to make me drive home drunk, are you? Could get a D. U. I. or crash my car and get hurt real bad, or even get killed. Now, Babe, you don't want that happening to me, to you?"

"Get out!"

"Now Sweet Heart, what is the big rush?"

"You have to go. I have a roommate."

"Who is he? I'll kick his ass. Cutting in on my woman."

"It's not a him. And I'm not your woman. Get it through your thick head, it's over between us."

"Not a him? So you have a lady friend? How about a three-some"

"She's not that kind."

"She like women?"

"No, she is a nice white lady, who would not want to have sex with a drunken black man."

"So, that's it? Isn't it. You want to be white. You always wanted to be white. Am I not right? I should have seen it coming. Your mom told me that you always wanted to play with white dolls. You always want to be around whiteys. Well woman, I have news for you. You are black and you will always be black."

"Get your ass the hell of out here, and don't you ever come back." She picked-up the phone and called 911. "Police can you send a car…."

"Never mind, I'm out of here. You aren't the only ass in town. That's for damn sure. And let me tell you woman, if you have a baby with one of your honky boyfriends he will still be black. The only thing is that he will be screwed-up as much as you are. You should stick with your own kind."

"Like you?"

"Yeah, Babe, that's what I'm trying to tell you, like me."

"Get the hell out of here!" With all of her might, she shoved him through the door and slammed it closed.

From the other side of the door she could hear Austin's muffled voice calling out, "Listen to me, you will be sorry."

"Aren't you going to invite me in?" Max begged Desiree.

Tenderly she stroked his face with the tips of her fingers and with a look of pity she told him, "Honey, I would love to. God knows that I would love to, but I made a promise to Dick. And I know if you come inside that I might not be able to keep my word. You wouldn't want me to do that would you?"

"How in the hell would he know? Not from me."

"I know, I know. I want you so bad myself, but a promise is a promise. Soon as we get the test results back then we will go wild, and I mean wild." She gave him a long and passionate kiss. His hand slid under her brassiere. She let him massage her breast as they kissed, then she slowly pulled away and with a big smile she said, "Oh, you're a naughty boy, aren't you?" She got out of the car and kissed him again through the window. "See you tomorrow night?"

"Sure, tomorrow night." he said with the sound of disappointment in his voice.

She walked to the building and rang the doorbell. 'I hope that he isn't wondering why I don't have a key,' she thought to herself, as she smiled back at Max. She rung the bell over and over, it seemed like an eternity before she was buzzed in.

"Do you know what time it is?" was the greeting that Nicole gave her.

"Yes Mother," was Desiree's sarcastic reply.

"Shit, it's too damn late to go back to bed. We sure in the hell have to get you a key. I'm not going to be getting my ass out of bed at all hours to be letting your ass in. Well, now that I'm up, I imagine that I should make breakfast. Are you hungry? Have you been eating or been doing something else?"

"Something else?" She laughed. "You know that I am just an innocent farm girl? I would never do anything that my God fearing Mother wouldn't approve of."

"I'm sure that you are innocent as a new born baby, but tell me what in the hell happened."

"I've been making that poor sap fall in love with me."

"And you?"

"And me what?"

"Are you falling in love with him?"

"Am I falling in love with him? Am falling in love with the man who murdered my sister? Hell no. I said that I was going the make that bastard pay for what he did to Hope, and he will."

CHAPTER 45 ━━━━━━━━━━━

On Michigan Avenue, which over looked Grant Park and Lake Shore Drive, which runs along Lake Michigan, near to the Art Institute and the Civic Center was a private art gallery by the name of The Mnemosyne Art Gallery. It occupied most of the third floor. It was a place where the patrons of the arts would come before or after they had seen the Chicago Symphony Orchestra play. Each of the visitors would be offered a glass of wine while they observed the works of art that were on display. On this day there were three artists being shown; one who specialized in black and white photographs, another one was trying to mimic Picasso, and in between them were the large paintings of Lenny Chopin. There were four pictures. All of them were works that were done by an artist that had great skill. One of them was of an orchestra playing in the clouds with ballroom dancers flowing to their music. Another one was of a little boy sitting on stair steps, blowing bubbles. In each of the bubbles were things that he would like to be; a policeman, a fireman, a cowboy, a doctor, an astronaut and an artist. There was one painting of people ice skating on a lake. But the painting that received the most attention was The Bathers. It was of young ladies bathing in a pool at the bottom of a water fall.

It was Lenny's first show, and he could hardly restrain his excitement. He heard nothing but praise for his work. Men and women of high social standings were shaking his hand and telling him how great his work was. This was more then what he had ever hoped for. The price tag that the curator placed on his work exceeded beyond his wildest expectations. Even with the gallery's commission it would leave him with enough funds that he could paint full time. Plus now he would be recognized as a respected artist. The future belonged to him. He would be able to escape from Dick's clutches. Yes, he would be a free and independent man. He would be able to devote all of his time to his art. His life would now have real meaning.

At that time in walked Grant. He took a glass of wine and moved around the room, nodding at the patrons as if he was one of them. In a loud voice, loud enough that everyone in the room would hear him, he said, "Tell me Mr. Chopin, were any of your models filmed while they were being raped?" A hush came over the room then a complete silence. "Like you did at Coldman Studio? Don't you remember? That is where you watched Dick Coldman and Max Springer rape Hope Adamsen." A man grabbed his arm and pulled him towards the door. "Tell these fine people what happened to her." He broke away and hollered, "She committed suicide, didn't she? Why? Because you watched your buddies rape that innocent girl and you didn't have the guts to do anything about it. Am I not right?" He smiled at the man that he had broken away from and he let the man escort him out of the studio.

After Grant was escorted out of the room, everyone moved away from Lenny. He saw a look of disgust on their faces as they backed away from him. He watched them as they started to file out of the gallery, leaving him alone in the now empty room. His moment of pride had quickly turned into a moment of shame. His fear, the thing that he tried to lay to rest, the thing that he tried to bury, came back to life. His sin, his moment of weakness was coming back to haunt him. The memory of watching Hope being raped by his two companions was always with him. Now he was faced with the real possibility of paying the price for his cowardly deed. At what cost he did not know. His secret had been exposed.

Shortly the curator of the gallery entered with a stone face. "Mr. Chopin," that was the first time that the curator ever called him by his sir name, "Are those allegations that that man made are they true?" Lenny did not answer the question. "Did you film a girl that was being assaulted, and do nothing about it?" Again he did not defend himself. "Can you explain the allegations that that man made against you?" Lenny just stood there. "Well, I'm waiting."

"The charges were dropped."

"Why?"

"No witness."

"Why? Because she committed suicide? Please remove your paintings as soon as possible. We are done with you, along with all the other studios in the city, if not in the country."

Lenny felt as if he was a mountaineer who was on the verge of reaching the summit but had slipped and was falling into an abyss where he would forever be. Never again would he be able to climb to the top of the mountain. His lifelong dream was finished. A feeling of remorse flowed over him. 'I should have gone to the police as soon as she was raped? I could have given the memory clip to the police when they came with the search warrant. But I didn't'. His dream had been destroyed. Again he was back in the clutches of Dick. He felt that there was no escaping, He was trapped in a situation with no way out.

"What in the hell are you doing here?" Dick asked when Lenny entered the studio. "I thought that you were having your big show."

"They closed it," mumbled Lenny.

"After one day? They must not like your paintings."

"No. They loved my paintings. It was us that they didn't like."

"Us? What in the hell are you talking about?" demand Dick.

"You and Max raping that girl, which is what I'm talking about." Lenny said with a voice that angry.

"Shit, the charges were dropped. Didn't you tell them that?"

"Only because she committed suicide."

"Still the charges were dropped. That is what counts. It shouldn't make a damn bit of a difference to them."

"Well. It does. They don't want to be associated with a rapist, and that includes me."

"We just were teaching her how to show respect, and what it's like to be a woman. That's all. She called it rape, but it wasn't, the ungrateful little bitch." There was a long moment of silence before Dick asked. "How did they know about it? I don't think it was in the papers."

"One of the bartenders from The Garden was there. He told them."

"Which one?"

"The old one. The tall thin one with white hair."

"Someone should teach him to keep his God damn nose out of other people's business."

"That's for damn sure," Lenny agreed, still feeling sorry for himself. Not wanting to linger on the subject any longer, he asked, "Where is everyone?"

"You weren't here and that Max is so God damn in love he is completely worthless. So, what the hell, I kicked everyone out so I could catch-up on some of my paper work."

"You say that Max is in love? That's hard to believe."

"Yeah, that little blond that was in here the other day. Dee Dee, or whatever in the hell her name is. Anyway, he sure has it bad. Just what we need, a love sick puppy running around here."

"That's hard to believe that Max could love anyone other then himself."

"You know," Dick replied before he changed the subject back to the sabotaging of Lenny's career as an artist. ""If that bartender went after you, and you didn't do anything, what in the hell has he planned for me?" Dick pondered.

"And Max?"

"Yea, and Max too. We need to know who in the hell this guy is. I'll tell you what. We will call that place and find out what time it closes and you will go there and get his license number. With that we can find out every God damn thing about him. If you mess with the bull you will sure in hell get the horns."

CHAPTER 46 ━━━━━━━━━━

Nicole got up and took her drink and sat on the other side of Grant, leaving a gap between then and the other two who were having their night caps too. "They called me today. They want Desiree and me to make a movie tomorrow," she said softly to him so the others would not hear.

"You don't sound like you are all that enthusiastic about it. You sure that you want to go through with it? You know that it will be awfully dangerous."

The word, 'Dangerous' caught Davy's ear. He walked over and stood by them. "W-what will be dangerous?"

"Nothing," Grant said.

Seeing that he was not buying that, Nicole replied, "Me and Desiree have some little thing planned. That's all, it's not important."

"And th-this little thing is dangerous? It doesn't sounds like an l-little thing to me."

In unison they looked towards the office to insure that the owners were still there. Yvette join them, making a circle. "Well," Grant said as he was coming to Nicole's aid. "Desiree and Nicole are going to try to get the ones who raped Hope on statutory rape, by having the police catching them having sex with Desiree."

"Is that true?" Yvette confronted Nicole.

"That's what we decided on at Ruben's, didn't we?" Nicole tried putting the others on the defense. "You weren't there, but we all decided to make them pay for what they did to Hope. But I guess that you guys were just blowing hot air out of your asses."

"Whose idea was this?" Yvette inquired.

"All of ours," said Grant.

"W-wasn't it Desiree brought it up in the f-first place?"

181

"It's irrelevant," Grant said. "For we all decided to make them pay. I went after the photographer. Now Nicole and Desiree are going after the other two."

"What did you do?" Yvette asked Grant.

"I told the art community what he did. It's up to them if they are going to ostracize him or not."

"So, you two are going to make a porno movie in hopes that the police will rush in and arrest them just before you'll have to do the act. That's dumb. Don't you know that if you're going to do porno then you have to have sex? Are you willing to do that?"

"Desiree said that she is." replied Nicole.

"And you?" asked Yvette.

"I guess so."

"That sounds like a no to me."

"I'll do whatever it takes to make those bastards pay. Yes, I will screw them if I have to."

"But you don't want to?" Yvette grilled Nicole.

"Of course not." In a softer voice she added, "If I have to, then I will."

"So, how are you aiming on doing this?" Yvette wanted to know.

"Maybe I can leave and call the police. And they will catch them in the act."

"And you really think that that is going to work?"

"Do you have any better ideas?" Yvette had no answer. "Then we're going to do that, for I don't see any other way."

"Maybe you should see Joan and Jack? See what they have to say."

"It's out of their precinct," Grant said, "but they might still able to help. They must know other policemen in that precinct."

"They are afraid that they might get arrested for statutory rape themselves," Nicole said.

"How is that possible?" Yvette asked.

"Because they would be part of the conspiracy to lead to statutory rape," Grant answered.

"If that is the case, then Nicole would also be guilty of statutory rape herself," stated Yvette.

"But I'm a woman."

"It doesn't matter. You will still be guilty."

"I'm afraid that Yvette is right," Grant agreed with Yvette. "They could get you on statutory rape."

"Maybe she won't be there wh-when the police get th- there," Davy interjected.

"I can go in with Desiree and then gave some reason for leaving; then I'll call the cops. That should work, shouldn't it?"

"Maybe," Grant said slowly. "It will be risky. We should be there in case things don't work out."

"I don't w-want to cop out. But I can't get out of w-work," said Davy.

"After I drop the kids off at school…."

"No!" Grant interrupted Yvette. "You have a family. You've got too much to lose. I'll go."

When Lenny drove into the parking lot there were only five cars there. Assuming that one of them belonged to Grant, he jotted down all of the license numbers and then he pulled back on to the street and waited in the dark. He felt as if he was a thief that was stalking his victim.

About an hour later the employees came out and headed to their cars. He spotted Grant walking to his. He was talking with a black woman. His mouth dropped open and his eyes widened. "My God! That's the girl, the one that was at the studio," he said to himself. Was the Coldman Studio being set up? If one of the bartenders went after him, and he was not one of them who actually raped the girl, would they not go after Dick and Max as well? But then the blond had to be in it too. Did she also work at the restaurant? He hadn't remembered seeing her there the night that the three of them went there. "Sister?" he mumbled to himself. 'Could it be? It must be. It had to be. The two do look somewhat alike,' Lenny thought.

CHAPTER 47 ━━━━━━━━━━

When Dick got to the studio he found Lenny waiting. "Well, there is the first time for everything. You beat me here today. Did you get his license plate number?"

"Much more than that. We are being set up."

"What?"

"That black girl...."

"Nicole?"

"Yea, Nicole or whatever her name is. She was there. She works at The Garden. And to top that, I figure, that the other one, the blond one, must be the sister of Hope Adamsen."

"So, Dee Dee is trying to play us for suckers. We will see who the suckers are, won't we?" Dick strolled through the office to the room where they made the movies, pulled the heavy curtains back from the window and looked out onto the street. "Do you think that the police are involved?"

"Maybe." Lenny replied. "I don't see how. We are legit."

"Do you really think that they are sisters?"

"Well, they do look a lot alike, and we didn't see any driver's license, did we? I think they are setting us up. Don't you?"

"Yea, you're probably right. They are trying to screw us big time. But I don't know how they could hurt us, but you're probably right. They will try and pull some shit. But I can assure you that it won't work. Maybe it's time to teach those little bitches a damn lesson. Mess with the bull and you sure in the hell going to get the horns."

"Don't put us in jeopardy."

"Us?" Dick laughed. "Don't you mean you, Lenny? When in the hell are you going to grow some balls? My God, you're still hanging on to that damn chip, aren't you?" He waited but there was no response. "You are not going to run off this time, that's for God damn sure. Whatever we do you are going to be a part of this. Is that clear?" Again no response. "Good."

"Where are the others?" asked Nicole after she and Desiree had arrived at the studio.

"Today we are going to do something different. First things first. Take off all of your clothes and put those on," Dick said as he tossed them bikinis.

Nicole sensed that something was wrong. Max was still in his street clothes, and as they were stripping down, the other two men were watching. She wondered if they were looking for a wire. Next to her Desiree was acting like a little girl that was changing her clothes to go to a party. 'What is he up to?' keep running through Nicole's mind. 'Does he know that something is up? Does he know that Grant is outside, waiting to get the police when I call to him. How could he possibly know that?'

After they put on the bikinis, Dick told them, "You ladies are looking good, but now we have to go. You can leave your purses there. They will be safe here."

With their purses locked up they would not be able to communicate with Grant. They would be on their own. No one would be able to come to their rescue - not Grant nor the police. "I like to keep my purse with me at all times," Nicole said as she reached for it.

"I said that you won't need it." He snatched up both of the purses and locked them in his desk. "Now, should we be off?" With that the five of them left the studio and climbed into Dick's Lincoln. He was in the driver seat with Lenny riding shot gun. In the back, Max sat in the middle, between the two young women, who were trying to hide their fear for what may lay ahead for them.

"Where are we going?" asked Nicole as the car pulled out of the parking lot and headed south.

"We, my little pretties, are going swimming. I assume that both of you like to swim, don't you?" Dick asked.

"I love swimming," Desiree spoke-up.

"In the nude?"

"Skinny-dipping? When I was a kid, we used to go skinny-dipping all of the time. It was fun."

"And where was that?" Dick quizzed her. Nicole, who was already in a state of anxiety, was afraid that she would say Wisconsin.

"LaSalle. You know, by Starved Rock."

'How in the hell did she come up with that?' Nicole wondered as she took a breath.

In the rear view mirror, Dick looked at Nicole and asked, "And you?"

"I don't swim."

"Not even a little?" he asked as they turned on to Ontario.

"Maybe a little."

In his old green station wagon, Grant pursued them onto Ontario, which turned into a spur ramp to the Dan Ryan Expressway. When they drove south onto the Stevenson Expressway, he followed at what he thought was a safe distance as they were heading southwest.

"Where are we going?" Desiree asked.

"We are going swimming. Does that not sound like fun?" Dick replied as pulled onto the Pulaski ramp, and then he turned south, watching a green station wagon do the same. He drove through a few lights before turning on 47th Street, an industrial area, where he pulled over and watched the other car pass him. "There goes your friend." He smiled as he dialed 911 on his cell phone. "I would like to report an impaired driver going west on 47th Street, west of Pulaski." He pulled back onto the industrial street and passed Grant, who had parked on the side of the street, and then he started to follow the Lincoln again. "Yes, it is a green station wagon with a license that start out with B T then some numbers….You're welcome."

As they drove past Cicero Avenue they saw Grant being pulled over by the police. "Did you know that your friend has a drinking problem?" Dick laughed as he took Central Avenue back to the expressway.

"What's the matter officer?" the bewildered Grant asked.

"Let me see your driver's license and proof of insurance."

"What's wrong?"

"Your driver's license and proof of insurance!"

Grant gave them to the young policeman, who examined the items before running them though the computer.

"Get out of the car!" demanded the officer. "Stand with your arms outstretched, and touch your nose with your right index finger."

"I'm not drunk," he protested as he replied to the commands. "Give me a Breathalyzer if this will hurry things up."

"Why are you in such a big hurry?"

"That car, the one that I was following, the one that probably claimed that I was drunk. He is holding two girls against their will."

"You saying that they are being kidnapped?"

"I'm saying that they are in great danger. Look. Do you know Officer Joan Fisher?"

"She's not on duty. She's on nights."

"Call and tell her that Coldman has Nicole from The Garden. She will know what I'm talking about."

"First things first. Blow into this," the officer said in a condescending manner as he gave Grant a Breathalyzer test. After he had blown in it the reading was .02. -Well under the legal limits.

"So, what does it read?"

"It's inconclusive."

"I told you that I haven't been drinking. Now, will you call Joan Fisher before it's too late?"

Another squad car pulled up with his lights flashing. "Wait here and don't move," the officer demanded as he walked back to the other car. Grant watched them talking as he felt himself getting more and more stressed out. He could feel that time was slipping away. Every minute that passed was putting Nicole and Desiree into more jeopardy.

An older officer got out of his car and approached Grant. "Let me get this right. You were following a car that had kidnapped two women? Is that right?"

"I said that they were in danger."

"But not kidnapped?"

"No, not kidnapped. Maybe. I don't know. But they are in great danger, that I do know."

"You haven't been drinking?"

"He was point two," the younger officer stated.

"You sure?" the second officer asked.

"No!" Grant shook his head in frustration. "I have not been drinking. I have not had a drink all day. Coldman called you to get me off his tail. Please call Joan Fisher and tell her that Coldman has Nicole from The Garden. She'll know what I'm talking about."

"I told him that she wasn't on duty," the first officer said.

"Are you talking about the case of the rape victim that committed suicide?" the second officer asked.

"Yes! Yes. That's right."

"Who does he have?"

"Nicole Harris and Desiree Adamsen, the sister of Hope Adamsen, the girl that they raped."

"How come she is with him?"

"Desiree? That's not important."

"If you want us to get involved, we need to know what is going on. Why is she with him?"

"Is it really necessary?"

"If you are withholding information about a crime that has been committed or one that is going to be committed then you are obstructing justice. And you are also putting your friend in more danger."

Grant took a deep breath and then exhaled slowly before he told them, "Nicole Harris and Desiree Adamsen, remember? The sister of the girl who got raped and committed suicide, were trying to get them on statutory rape. The guys from Coldman Studio must have figured out that something was up. Where they are taking them to or what they going to do only God knows."

"God damn amateurs," the first police officer said.

The second one motioned for Grant to follow him back to his car. "Do you know what his first name is?"

"I believe it is Richard, Richard Coldman. He goes by the name of Dick."

"There are three Richard Coldmans in Chicago and two more in the area," the officer said as he read his computer. "What kind of car was he driving?"

"A Lincoln."

"There's a Richard Coldman that lives in unincorporated Cook County. We have a Lincoln registered in his name. Let's see. He was investigated on a charge of rape about two months ago."

"That's got to be him."

"Okay, we will take it from here," the second officer said as he returned Grant's license to him. "Go home. There's nothing you can do."

Grant got back into his car and watched the policemen pull away. The feeling of despair overwhelmed him. There was nothing he could do. Everything was out of his hands. The fate of Nicole and Desiree had been set in motion. Whatever the misfortunes facing them were his fault. He could have refused to be a part of their scheme. Somehow he could have persuaded them to take another course, but it was too late. The dice already had been cast. He felt helpless for he knew that there was nothing that he could do. It was out of his hands.

A one-legged old man in a worn army uniform hobbled along on crutches. When he came along side of the car he held out a large dirty soda plastic cup. Grant started to put a dollar bill in the cup, but he saw in the old soldier's eyes, the look of hopelessness. The look that said that he was still engaged in fighting the war of his youth, although his country had declared the war to be over years ago, but to him it was still lingering on. In those sad eyes Grant saw the reflection of his own soul. He knew that they shared secrets that only those who have experienced war have knowledge of. With this he emptied his wallet of all of its cash and gave everything he had to the veteran, his comrade-in-arms.

The pool was enclosed in a greenhouse that was attached to the mansion. It was surrounded by flowering plants. The flowers gave a feeling of tranquility. A place that one would always want to turn to, with a tall fence that shielded the lawn from the outside world. It was a place that one could freely do nearly any activity without fear of reprisals from the neighbors, a place that all apprehensiveness of the outside world would be dismissed.

Dick had insisted on everyone, except for him, put on one of his swimming suits from his abundant collection. As they were changing, he made drinks and put them on the poolside table. He was playing the role of the perfect host. When they came out wearing their revealing attire he whistled at Lenny's skinny legs. "Maybe we should rethink this, and have you and Max trade roles. Have him shoot and you be the stud." They all laughed, except for Lenny. Even the two young women laughed for comic relief.

"Yes," Desiree said as she rubbed his head, messing up his hair. "He's a real cutie."

"I would love to accommodate you," he said as he tried to straighten his hair with his fingers, "but I don't think that he is intelligent enough to operate a camera."

"Who in the hell is he trying to shit," Max struck back. "He couldn't get it up for one, how in the hell is he going to get it up for two, the damn fag."

"Now, now, kids let's play nice," Dick said as he smiled. "We don't want these ladies thinking that we aren't gentlemen, do we?"

"Gentleman?" Lenny replied as he looked at Max with disdain. "I strongly doubt that you should use that word to describe him."

"Let's kiss and make-up. And now on with the show." After Dick told them that he discretely walked away and went back inside the house, as Lenny set-up the cameras.

"You look nervous," Lenny said as he looked at Nicole. "Relax, there isn't anything to be scared about. Just pretend that the camera is not real, just a toy. It will be fun. You'll see."

"I know, I know. But I still can't help but think of what others might say."

"I see. The old evil eye. Who is it? Your mother? Grandmother? Your father?"

"Everybody. I can't help it. I can't stop thinking what the ones that I went to school with and the ones that I go to church with will think."

"They could be envious of you when they see you with Max," Dick said as he returned to join them. "You aren't going to back out on us now, are you?"

"She's just having little second thoughts, that's all. It's natural," Lenny said as he turned to Desiree. "You aren't, are you?"

"If I give a damn about what other people think, I wouldn't be here in the first place, would I?" Desiree laughed. "Like what Dick said, on with the show."

"That's the attitude, when you see how much fun that Dee Dee and Max are having you will want to join in," Lenny tried to assure Nicole.

"And you won't have to worry about paying me back." Dick added. "You can start thinking on how you're going to spend all of the money that you will be making."

"Is everyone ready to get wet?" Lenny said. "This is what we are going to do. Dee Dee will dive into the pool and then Max will walk up to it and say something smart and then you will splash him. He will act like he was pretending to be mad and he will do a cannonball, next do you. And when he comes up you will push his head back down under the water again. Then you will head for the side. As you get there he will grab the bottom of your bikini and pull it off. Then we will see how it goes from there."

With enthusiasm Desiree strutted to the pool. She turned and smiled at the men, seeking approval. Lenny gave her a nod and she gracefully dove into the water and swam to the center of the large pool. As she began to tread the water, Max walked to the edge and said, "That wasn't too bad, but it would have been better without the bikini." She playfully splashed water towards him as she was instructed to do. He jumped as high as he could and curled up into a ball and came down next to her.

At that time the front door bell rang. Dick got up and went to answer it as the others began to carry out Lenny's instructions. At the front door were four Sheriff Police. When he saw them his blood ran cold. 'Lenny was right, this is a set up.'

"Are you Richard Coldman?"

"What is this all about?"

"Are you Richard Coldman?"

"Yes, I am. What in the hell is this all about?"

"We are investigating a report of illegal activity in progress at this location."

"I can assure you that nothing illegal is going on here."

"That we will have to see for ourselves."

"Do you have a search warrant?"

"We have cause." With that the four officers pushed past Dick and went through the mansion, checking out the rooms on the first floor before they came to the door that opened into the greenhouse. They saw Max and Desiree on the other side of the pool, in a compromising situation, with Lenny filming them. The officer in charge demanded, "Everyone stay put!" He walked around the pool to the naked couple. He took the camera out of Lenny's hands as Desiree put back on her bikini, as Max stood naked. The officer asked her, "What is your name?"

She smiled and said, "I'm Desiree Adamsen. And I am seventeen."

CHAPTER 48 ━━━━━━━━━━━━

"What!" Ruben tried to comprehend what Nicole was telling him over the phone.

"They have us in jail."

"Who?"

"The police."

"I figured that. You said us. Who is us?"

"Me and Desiree."

"Where? What jail?"

"County."

"Why are you in jail?"

After a long pause Nicole replied, "It doesn't matter. The only thing that matters is that me and Desiree are locked-up and we need a lawyer. Are you going to help us or not?"

"Why are you locked-up?"

"I said it doesn't matter."

"I'm afraid that it does. If I call Greenfield or someone else, he is going to want to know why they locked you up. What am I going to tell him? I need to know."

"Just tell him that we got in a little trouble, that's all."

"That won't be good enough."

"Yes, it is."

"No, it's not."

"Well, if you must know, we went after the ones that raped Hope, and one thing led to and other, and now we are locked-up. Are you going to get Greenfield or not?"

"What did you do?"

"We decided to go after those who raped Hope and who made her commit suicide, right?"

"Go on."

"Well Desiree thought that we could get them on statutory rape. She's not eighteen yet. So we made a false I.D. and got them to use us…"

"Use you for what? To make porno? Did you screw them?"

"No, not me, but Desiree did. Max and she was going at it when the cops came in. She told them that she was only seventeen, so they arrested all of us."

"So Desiree was screwing this Max guy, you didn't. Although you would have if the police didn't come in, right?"

"I wouldn't have wanted to, but I would have to, yes"

"Sure," he replied sarcastically.

"Please don't be mad at me, I didn't want to hurt you."

"What do you mean that you didn't want to hurt me?"

"Because I….I just don't want you to be mad at me, that's all."

"But you were willing to screw them."

"Only to get justice for Hope. The law wasn't doing anything, right?"

For a long time the phone was silent before Ruben told Nicole, "I'm not a lawyer, but I can tell you not to say anything. Do you hear me?"

"Yes, I know. And I told Desiree to keep her mouth shut, and we told the police that we weren't going to say anything until we get a lawyer."

"That's good, but they are going to work on her, that's for sure. Tell her don't say anything until we get you a lawyer, okay? It's very important."

"I know, I know. If they let me see her, I will remind her. Do you think that you can get us Greenfield?"

"He charges five-hundred an hour."

"But he did your case for nothing, maybe he will do the same for us."

"I don't think so."

"Why not, isn't it part of the same case?"

"Well, yes, in a way, but he owed someone a favor, I don't know who, but someone. That's the reason he helped me. But, I'm assuming, the debt has been paid."

"But won't you try? Talk to him. Maybe he will help us. We are in trouble, and we do need a good lawyer to get us out of this mess."

"This is Greenfield," the lawyer answered his phone in his interoffice.

"Mr. Greenfield, this is Ruben Garcia."

"Ruben, how can I help you?"

"Do you remember Desiree, Hope Adamsen's sister?"

"The young blonde? Yes," answered Greenfield.

"And do you remember Nicole? She is our black friend."

"I believe so, why?"

"They are in the County jail." said Ruben.

"They're at County? What for?"

"They went after the ones that raped Hope, trying to get them on statutory rape. Well, both of them are locked-up now."

"Was a sex act performed?"

"Desiree, Hope's sister, did. She is seventeen, but they arrested all of them."

"Arrested or took them in?"

"I don't know. Nicole told me that she and Desiree were locked-up."

"You do know that my rates are five-hundred an hour?"

"I know," Ruben said as he felt that the lawyer was going to be out of reach.

"Never mind. We will work something out. What can you tell me about what happened?"

"Basically, I know nothing. I guess that they were making a porno and the police walked in on them."

"And Desiree was participating in a sex act?"

"That's the way that I understand it."

"That can be bad. Nicole can be charged with statutory rape herself."

"I know," he answered soberly.

"We will see what we can do. It might get a little complicated, but we still might make it go away."

After Ruben hung-up Greenfield made another call. "Dan, this is Ira Greenfield, I'm calling about Hope Adamsen's sister Desiree. She and a friend have been locked-up."

"Locked-up? What for?"

"Statutory rape. They were trying to get Hope Adamsen's rapists arrested on statutory rape, but it looks like they might have only succeeded in their friends being arrested."

"Who arrested them?"

"That is something that I was not told. What I need you to do, if you can, is to see if you can find out who arrested them. And see if you can get them to hold off on Nicole Harris being charged. She doesn't need to have a sex crime arrest on her record. She was only trying to bring the men of Coldman Studio to justice."

"I see."

"Maybe we can nip this in the bud. We have to do what we can to make this to go away."

"I'll see what I can do. No promises, but I'll look into it."

Chapter 49

"Before we can let you go we first have to get a statement of what happened," the young male officer said to Desiree, who was still in a bikini. She stared without a reply. "We need to know if Miss Harris knew that you are a minor, and as soon as you confirm that you will be free to go."

"Do you think that I am sexy," she said as she twisted her body in a sexy manner. The question took the young officer by surprise. He did not know how to respond, as his face became red.

"I don't know what in the hell you are trying to pull," said the female officer who was in the room, "but I don't find you being funny. This is a serious matter. You can cooperate with us or we can hold you as a material witness. That can be until the trial starts, which might be a year away. So, are you going to cooperate or are you willing to spend a year in jail? I'm sure that they won't find you sexy in there. So what will it be? You're going to cooperate or not?"

"When they put us in the car we told the policemen that we weren't going to say anything until we talk with a lawyer. You trying to make me talk, isn't that screwing with my civil rights or something?"

"You have not been arrested. So we can tell you anything we want to, and we just want you to know what you're up against. Being a smart-aleck isn't a wise move. What will be a wise move is to cooperate with us."

"If I don't you're going to throw me into jail for a year?" she said with a mocking smile.

"We can arrest you on obstruction of justice. So, Miss Adamsen, you better get your act together and start cooperating with us."

"So you can use me to get to Nicole? I'm sorry, but I'm not going to let you bully me into helping you get to my friend. Would you let someone bully you into hurting one of your friends? I hope not."

"We are only concerned for you. We have no desire in having you arrested. We only want to know if Harris knew that you are a minor or not."

"I don't have any idea what she knows."

"Your attitude is going to get you in a lot of trouble, young lady. You think that you are hot stuff, but you're not, that's for damn sure. We are going to leave now and let you think things over. Hopefully you will come to your senses and decide that it is best to cooperate with us. I'm sure that your so called friend will." With that the two officers left the room, leaving Desiree all alone.

"I'm Ira Greenfield, an attorney. I'm here to see my clients, Nicole Harris and Desiree Adamsen," he told the officer at the desk. He was led to a conference room. In a few minutes they brought in Nicole, who was still in a bikini. He asked the officer, "Where is Adamsen?"

"She isn't being charged."

"Has Harris been charged?"

"Not yet."

"Good, I want to see both of my clients." As soon as the officer left the room, he asked her, "Did you tell them anything?"

"No, not a word. They tried to trick me into making me confess, but I didn't, I didn't say anything."

"That's very good. They are good at making people confess to some things that they didn't want to confess to. What about Desiree? Do you think that she might have told them anything that would hurt you?" Greenfield asked.

"I hope not. You can never tell about her. Sometimes she seems so flaky and other times she seems like she is real smart. You never can tell about her."

Soon Desiree entered the room, giving them a big smile. "Well, Mr. Greenfield, it's nice to see you again. Do you like my bikini?"

"Yes, you look very lovely, but now we have to get down to business. Tell me what happened and I need to know everything, don't hold back, I'm not here to play games and neither will the District Attorney. So, tell me what happened."

"They raped my sister that drove her to commit suicide and they got off scot-free, so we decided to make them pay. We set those ass-holes up to be arrested for statutory rape, and it looks like we did it."

"I wouldn't be too eager to pat yourself on the back. Your friend might go to jail for statutory rape herself." He turned to Nicole and asked, "Did you know that she is under age?" She nodded her head. "Did they?"

"You mean the ones that raped Hope?"

"Yes, them."

"No," said Nicole, "I don't think so."

"I had a false I.D.," said Desiree.

"A false I.D.? Where did you get it?"

"I made it," Nicole said before Desiree could answer.

"No, I made it."

"So, was this I.D. a driver license?"

"No," Desiree said with pride. "We made a college I.D. The University of Illinois at Chicago. It had my age as twenty-one. We didn't know what the age limit is on making porno, so we put on it that I was twenty-one, to play it safe."

"To play it safe," he mocked.

"And get this, when I was little they used to call me Dee Dee, so he put on it that my name was Dianne Johnson, so they would call me Dee Dee, like when I was little, very smart, yes?"

"Yes, very clever, but you said he."

"No, we. I meant to say I made it by myself." Desiree was trying keep Grant out of the picture.

"He, we or I. That is something we're going to get straightened out later. But now I want to know is did you have sex with them?"

"With Max. Lenny was filming us then the police came in. They took the camera away. So they have it, they have Max screwing me on it. They don't need anything more. The mission is accomplished. Now they are going to pay for what they did to my sister."

"So will Nicole, and who ever made that I.D. He might be in serious trouble too." He looked at Nicole and said, "Do you want to tell me from the beginning what happened?"

"Well, we decided to make them pay for what they did to Hope."

"They raped her and because of that she committed suicide," Desiree said, interrupting Nicole. Greenfield motioned for her to be quiet and for Nicole to continue.

"She wanted to see them, wanted to see what they looked like. And, also, we wanted to know if they would recognize me or not. They might have seen me at The Garden. I didn't know if they did or not. So I put on my old bike messenger outfit."

"She looked hot in it." Again Greenfield motioned to Desiree to be quiet.

"I acted like I was at the studio by mistake, and they didn't recognize me, and they offered me a job making porno."

"I told you that she was hot."

"I told them that I had a good looking friend, and they said to bring her in. The next day we went there with her false I.D. and they sent us to get a physical. They didn't make Hope get one, but we had to."

Greenfield smiled and said, "Guess one of them must have come down with something."

"Maybe, anyway, they called us yesterday and told us to come in today. But when we got there we were the only ones there. Just me and Desiree and those guys. You know; Dick, Max and Lenny. Dick made us get into these bikinis."

"By force?"

"No, he just told us to get in then. He locked up our purses up in his desk drawer. I told him that I wanted it, but he said no. Then he took all of us to his house. It was a big house with an in-ground swimming pool. I told him that I couldn't swim. They told her to jump in the pool and for Max to jump in after her, and for him to pull her bikini off and do it. As this was happening the police came in. And that's about it."

"What did the Sheriff Police see?"

"They saw Desiree and that Max guy going at it."

"Going at it?"

"Yea. You know, the big nasty."

"And you?"

"They were on the other side of the pool, all I was doing was watching, that's all. I sure in the hell wasn't going to screw him if I didn't have to."

"So that is when the Sheriffs Police walked in?"

"Yes. And then they brought us here. But first, soon as we were in the police car, the Sheriff car, I told her to keep her mouth shut. I told her not to say nothing."

"I didn't tell them nothing. They tried to get me to say that she knew that I was underage, but I told them that I didn't know what she knows."

"Do you remember what their names were?" Greenfield asked Desiree.

"Who?"

"The ones that were trying to make you talk."

"No. It was a man and a woman."

"Did you…. Neither one of you told them anything that they didn't already know?"

"I told them right up front that I wasn't going to say anything till I talk to an attorney." Nicole said.

"They said that since I wasn't under arrest that I wouldn't need a lawyer," Desiree

explained. "But then they tried to get me to make her look bad, but I didn't."

"I'll see what we can do. First things first, we will talk to the District Attorney, and see if we can work something out. We might be able to come up with a deal."

"How about my things?" Nicole asked. "My purse and clothes."

"I'll see if we can get them for you. There is no need for them to be kept as evidence. Maybe we will get an understanding D.A. and a reasonable judge."

"Do you think that we will?" Nicole asked.

"I don't know, but let's hope so."

"What we have here is a simple case of two young and innocent ladies trying to bring some criminals to justice, something that your office failed to do," Greenfield said to the Assistant District Attorney. "So, let's try to come to an agreement that won't embarrass your office."

"I was told to watch out for you. So, tell me how you are going to 'embarrass' our office."

"Does the name Hope Adamsen ring a bell?" There was no reply. "And that is what this is all about. You cannot prosecute anyone without establishing a motive first, and that means that the Hope Adamsen case will be brought up. How did this naive beautiful young farm girl come about to commit suicide? Yes, everybody will wonder why her rapists weren't prosecuted. Was it because one of them was named Coldman? I always assumed that was the reason, and so will the public."

"You think that we will roll over and play dead just because you are making a threat that you will make our office look bad? Get real, you have to do better than that."

"Okay, I will get real. You are going up against deep pockets. They are going to throw an army of top lawyers at you. I don't know what your budget will be, but I can assure you that theirs will have at least three times as many attorneys than you will have. If you're going to win you will need the cooperation of my clients. Did I mention that I have lots of friends in the news business that are always looking for a good story about how their government officials dropped the ball?" In sales there is a saying, 'He who speak first loses.' This was something that Greenfield was aware of, so he waited and waited for the young Assistant District Attorney to speak.

"What are you looking for?"

"I don't think that the state has anything to prove by prosecuting either one of my clients. Do you? We are looking for complete immunity for both of them."

"Immunity for both of them? I don't see that as a reasonable request. I can't go to the D. A. and asked him for immunity for both of them. It doesn't work that away."

"It doesn't? Let's examine the case. You have a seventeen year old girl, which will mean that you going to be tried as a juvenile, so if you hurry you might get a hearing before she becomes eighteen. And may I have your honest opinion on your odds on a conviction? Especially after the jury finds out what her motive was. I would say that things won't look all that good for your case, wouldn't you agree?" He did not respond. "Let's discuss the other case, Nicole Harris. She is a very attractive young black lady that will be going in front of a Cook County jury. I think that it might be to your benefit to have her on your side. One thing that you can count on is that under no circumstance will one of them roll over on the other. But both of them will work with you to get the real criminals convicted."

"So, you want full immunity for Harris? We will drop the statutory rape charges for her testimony? I don't think that you are being very realistic about it. According to the law she is as guilty as the men are. No way that we can let her walk."

"Why? Because you don't have enough blacks locked-up?"

"You aren't going to try to play the race card, are you?"

"I will tell you what I will do, I won't bring up race if you agree to not bring up the statutory rape charges."

The Assistant District Attorney laughed. "Are you being serious? She is as guilty of statutory rape as you are as being guilty of being a defense lawyer, and you want us to drop the charges?"

"Let's keep this on a professional level." said Greenfield.

Knowing that his statement was not called for the embarrassed attorney felt the need to be more cooperative. "Okay, for her testimony we will agree to cooperate with you by dropping the charges down from statutory rape to contributing to the delinquency of a minor."

"A felony to a misdemeanor?"

"That would be the best that we can do."

"And there wouldn't be sex crimes charges attached to it either. With our arcane laws she wouldn't be able to walk her children to school. I don't think that it is necessary to ruin her life, do you?"

"We will have to have her full cooperation, or we will amend the indictment to statutory rape."

"That's understood," Greenfield agreed. "I don't see any need to have any bail, do you."

"I think you are pushing the envelope a little far, don't you?"

"Look, she put herself in jeopardy for justice. She isn't going to go anywhere."

CHAPTER 50 ───────────

"Who is our next case? The judge asked.

"She is Nicole Harris," the bailiff announced.

"Does she have an attorney?"

"Yes, your Honor, I am her attorney."

"Well, Mr. Greenfield, it is always good to see you. Sometimes I think that you are here more than I am."

"It's the nature of the beast."

"That's for sure," the Judge said and then asked, "What are the charges?"

"Your Honor, she is being charged with the contributing to the delinquency of a minor. She was involved in a case of statutory rape." the Assistant District Attorney stated.

"Statutory rape? Can you explain to the court what she did?"

"Your Honor, she was involved in making a porno film. She took a minor with her, who was caught in the act by the police."

"Shouldn't she by charged with statutory rape instead of delinquency of a minor?"

"She is agreeing to cooperate with the State."

"I see," the judge looked at Nicole, who was then wearing the clothes that she started off the day in. "Young lady, do you understand the charges against you?"

"Yes, Your Honor, I do."

"How do you plea?"

Greenfield whispered to her, "Guilty."

"But, if I plead guilty then I'm saying that what we did was wrong."

"We can always change the plea."

The young black lady looked at her lawyer as she questioned his advice. She knew that he was one of the top defense lawyers in the Chicago area. She had to trust his opinion, but still she was apprehensive about admitting to a judge in a court of law that she was a criminal. Reluctantly she said, "Okay Your Honor, I plead guilty."

"Your plea of guilty is noted."

"Your Honor," Greenfield said. "We request her to be released on her own recognizance. There is not any reason to make her pay bail. She has already agreed to cooperate, there is no need for bail."

"Your Honor, we still feel that there is still a chance that she might get cold feet. We are asking for a bond of hundred thousand."

"I thought that we had a deal," Greenfield said as he glared at the assistant D.A. "A hundred thousand! Your Honor, a hundred thousand is highly unreasonable. That is far beyond what she will be able to raise. I find it most unreasonable to have any amount, especially if you consider her motive." As soon as the words came out of his mouth he knew that he had made a big mistake.

"May you please tell the court what her motive was?" The judge demanded to know.

'What was her motive?' How could he put it in words to make it sound like something other than revenge? "Your Honor, ill-conceived as it may have been, my client was trying to bring justice for her friend who was raped by Richard Coldman and Max Springer. The innocent young lady, whose name was Hope Adamsen. I used the past tense when I referred to her, because after the rapists' charges were dismissed, the words of an innocent young lady were rebuffed by the two men who brutally raped her. There was no doubt that she was raped, but never-the-less, they weren't ever prosecuted for their crimes against her, leaving her in a state of despair. Because of the lack of justice for her she was living a life of agony that led her to commit suicide."

"Your Honor," the assistant D.A. broke-in, "what he is stating has not been substantiated. What is the simple fact is that Mr. Coldman and Mr. Springer were never convicted of any crime. The charges that he is alluding to were dropped."

"So, do I understand this right? In every case that is dropped is it because the accused were innocent? My client, Nicole Harris, the friend of Desiree Adamsen, was seeking justice for her deceased friend, because her friend never got justice while she was alive."

"How was she going to get justice?" the judge asked.

"On statutory rape," replied Greenfield.

"Statutory rape? How old are you?"

"Twenty-two," said Nicole.

"She is a little old to be a victim of statutory rape, isn't she?" asked the judge.

"The young sister of the rape victim is under age."

"So, they were setting them up on rape charges? She was trying to use the law for her revenge? Young lady, I don't know what made you think that you had the right to give out justice. We have a legal system to do that. If everyone took it in their own hands to deal out justice then we would have anarchy. Then there would be no justice for anyone. Do you understand?" Nicole nodded her head. "By all rights you should have been charged with statutory rape instead of delinquency of a minor. I'm going to leave that up to the trial judge to decide." He turned to the Assistant District Attorney. "Do you have anything to add?" When there was no reply he said, "We will compromise. The bail is set at fifty thousand. You are required to put up ten percent."

"Thank you," Greenfield said as he started to lead Nicole away.

"I don't have five-thousand."

"Maybe your family can be raise it."

"My family? You're kidding? I don't want them to know."

"They will know sooner or later. I think that you should give them a call. You said that Hope lost her job because she didn't go to work. Do you want the same thing to happen to you?" She shook head. "Call your parents."

As the attorney and his client were being escorted down the corridor, away from the court room, they were approached by the three men and their lawyer who was also being escorted by two officers. "Nicole, did you tell the judge how you lied to set us up, you little whore? You do know what goes around comes around."

Greenfield stepped in between the two men and his client, Nicole. He looked at Dick and said in a forceful tone, "Are you threatening her?"

"Am I threatening her? Did I say to her that she's liable to suffer great harm if she isn't careful what she says in the court? No, I didn't" He give her a sinister smile. "Isn't that right Miss Nicole Harris of Summit, who works at the All Right Apartment Store?"

"Officer!" Greenfield yelled. "Put a muzzle on him."

"What did I say?"

"It is a felony to intimidate a witness."

"Nothing that I said was a threat, was it? All that I told her is that I know her name and where she lives. She gave that information to me when her and her little friend filled out their application."

"That can be taken as a threat."

"A threat? My God all of you lawyers are the same. Shakespeare was right, 'The first thing we should do is to kill all of the lawyers.' If I made a threat you would have known it."

An officer grabbed hold of Dick's arm and started to pull him down the corridor, as Greenfield took Nicole in the other direction. "Don't let what he said get to you. A guy like that is nobody to worry about. He is all talk, no bite."

"I'm not all that sure. I didn't put down where I really work at, but he still knows. How does he know? Tell me how does he know?"

"We will get a restraining order against them," Greenfield said trying to calm her down.

"I once had a friend that was a witness to a murder and they killed her. They know where I work and they know where I live."

"You aren't the only witness, what are they going to do? Kill all the policemen that were there? But, never-the-less, we will get a restraining order. I don't think that they will bother you."

"You're maybe right, but I'm not all that sure," Nicole said with a nervous tone in her voice.

CHAPTER 51 ━━━━━━━━━━━━━━

"Hello," the middle aged woman answered the phone as she rolled over in bed, trying not to wake-up her husband.

"Momma, it's me."

"Nicole, do you know what time it is? It's half past eleven."

"I'm sorry, but I'm in trouble, and I need your help."

Swinging her feet on the floor, sitting up-right on the bed she said with a concerned voice, "What's the matter, Sweet Heart?"

"I'm in jail...."

"What!" Her loud voice finished waking Nicole's father up.

"I need to be bailed out. Will you help me, Momma?"

"What are you doing in jail?"

"Who's in jail?" he asked.

"Nicole."

"Nicole? Nicole in jail? What is she doing in jail?"

"Nicole, what are you doing in jail?"

"I don't want to talk about it now. I need you to bail me out. Will you?"

"You in jail and you don't want to talk about it? But you want us to bail you out?

Just like that?"

"Momma please, I don't want to talk about it now. Will you get me out of here? Please? I will tell you everything when I get out."

"How much do you need?" Her mother said reluctantly.

"Five-thousand."

"Five-thousand?"

"Five-thousand dollars," he repeated his wife. "That's a hell of a lot of money,"

"Momma, I need it to get out. I have to go to work, and I can't do that in here, can I? You know that I'm good for it. And we will get it back when the trial is over. I always have paid you back, and this time I will too."

"I know Sweet Heart, I know. But I still would like to know why my daughter is in jail."

"It's a long story. I'll tell you when you get me out, okay?"

"What is she in for?" her father, Henry, interrupted.

"I don't know. She won't say."

"Won't say? What do you mean that she won't say? She wants us to come up with five-thousand and she won't tell us what she is in for? Give me that phone!"

"Just wait," she said over her shoulder as she stepped away from him. "I'm talking to her.

"Now Baby, where are you?"

"Cook County, Twenty-six and California. Please hurry."

"We will as soon as we can get the money, don't worry your little head."

"I love you, Momma."

"I love you too, Sweet Heart."

Before she could hang-up Henry grabbed the phone from her hands, "Nicole, what in the hell are you doing in jail? I never raised no daughter of mine to be thrown in jail like a common criminal. What did you do?"

"I didn't do nothing. I swear to God."

"Don't lie to me young lady. And don't try to use the name of God to make it sound like you are innocent. Now tell me what you did to get your ass thrown in jail?"

Nicole began to cry, making sure that her father could hear. "Daddy, oh Daddy, I was trying to do the right thing, just like how you always taught me. You know that there isn't anyone on God's Earth that I respect more then you, you know, don't you?"

"Go on child, and tell me what happened."

"You always taught me to do the right thing, didn't you?"

"Go on."

"Sometimes you need to put your friends and family ahead of yourself, even at your own risk, right? Well, that is what I did. I put my friend ahead of myself and that is why I'm here."

"So, what did you do?"

"I sought out justice for Hope."

"Who is Hope?"

"You know, she was my white friend. You had met her, she had been at the house."

"Her? What do you mean justice for her?"

"Oh Daddy, she was raped and nothing happened to the ones that raped her. She ended-up committing suicide."

"Are you talking about the girl that you went to Wisconsin for her funeral?"

"Yes, Daddy, that's the one. I wasn't going to let them off scot-free."

"You shot them?" asked Henry

"No Daddy, I didn't kill them, but I'm making them pay for raping her."

"You are in jail for trying to get even for a white girl? You're not playing with a full deck, are you? You were seeking revenge for a white girl."

"She was my best friend. And you always say that racism is going against God's will, no matter which race you are talking about, right? Racism is racism, now you are acting like you are a racist. If she was black would you still feel the same?"

"That's not the point."

"Yes it is."

"No it isn't. It's…..It's just that I don't want to see my little girl hurt, that's all."

"Then Daddy, come and get me out."

"We will. Hang in there," he was trying to give his daughter a word of encouragement before he hung up the phone.

"What did she say?" Mrs. Harris asked her husband.

"We have to bail her out."

"Why did they lock her up?"

"I don't know, she didn't say. Only that we have to get her out of there."

"Five-thousand, that's lots of money. Where are we going to come up with that amount this time of night?"

He shook his head, "I don't know. There must be someone that we know that can help us, but who?"

"Maybe the church?"

"No. They don't need to know our business," he said.

"How about Jake?"

"Your brother?" asked Henry.

"Why not? They are close. He was always more like a big brother than an uncle."

"He's going to find out."

"Yes, Henry, of course he's going to find out, sooner or later. You can't keep something like this a secret. In time everyone will know."

"Our little girl is locked-up like a common criminal."

CHAPTER 52 ━━━━━━━━━━

"Mr. Sparks," the Judge looked down from the bench at a battered defendant, "I have lost count of how many times you have been here, and if my memory serves me right, you have never won a fight."

"No, Your Honor. I beat-up Bobby Miller and that fat guy," the court room broke out in laughter, "and I could have won this one too if there wasn't any spilled beer on the floor. That's how come I lost. I slipped on that God damn beer, or I would have won. I would have beat his ass if I did not slip on that damn beer. Say, Judge, can I sue that damn bar for having a wet floor?"

"Why was the beer on the floor?"

"I don't know. Probably because they were too damn lazy to mop it up."

"Or could it be because you were fighting? And that's the reason there was beer spilled on the floor."

"Maybe, but I still think that I should be able to sue their asses."

"Mr. Sparks, my advice to you is to get another hobby other then fighting."

"They always start it."

"I'm sure they do, and all the witnesses are lying, but I'm inclined to lean in their favor. The court sentences you to seven days."

""Your Honor, shouldn't the defendant have a financial option?" the young Public Defender asked.

"Yes, you are right. Seven days or a thousand dollars. Mr. Sparks, do you have a thousand dollars?"

"No, Sir."

"Do you think that you will be able to get it, say, from a friend or a family member?"

"No, Sir."

"A bail bondsman?"

"A bail bondsman? Are you shitting me?"

"Mr. Sparks! I don't allow foul language in my courtroom."

"I'm sorry Your Honor Judge Sir. I try not to use any bad language, I don't want you to get pissed you off at me."

"You did it again."

"I did, didn't I? I'm sorry Judge. Some of the guys that I hang around with have pretty bad mouths. You know what I mean? Their bad language must have rubbed off on me. I'm from a good Christian family."

The judge gave a stare at the accused, trying not to laugh. "Are you saying that the bail bondsman are out of the question?"

"Yeah, they say that my credit isn't any good."

"How about your lawyer? He surely has a thousand dollars that he can loan or give you?" Both the judge and the defendant looked at the embarrassed lawyer. He slowly shook his head 'no'. "Then the sentence is seven days.

"Next."

Arthur Banks came in front of the bench with his three clients, Lenny Chopin, Richard Coldman and Max Springer. "Well, what do we have here?" the judge asked the Assistant District Attorney.

"They are charged with statutory rape."

"Statutory rape? Would this by any chance have anything to do with making porno?" the judge asked.

"Yes, Your Honor, these are the men that were apprehended by the police while they were having sex with a minor." the Assistant District Attorney stated.

"Your Honor, when my clients were participating in a legal activity, except for the fact that one of the women falsely represented herself. She claimed that she was someone that she was not, and she backed up her lie with a false I.D. My clients are honorable men. They would not knowingly break the law. They were victims of a malicious act by a misguided young lady who had the false impression that these fine men caused the death of her sister. We do not believe this was the case. Her sister was fired from her place of employment. We do not know the reason for her dismissal, so we cannot say that it was due to thievery or spreading rumors…."

"Your Honor, my colleague is trying to demonize the victim's deceased sister, with allegations that they have no proof of."

"Your Honor, we just feel that my clients are the real victims. They were being set-up in a sting operation that was not approved by a judge. On that ground we feel that all of the charges should be dismissed."

"Dismissed? Your Honor, they were caught in the act of having sex with a minor by the police; an act that they do not deny. Dismissal would be a miscarriage of justice."

"I don't see any reason not to set bail of one hundred thousand a piece," the Judge said.

"Your Honor, we request that they handover their passports."

"I don't think that will be necessary," Banks said.

"Richard Coldman has the means to travel and live anywhere he wants to."

"Is this true," the judge asked.

"The question should not be can he, but will he. He is a businessman with interest in this area. He is not a flight risk. He might need his passport to go on a business trip."

"And he might not," the judge said. "You will relinquish your passports and you are not to leave the state. The bail is set at a hundred thousand a piece that will be ten per cent in cash. I'm sure that a big businessman like you can come up with thirty thousand."

Chapter 53 ————————

"Jake, your sister is on the phone."

"That's good," he said as he rolled back over in bed.

"She needs to talk to you."

"Can it wait until morning?"

"If it wasn't important Dolly wouldn't be calling in the middle of the night."

"Dolly?" He took the phone and asked, "What's up?"

"I hate to call you at this time of the night, but it's important, and I don't know anyone else that I can count on. We need a big favor from you."

"What?"

"We need five-thousand dollars."

"Five-thousand!"

"What with five-thousand?" Jake's wife asked as he motioned for her to be quiet.

"We have about two-thousand, we need three more."

"Three-thousand? I don't have that kind of cash lying around here."

"They want three-thousand dollars?" His wife, Juanita, asked. "What for?"

"Why do you need it?"

"For Nicole." Dolly paused, knowing that he had always been close to her. "She needs to be bailed out of jail. Will you help?"

"That's lots of money, five-thousand. "What is she locked-up for?"

"Who's locked-up?" Juanita demanded to know.

"It's Nicole," Jake said as he covered the phone with his hand.

"Nicole? Nicole is locked-up? I don't believe it. Not Nicole. She is always the good one. What was she locked-up for?"

"Dolly, Juanita wants to know why she needs to be bailed out."

"Because she is in jail."

"No, no, no. I mean why she is in jail."

"I don't really know what she did for sure, only she was trying to get back at some guys that she thinks caused her friend's death. Now we need to get her out of there so she won't lose her job. Will you help?"

"I guess that I can help some, but not all. Maybe Dad and Mom can help. They always have a rainy day fund. I'm sure that there won't be a hell of a lot in it, but maybe enough."

"I hate to get them involved, but you might be right. It will be best if we talk to them face to face. I will call them and let them know that we are going over there. Will you meet us there?"

"I guess that we don't have any choice," he replied.

"Let's get this right," the elderly man said as he tried to comprehend what the members of his family were telling him, "They have Nicole in jail?"

"That's right Dear," his wife patted him on his hand, "and they need money to bail her out."

"To pay her fine?"

"Yes, something like that. We can gave them some, but not all they need."

"She is one of our grandchildren?"

"Yes, she is Dolly's daughter." She could see that her husband was having a hard time placing Nicole. "She is the one that sings in the church choir, the pretty one."

"Nicole." The elder man smiled with his mouth open. "She is a good kid. Is she still in school?"

"No, Dear, she's out of school. She's in trouble and needs our help. That is why Dolly and Jake are here, asking for our help." She turned to the others at the table and told them, "He now is what they a call Sun Downer. He is good in the morning, but as the day goes on he looses some of his sharpness. In the morning you can't tell that anything is wrong, but as the day goes on." She did not finish the sentence. She did not see any need to. She asked her husband, "Are you tired, Dear?" He looked at his wife, trying to comprehend what she wanted to know. "Do you want to go and lay-down for a while?"

As the couple got up from the table Dolly told her father, "Good night."

"Did you know about this?" Henry questioned his wife.

"Momma said that sometimes Daddy has a little trouble remembering things."

"A little trouble? Shit, he couldn't place Nicole. I'm not even sure that he even knows who we are."

Dolly motioned for him to lower his voice as their mother returned. "How is he doing?"

"He went right back to sleep. In the morning he probably won't remember you being here."

"How long has he been this way?" Henry asked.

"Well, it is hard to say. The truth is that I don't really know. It just came on so slowly, I hardly noticed. He was having trouble remembering names, then he was having trouble keeping up with the TV shows."

"What's going to happen to him?" asked Dolly.

"That's in God's hands. The doctors say medically there's really nothing that they can do. He will gradually get worse. Eventually I will have to put him in a nursing home."

She rubbed her eyes. "But that still might be a long time off."

"How long?" Henry asked in a sober voice.

"No way of knowing, might be a couple of weeks, or a couple years. There is no way of knowing."

"And we came to you for help," Dolly said as she hugged her mother.

"Now, now, first things first. Right now isn't the time to worry about your dad, it's the time to take care of Nicole. We have to get her out of that awful place. How much do you need?"

"We have sixteen-hundred and Jake is saying that he is good for another twenty-two, that means that we will need another twelve-hundred. Can you help us?"

The elder woman looked at her daughter as she was calculating in her head if they could afford giving her the money or not. She got up from the table and walked over to her purse and took out her ATM card and handed it to Dolly. "The number is one, two, three, and four."

"That is the most common number," Jake said. "You should change it to another number."

"That might be the most common number, but it also the easiest one to remember."

"Thank you Momma," Dolly said as she hugged her.

"I'm just glad that I can help out." She was thinking that it was still good to be able to help her family out.

"You're free to go," the black female guard said as she unlocked the cell door. As they walked past the others who were incarcerated, most were asleep, Nicole could hear them snoring, some were moaning, others were talking, while some were just staring into space. She had not gotten used to the smell. In her short time there she observed how the strong, physically or mentally, took advantage of the less fortunate ones. Was this going to be her future? Is this what awaited her? What she and Desiree did she felt was a noble thing, but now her reward for her valiant act might mean imprisonment. Now she was beginning to question if she was going to pay too high a price for her noble act.

Soon she was in the presence of her parents, and her mother's face had a look of concern, while her father was more judgmental. "My daughter has been arrested. How do you think that makes me feel? My own flesh-and-blood is a jail bird?"

"Henry! Be quiet. She don't need you to be yelling at her." Her mother took hold of both of her hands. "Now do you feel like telling us what happened now?"

"Being honest with you I really don't want to discuss anything now, if it's alright with you."

"I think that we have the right to know what's going on," her father said.

"I agree with him. We put up the bail money and that give us the right to know."

"Not here."

"Where?"

"Any place but here."

After they picked-up Nicole's car the family reunited at a twenty four hours restaurant. They sat as far away from everyone as possible, where the parents had coffee and pie as they watched their daughter scoff down a hamburger and fries. It had been hours since Nicole had anything to eat. She didn't realize how hungry she was. "Now, are you going to explain what you did?" her father asked.

"If you promise that you won't make a scene." Her father looked at her without a reply. "Well?"

"Okay, I'll control myself. Tell us what happened?"

"You know the story behind Hope killing herself? I've told you that. Anyway, we decided to make those bastards pay for what they did to her. The law wasn't going to do anything that was for damn sure. So, we decided to do something on our own, to make those ass holes pay."

"Who are we?" her mother asked.

"Does it matter?"

"Yes, it does, it will let us get a clearer picture, Sweet Heart."

"Someone that works at The Garden and Hope's little sister, Desiree. Well, Desiree thought that we should get them on statutory rape."

"Statutory rape!" her father's voice was loud enough that the few that were in the restaurant looked their way.

"Daddy, you promised."

"How were you going to get them on statutory rape?" he asked. "You are of age."

"Yes, I know, but Desiree isn't. The ones that raped Hope are in the porno business. She didn't know that. She thought that she was going to pose for a painting, not for porno. Because she wouldn't go along with them they raped her. Now do you understand why she did what she did?"

"What are you saying?" her father asked. "She killed herself because she was raped? That don't make any sense at all."

"Henry, have you ever been raped?" His wife challenged him. "No, you haven't, have you? Until you do keep your trap shut. You guys always feel like you know what it is like to be raped. I can tell you that you don't have any idea."

Henry looked at his wife with astonishment. "You have been raped?"

She turned her back to him as she motioned for her daughter to continue.

"So we decided to put their asses in jail, where those bastards belong, and that is where they are now, right where they belong. That's right, we set those suckers up. We were making a porno film when the police came in. They caught them in the act with Desiree, and they arrested their asses."

"You made a porno film?" her father wanted to know.

"No, the police came in before I had to."

"Before you had to? You mean that you would have screwed them if the police didn't show up? On camera and everything."

"I wouldn't have any choice. I would have to. If I didn't I don't know what they would have done. I'm not a whore, but sometimes you must do what you have to do. Yes, I would have sex with them, I wouldn't have any choice, would I?"

Henry looked at his daughter in a way that he had never seen her before. She was no longer his little girl. She was a grown woman that demanded to be her own self, to decide for herself what was right and what was wrong.

"What did they arrest you on?" her mother asked.

"Contributing to the delinquency of a minor. First they were going to arrest me on statutory rape, because I took her there. How can I rape her? We are both women, and we didn't have sex. But they claimed that I was a part of it, so I was guilty. Mr. Greenfield got them to drop the charges down to delinquency of a minor."

"Who is this Mr. Greenfield?" her father asked.

"He was Ruben's lawyer. He is one of the best."

"You say he is one of the best?" Her mother asked.

"Yes, he is."

"How much does this top lawyer charge?" Her father wanted to know.

"His price is five-hundred an hour."

"Five-hundred an hour! My God, that's as much as I make in a week. Five-hundred an hour. How are you going to pay him?"

"I don't know, Daddy. He might gave me a break. He didn't charge Ruben anything. But Ruben told me that he said that he owed someone a favor. I don't know who, but someone, he wouldn't tell him."

"I don't know," her father said as he shook his head. "You are in a mess, I'm afraid that this might haunt you for the rest of your life."

"Don't be so pessimistic," her mother said as she held Nicole's hand. "Have faith in Jesus that things will work out."

"Oh, God. You don't know how hard that I've been praying. Momma, I've seen the inside of that jail and I don't even want to go there. It's awful. You couldn't believe how bad it is. You wouldn't keep animals like that. Thank God that you bailed me out."

"You're out now and hopefully you won't have go back in that place."

"Momma, I pray to God that you are right."

"Listen Sweet Heart, it's getting late, we have to go to work now," her mother said. "What are you going to do now?"

"I called Desiree, and she is still at County, waiting for someone to pick her up to take her back to Wisconsin. So, I have to go there. She still has her things at my place. She moved in with me."

"I don't think that you should associate with her," her father told her.

"She is my friend, like it or not, and sometimes I don't, but she is still my friend and I will always stand by my friends."

CHAPTER 54 ━━━━━━━━━━━━━━

While the city was still in darkness Chuck entered the Cook County jail. He saw his sister sitting on a bench with Nicole, in the lobby. They both were in the clothes that they started off wearing the day before. "You're okay?" He asked his sister as he nodded to Nicole. He looked around the room. He had never been inside of a police station before. There was a uniform officer standing next to the metal detector. He appeared to be the person in charge. He told him, "I'm here to pick-up my sister."

The officer looked at him and then at the young blonde across the room. He could see the family similarities. "Where are her parents?"

"They couldn't make it."

"Why?"

"Health reasons."

"I see, and you are her older brother?"

"Yes."

"How old are you?"

"Twenty-four."

"You got an I.D.?"

He handed the office his driver's license. After studying the license the officer give him a form to sign, then he made a phone call. "The Lieutenant wants to talk to you," he told Chuck.

Soon a veteran officer entered the lobby. The policeman behind the counter pointed to Chuck. "Mr. Adamsen, I'm Lieutenant Holzman. I was informed that you are here to take your sister back home to Wisconsin, right?"

"Yes, Sir, that's right."

"Do you know why we have her?"

"We were told that she was involved in illegal activity."

"She is a minor and she was participating in making porno."

"Porno?"

"Yes, I'm afraid so. We were tipped off, but when we got there she was in the act. The others were arrested on statutory rape. She will have to be a witness at the trial."

Chuck quickly crossed the room and angrily confronted his sister. "He said that you were making porno, is that right?" She did not answer him. "Why?"

"Because they are the ones that raped Hope, that's why. Yes, I did. And I would do it again to make those bastards pay for what they did to our sister. Wouldn't you have done the same?"

For a moment Chuck did not speak, then he walked back to the Lieutenant and asked, "Is she being charge with anything."

"No, she's not. But needless to say that was a very dangerous game she was playing." He said loud enough so Desiree would hear. "She is lucky. Although she might not be out of the woods yet, there still might be repercussions." He turned to Desiree and told her, "You're free to go young lady."

"Thank you Officer," Chuck said as he give his sister and her companion a cold look. "Let's go." After they were outside he confronted the two young women. "What in the hell were you two thinking? You didn't think it through, did you?"

"Of course we did." Desiree defended themselves. "We knew exactly what we were doing." She looked at the policemen that were entering and leaving the jail. "Let's get out of here."

"Did they give you anything to eat?" Nicole asked.

"Yeah, not much."

"You were lucky. They didn't give me a damn thing, I was starving my ass off. I did a burger with Mom and Dad, but I'm still hungry."

"Let's grab something to eat," said Desiree.

"There's got to be a restaurant around here, somewhere," Chuck commented.

"There's one by my place," Nicole said. "If you are going back to Wisconsin you're going to have to get your things anyway."

"Yea, it looks like I'm heading back home. Are you going to go to work today?"

"Hell no. Are you crazy? I haven't had any sleep in the last twenty four hours. Say, do you have that I.D.?"

"Sure, it's in my purse. Everything is in it. They didn't take anything out."

"Thank God. Soon as we get home we will burn that damn thing. We don't need to have the police find it. I can't believe that the police didn't keep it.

"I think that I'll keep it, as a keepsake."

"Like hell you will." Nicole said as they walked up to their cars.

"An I.D.? Let me see it." Desiree handed it to her brother. "Dianne Johnson, University of Illinois at Chicago. Very good," he said, trying to make peace with his sister. "How did you get it?"

"Don't tell him!" Nicole said harshly to Desiree, and she smiled at him and said, "That's our little secret."

"I also want to swing by Ruben's before we head home. I want to say good-bye to him."

"Don't we have to stop there anyway, to get your things?" Chuck asked.

"I moved in with her. First we eat, then we pick-up my stuff from her place, then we will go and say good-bye to Ruben."

"That sounds like a plan," Nicole said. "But I'm going to follow you over to his place."

"Okay, but it will be getting late by the time we make it back home," Chuck commented.

"You said that Mom and Dad are sick?"

"No, not really. We just thought that it will be best for me to pick you up. You do know that we are moving?"

"What?"

"You knew that we were losing the farm."

"I know that the bank was trying to take it away, but I thought that it wouldn't really happen."

"Well, they did. It really happen, and now we are moving into town."

"Into town?" Desiree never wanted to live on the farm, but she still always wanted it to be there.

"Are you going to tell them what we did?"

"I think that they might already know. When Mom sent me to get you she acted angrier then concerned."

"If they don't know then you don't have to tell them, do you?"

Standing on his crutches, Ruben open the door for his three guests. The two young ladies gave him a hug and he shook hands with Chuck. "This is an unexpected pleasure. What's up?"

"Can't we just stop in and see how our favorite patient is doing?" Desiree teased.

What he wanted to say was, 'You two always can come by to give me a sponge bath.' But he restrained himself. "Likewise, you two are my favorite nurses."

Lucy came out of her bedroom, wearing her night clothes. "I have to see what all of the racket is about," she said with a smile. "Who is this?"

"He is my brother, Chuck," Desiree said, "And this is Ruben's mom, Lucy Garcia. He came to take me home."

"You are moving back home?" Ruben asked.

"I'm afraid so."

"But you just moved in with Nicole. Things didn't work out?" Lucy asked.

"Yeah, she snores," Nicole laughed.

Desiree smiled at Nicole then said to Lucy, "My parents think it is best."

"Well," Lucy said. "Parents usually know best. We will miss you."

"And I will miss you too. But Nicole will still be here, and I will come back to see you."

"Well, I'll still miss you. But now I'm going back to bed. It is too damn early to get up." She gave Desiree a hug and told her, "Take care of yourself and come back and see us, do you hear?"

"You can count on that Mrs. Garcia."

"I'm going to crawl back into bed, you guys keep it down, okay?" She give a forced smile to Nicole as she left.

"So, tell me what in the hell is going on?" Ruben demanded as he stared at the two young ladies.

"They charged me with aiding to the Delinquency of a Minor," Nicole said. "And I will have to testify against those bastards."

"Aiding to the Delinquency of a Minor? That sounds bad, what is the penalty for that?"

"Up to a year in County and ten thousand dollars fine."

"A year and ten thousand?"

"Yeah, they say that I'm lucky. They could have charged me with Statutory Rape. That would have been much worse. They would send me to prison for a long time and call me a sex offender. Greenfield said that I might get off with probation. I will still have to testify against them, but that will be a pleasure. I'm not scared of those bastards."

"Maybe you should be," Ruben turn to Desiree and asked, "What about you?"

"Me? They're sending me back to Wisconsin. If needed me, I'll have to testify against those rapists. That will be fun."

Ruben looked at Chuck in a way as to ask if they were free to talk in front of him. "I also would like to know just what happened." Chuck said.

"What do you want me to tell you? Every little detail?" Desiree tried to shame them out of asking embarrassing questions, especially in front of her brother. "We agreed to go after those ass holes that raped and caused Hope to commit suicide, did we not? And that is what we did. We got their asses thrown in jail, where they belong."

"Just what did you do to get them thrown in jail?" Ruben wanted to know.

"I did whatever it took. They wanted an actress for their porno film, and they got a damn good one. They got me. And the police got them just before I lost my virginity."

Nicole laughed. "Before you lost your virginity?"

"Did you lose your virginity?" Ruben asked Nicole.

"No." She looked at her companion. "But I would have if the police didn't get there when they did." She looked at Ruben and added, "I wouldn't have any choice, would I? Like what she said, we had to do whatever it took. If we tried to back out it is hard to tell what might have happened. They could have even killed us." With her eyes beginning to tear-up as she was pleading for Ruben to understand why she did what she had done, and to forgive her, but he looked away. She grabbed his arm, making him look at her. "What I did was for you, and for Hope and your unborn child. Now you're acting like what I did was wrong. Out of all that I have done for you and still you can't see it in your heart to understand why I did what I did, do you? Don't you know that I love you?"

What he heard confirmed his suspicions. This lady of a different race was in love with him. He was taught that it was wrong to have relationships with one other than whites. He felt that he could be faced with ridicule and even ostracized by his friends and family. But still he had to admit to himself that he also had strong feelings for her too. Now she was standing in front of him. She was close enough to him that he could smell her perfume and see the tears in her eyes. He looked at the trembling lips of the woman that had just told him of her love for him. Her quivering lips were like a magnet that was drawing him to her. He dropped his crutches and he kissed her. At that moment they were the only two in the universe. At that moment they were not aware of the brother and sister who were in their presence. Nor were they aware of the woman that was listening behind her bedroom door. When she heard the crutches hit the floor she cracked open the door, just in time to see her son embracing a black woman. She softly closed the door. With her back turned to the ones in the other room she took a deep breath as she asked herself why she let Nicole become a part of their lives.

CHAPTER 55 ━━━━━━━━━━━━━━━

On the long journey back to their home Desiree asked her brother, "Do you think that they know what I did."

"I'm going to guess so. I'm pretty sure that Mom knows."

"If Mom knows then more likely Daddy will know too. She tells him everything."

"Maybe not. She might think that it is best to let it ride," Chuck said. "He is going through pretty rough times. She might not want to make things worse."

"Mom keeping something from Daddy? I don't think so. If she did then it will be the first time."

"I doubt that."

"What do you mean by that?"

"Everybody has secrets, even Mom."

"Even Mom?"

"Yes, even Mom," Chuck told his sister. "She is human, isn't she? Then she has secrets. Everybody has secrets, even her."

"But Mom? That's hard to believe."

"Believe it or not, that is a fact of life, everyone has secrets."

"What are your secrets? What are the wicked things that did you do that you won't tell anyone about?"

"I'm the exception to the rule."

"Yeah, I know, you are innocent as a new born baby. So, tell me what is one of the evil deeds that you done that you won't tell anyone?"

"You want to know what my deepest and darkest secrets are." Chuck laughed. "Why should I have to tell you that?"

"It's all fair, you know mine now, don't you? I have the right to know yours."

"Everybody knows yours now." He smiled at her.

"Don't be an ass, and tell me, what are your deep dark secrets?"

"Do you really want to know?"

"Yes, I do."

"Okay, I will tell you one. I knew that you were lying. I knew that you were not a virgin."

"What!" Desiree tried to act shocked at her brother questioning her purity. "How do you know?"

"Because I saw you and Sammy. You wanted to know my secrets? That is one.

I watched you two going at it."

"You bastard," she said as she slapped him lightly on his shoulder.

"Am I? If I was a real bastard then I would have broken you two up and told Mom and Dad. But I didn't, did I?"

"But you watched me."

"Sure, I did. I'm only human. But the way that I see it is that you are not my responsibility. What you do is what you do. It's none of my business, is it? You are a big girl. If you want to screw someone that is up to you."

"I don't know if I should be mad at you or be grateful."

"Neither. Just accept things the way they are," Chuck told his little sister.

"So, you think that we were wrong by going after those ass holes that raped Hope?"

"That's not for me to say. Do you think that it was wrong or not? That's what counts. Not what I or anyone else thinks."

"Would you have done the same thing that I did?"

Chuck laughed. "I don't think that they would have sex with me."

"You know what I mean, would you?"

"That would have been a tough call. No, I wouldn't have wanted them to get-a-way with what they had done. Maybe I would have done the same as what Ruben tried to do, kick their asses."

"So what we did wasn't all that bad, was it?"

"I guess not. But don't go and brag about what you did to Mom and Dad."

"You said that Daddy is going through rough times?"

"Yea, he is taking the death of Hope real hard. He blamed himself. Everyone tells him that it was not his fault, but he still blames himself. And on top of that he's losing the farm. He's like Job, being tested by God."

"And if he finds out what I did it would be just too much for him?"

"Yea, something like that. That's why Mom sent me. He doesn't need to know what you did."

"So, what I did is our little secret?"

"I don't think that I would call it little."

Desiree leaned over and kissed her big brother on the cheek.

"What brought on that?"

"I don't know. I just felt like it, that's all."

Inside the house Desiree found that there were boxes filled with things that they had accumulated over the years; things that told the history of their family. It gave her an eerie feeling that she walked into a museum, other than her home. Her mother, who was standing by the kitchen door, give her a cold look. "I made it home."

"I see. I hear that that is not the only thing that you have made."

"What did they tell you?"

"Enough," Evelyn said as she turned her back to her daughter and went back into the kitchen.

Desiree put down her suitcase and followed her mother. "What did they tell you?"

"They told me that my daughter was a tramp. That you were making one of those dirty filthy movies. How could you? How could you disgrace our family like that? Don't you have any decency? Any respect? Shaming our family like that?"

"I did it for Hope."

"I'm sure that she would have been grateful that you did that in her name. Yes, she would have been really proud of you."

"Say what you want, but I did what I did for her, and I would do it again. I'm not going to let those ass holes get away with what they did to her. You might think that it is best to let them get away with it, but I don't. Yes, I did what I did, and I would do it again."

"You don't have any respect for yourself, do you?"

"If I didn't have any respect then I wouldn't have gone after those bastards, would I? No, I did what I did out of love and respect for Hope. After all, she was my sister, was she not?"

"What is done is done," Chuck said as the mother and daughter turned to see him standing at the door. "I don't think that anything is going to be achieved by you two arguing over what she did was right or wrong. So, kiss and make up."

The two women looked at each other and then looked away. After a while Desiree asked, "How's Daddy?"

"He seems to be taking things pretty hard. Sometimes I think that he just gave up. He spends all of his time just walking around the farm. I think that he is saying good bye to it. Sometimes I think that he loves the farm more than me. At night he will sit on that old wooden bench out there under those cottonwood trees, watching lightening bugs and looking at the stars." She shook her head. "I don't know what I can do. He sees his life passing him by and there is nothing that we can do about it. We can't get Hope back and we can't keep the farm. What can I do? I just don't know.

"Daddy." Desiree said as she approached her father. He turned and smiled at her and Sport. He had been gazing at the cattle in the pasture. He could remember when each one was born and how he or another member of the family name them. Not only did he milk them but he grew and harvested the food which he fed them. He knew that soon all of them would be taken away. His farm, which had been passed down through generations to him, will no longer be his. He will be removed from it forever.

His daughter wrapped her arms around him. He kissed the crown of her head and said "Well, hello Monkey. I didn't know that you had made it back."

"That's because I am sneaky."

"Your mom said that Chuck went to get you. Is that boy, Ruben, better now?"

"Yes, he's better. He doesn't need me anymore. He will be fine."

"I think that that was a good thing that you did for him. I'm proud of you. Most people just give lip service about helping others, but you didn't, did you? And that is why I'm proud of you."

"You would have done the same thing. You always help others out."

"I guess so. But I'm still glad to see my children do what they think is right. Not only that I'm proud of you but I know that Hope would be proud of you too. The most important thing in this world is family, and in their hearts they were family. Even though they were never married in a church, I feel like in the eyes of God that they were. At the time I didn't realize it, but he was a part of our family. And what he was trying to do was in a way the right thing to do. Jesus said to turn the other cheek, but I don't believe that he meant for us to have a blind eye towards justice for others, especially when it comes to family."

CHAPTER 56 ━━━━━━━━━━━━━━━

Dick entered the boardroom of Coldman and Company. Around the large oval table sat all of the board members. His white hair and bearded father, was sitting at his place of authority, at the head of the conference table, looked at him with a stone face. His sister Linda was sitting at his right side, the place that was always reserved for him. On the left side was his older brother, Lou. Also at the table were the others numbers of the board. There were no empty seats left there for him. He looked around the room for an empty chair, but there were none - they all had been removed. His watch read ten o'clock, the time that he was told that the meeting would start, but by the empty coffee cups he realized that they had been there for a long time. "I see that you've started without me."

"I called this meeting to discuss your conduct," his father said. "Your behavior has led to great embarrassment to this company. Do you have anything to say in your defense before we vote on your removal from the board?"

"Removal from the board? Why? I have not been convicted of anything, and Art said that there is more than a good chance that the charges will be dropped. The news is making a damn big deal out of nothing. They always do. It's not anything to be concerned about."

"The damage has already been done. Our stock has dropped precariously due to your actions. Already our sales are down. How much more in the long run? Only God knows. But in the short run it looks like the sales will suffer a great deal. Our reputation, which has taken us years to establish ourselves as a company with high morals standards, now is being questioned."

"I can assure you that nothing like that will ever happen again. That's something that I will give you my word on. And I don't give my word lightly."

"He is giving us his word," Lou said sarcastically. "Like that isn't something that he had never done before."

Dick turned from his older brother to his father. "This time I will promise that I will walk straight and narrow. I will never again take on a project that isn't first getting approval from the broad."

"That is what he said the last time," Lou reminded his father. "As if he had seen the light? He probably will say the same thing the next time too."

"So, you bastard," Dick gave a mocking laugh to Lou, "after all of these years, you're still trying to get even with me for taking Gloria away from you, aren't you? Boy, how long are you going to hold that grudge?"

"Go to hell, where you belong." he responded by standing up as his face grew red. "All that you ever cared about is your damn self, no one or nothing else. You sure in the hell never gave a God damn about your family nor this company, that's for damn sure. All you are is nothing but a Heffner wanna be."

"I have done as much for this company as you have, but what you can't stand is that everyone likes me more then you." Dick defended himself. "Isn't that it? You always felt that you never got any respect. Well, there is a good reason for that. You don't deserve any."

"I sure deserve a hell of lot more then you."

"That's enough!" the father said in a demanding voice. Then he looked at each one who was sitting at the table. "We are faced with a choice. Should we retain Dick? Should we forgive him and keep him as a member of the board? Or should we not? Was his action too detrimental to the company to allow him to stay as a member of the board, and a part of the company, or should he be dismissed?" He turned to his right and asked his daughter, "Linda, how do you vote?"

She glanced at everyone that was sitting at the table, then she looked at Dick and back to her father. "I sorry, but I cannot vote for him to stay nor can I vote for him to go. I have to abstain."

"Your abstention is noted. And how do you vote Mr. Reed?"

"He has done too much damage. He is too great of a liability."

"And you, Mr. William?" He asked the black man that was sitting at the conference table.

"I'm on the board as the representative of the union interest, so I am compelled to vote as if this is a union matter, and so I must demand that he is retained until he is convicted or acquitted, although I believe that a suspension without pay might be in order."

"Mr. Manning?"

"Outside of the family I represent the largest block of stockholders, I have a fiduciary obligation to vote for the best interest of the company. Without a doubt the company will be better off with his dismissal."

"Mr. Shoemaker?"

"I also vote for dismissal. This is the first board meeting that he took the trouble to show-up in how long? I don't remember. Evidently all he cares about is his compensation than about the company. I see it as we have no option other then voting for dismissal."

"And Lou, how to you vote?"

"With pleasure I vote for his dismissal."

The man with the white beard in a three piece suit stood and with a voice of authority told his son, "Dick, I warned you when that girl accused you of rape. I said that was the last straw. But did you listen to me? No, you didn't. Now it is too late. The board has voted, and it was nearly unanimous. As of now you are no longer a part of this company."

"But…"

"You will no longer be entitled to receive any compensation from this company. And I might add the house that you're living in is in my name. I'll give you two months to vacate the property."

"What am I supposed to do?"

"That's your problem. You still have your car and boat and the money you have in the bank. That is lots more than most people have."

"Just like that, you are kicking me out of the business and out of my house? What am I supposed to do?"

"You are going to be like most people. You are going to have to make it on your own. You have to leave now for good, you are never to return."

Without saying a word he looked at his brother's sinister smile, then back to his father's stone face. The others averted their eyes away from him. He was standing in a room that was filled with people but he was all alone. He was faced with the harsh reality that the life he had counted on and that he had enjoyed was a thing of the past - something that he might never be able to regain again. The outcast one left the building, taking nothing with him. His feeling of remorse turned into anger and he mumbled, "That damn Garden."

Chapter 57 ━━━━━━━━━━

"Tommy!" Dick yelled at the young bearded man, who was briefly his photographer. He stopped as he watched the big man in a suit hop out of his Lincoln and walk towards him. His first inkling was to run as fast and as far as he could away from this man, for he did not trust him. He felt that he could not turn around nor could he just walk past him either. He was trapped, and he felt that there was no escape. He stood still as Dick walked up to him and shook his hand.

"How are things going?"

"Okay, I guess."

"Okay? I was hoping for something a little more positive than that, but I guess okay is better than things not going too good, isn't it?"

"I guess so," Tommy said as he wondered what Dick was up to.

"Tell me, have you been able to find another job?"

"Not yet, but I have some irons in the fire, so to speak."

"I'm sure that you do. You do like to use fire as a metaphor, don't you?"

Tommy looked at Dick and wondered if he was going to offer him back his old job. He was facing with a dilemma. The little money he had was running out, and he had no real prospect of getting anymore anytime soon. On the other hand he knew that Dick could not be trusted. "Are you here to offer my old job back?"

"Is that what you're thinking? No, sorry, I have a good photographer. He is someone that I can count on, you know what I mean?"

"Like I said I'm not aiming to go back into prison because someone can't keep his damn dick in his pants."

Dick laughed. "Forget what that lying little bitch said. We didn't rape anyone. She was just trying to extort money out of me, that's all. But she didn't get away with it. She isn't anyone that we will ever have to worry about again."

"If you don't need a photographer then why are you here?"

Dick smiled at Tommy and said, "Can't a guy just stop by to say 'hi' to an old friend?"

"No."

"What do you mean, no?" He replied still smiling.

"I'm not buying whatever you are selling. You just happen to be in the neighborhood, and you just decided to drop-by."

"You are so suspicious, aren't you?"

"Why are you here?"

"Well, I do have a proposition for you, but I think it is best to discuss it somewhere other than here. I'm getting a little hungry. How about you? Could you go for a big juicy steak and some good wine, my friend?" Dick could sense Tommy's reluctance to go along with him. "You do like steaks, don't you?" Tommy did not reply. "Have you ever heard of a of a steak house by the name of Ed's Porter House? It's one of the best in town."

"Yeah, I've heard of it" Tommy said hesitantly.

"How does it sound?"

Tommy questioned that by going along with him would that not give Dick an advantage over him? He knew that it might make him feel obligated to Dick. In the short time he had known him he had seen how he would make people feel obligated to him. But going to one of the top restaurants in Chicago was something that was hard for him to pass by. He swore to himself that if he would go he would not let Dick take advantage of him. "Yeah, I guess that it would be okay."

"Then let's go." Dick opened the door to the Lincoln.

Dick asked and they were granted a table far away from the other patrons, where they could talk in confidence. After the waitress had taken their order he commented on how nice the place was.

"I don't think that you brought me here to show-off your taste in restaurants. What do you want?" Tommy wanted to know.

"Well," Dick said with a smile, "I have a little problem. It's like an itch that I can't scratch, you know what I mean?"

"You want me to scratch your back?"

"You could say that. Before I hired you I did a little investigation. And it seems that you like to set things on fire. Is that right?"

"That's what they say. Go on."

"Are you interested?"

"What do you have in mind?"

"Enough money that you won't have to worry about a job for a while."

"Just how much are we talking about?"

"Ten-grand."

"Ten-grand?"

"Yes, ten-grand. That's a lot of money. Have you ever had that much money at one time in your life? You can do lots with ten-grand."

"I can do a hell of a lot more with twenty."

"Twenty-grand is a little much. The itch isn't that bad." said Dick.

"Do you want the itch scratched or not?"

"Let's call it fifteen."

"Twenty."

"Twenty?"

"You're damn right twenty. I'm not going to risk having my ass thrown back into jail for anything less than twenty." Tommy said with resolve.

"No need to worry about getting caught, it well be easy. They only serve dinner. That means that they don't open up until five."

"A restaurant? Yeah, I think that I can handle that."

"Then we have a deal?"

"I guess."

"Fifteen?"

"I said twenty." said Tommy with a stone face.

"Twenty, uh? Okay, twenty it is. You drive a hard bargain. Twenty-grand is it." The two men shook on the sinister agreement. "It has to be Thursday afternoon. And not too late either. Say between one and four."

"You want it in broad daylight?"

"Is that something that you can't handle?"

"I can handle it, but I do want my money up-front."

"Fifty-fifty. Half now and the other half after the job is done, okay" Dick reached inside his suit jacket and pulled out an envelope and handed it to Tommy. "Ten-grand. You can count it when you get home."

"You're a bastard," Tommy smiled. "You were going to pay me twenty-grand all along, weren't you?"

Dick smiled and then he became serious. "I want to get something straight with you, I don't want you to come around looking for me to get the other half. That can get both of us into trouble, do you understand? The cops are going to be on my ass, and if you pop-up they will put the pieces together. Don't you worry your little head about your other half, I'm not dumb enough to run out on you. So don't come looking for me, is that clear?"

"Don't worry about me," Tommy said. "There will be no way in hell that they will be able to tie you to your little itch that you want me to scratch."

CHAPTER 58 ━━━━━━━━━━

"Welcome back," June, the owner of The Garden, said as Ruben limped into the restaurant with the aid of a cane. He smiled as she embraced him. "It's good to see you back."

"It's good to be back," he replied. "I hear that you were having a tough time without me."

"Yes, we were contemplating about closing up until you returned, but we managed to keep it open."

Standing in the foyer, which was at the head of the stairs that lead down to the Mediterranean banquet room, he scanned the up-stairs two rooms. The one on his left was the lounge. It was filled with cocktail tables and a small stage and a small dance floor. The other side of the room was the bar with the liquor bottles displayed. This was where he worked four times a week. In the other room that he could see from the foyer was the dining room. It was filled with tables that were covered with white table cloths. He had a feeling of euphoria and a little nostalgia. He never had admitted to it, but this was where he felt that he belonged. The lady next to him was reading his face as he give her a compliment, "It looks like you did okay without me."

"How do you feel?"

"Better, I will live."

"Then do you think that you will be able to come back to work?"

"I'm ready now."

"Now? Are you sure? You still don't look that good."

"You saying that I'm ugly?"

June smiled at the man with the scarred face and asked, "Do you feel like you're up to it?"

"I probably will move a little slow, but I think that I can handle it."

"Well, let's see what Gus has to say." With that the two started walking slowly to the kitchen. With every step Ruben took there was some pain, but he covered it up with a smile.

"Well, well, lookie who's here," June's husband Gus said as he was finishing prepping the food. There was a contrast between the couple's appearance. June was a well groomed lady who ran the front of the business. Gus was not that concerned about his own appearance as much as the appearance and the taste of what he served to his customers. He felt that was more important than his own appearance. His domain was the kitchen and the back of the house. His nickname was Froggy, a name that no one called him to his face, He was called that not because he was French, which he was not, but because of his appearance and his deep voice. He was short and heavy set. He had a round pitted face with large eyes. He had been known to have yelled at the help, like a father yelling at his children.

"How are you doing, Gus?"

"Better now that you are back. What happened to your hair? Did they cut it off?"

"No. I did it before I got hurt." replied Ruben.

"I think that it's going to take a little time to get used to."

"He says that he's ready to come back to work," June told her husband.

"So, do you think you can handle it?" asked Gus.

"I think so."

"That's my boy," Gus said with a smile. "I will tell you what. We can give it a try. If it is too much then we will just have to wait a little longer, that's all. But you can give it a try, okay? Don't be afraid to take it slowly. If you need to sit down for a while, then do, okay?"

"Okay."

"Go ahead and punch in," June said.

"I always thought that you were a good kid," Gus said soberly as Ruben hobbled across the kitchen. "Going after those low life bastards took guts. I hated to see what had happened to you. But at the same time I was proud of you. You went after them like a real man. Yes sir, what you did took guts."

"But don't you ever try that again," June admonished him.

Feeling a little embarrassed, Ruben just smiled.

"Yea, you better not do that again. We don't want to have to find a replacement for you," Gus joked.

"So, what do you need done?" Ruben said to change the subject.

"Well, I haven't done the beer order yet," Gus told Ruben. "Do you think you can do that?"

"I'll manage."

"That's my boy."

"Gus and I have some running around to do. Will you be okay?"

"Don't worry, I'll be okay."

She smiled and said, "It's nice to have you back."

"It's nice to be back," said Ruben.

Ruben put the empty liquor bottles from the night before, along with a note that told what beer and bar supplies were needed, onto a cart. He pushed the cart through the kitchen to the service elevator, where he pushed it inside and closed the door, for there was a policy that no one was not allowed to ride in the elevator. He walked down the stairs in the service area.

While Ruben was replacing the empty liquor bottles with full ones in the liquor room he was not aware of a man pulling in front of The Garden. The man got out of the car and waited until there were no cars passing by. Then he lit a piece of cloth that was in the neck of a bottle that was filled with gasoline, and he threw it through a window of the lounge. When it hit the floor, it exploded, sending the flaming gasoline across the carpet. The flames raced quickly towards the bar as another Molotov cocktail went through the dining room window. The smoke quickly filled The Garden as the raging flames set off the fire alarm. At first Ruben did not realize what was happening. It took him a second to recognize the sound of the alarm. By then he could smell the smoke and hear the fire roaring. With his cane he went as fast as he could move through the Mediterranean Room. Before he could cross the banquet room he could feel the heat from the fire. As he started towards the stairs when his leg gave out. Falling on the floor, he pulled himself up with his cane and grab the banister and pulled himself up the steps. He was able to see over the top of the stairs at the roaring fire. He could feel the heat of the flames and its choking smoke that prevented him from reaching the top. He could hear the liquor bottles behind the bar exploding. Over the top steps he could see the blue sky through the windows and the front door beyond the blaze and dark gray smoke that the fire was casting off. The heat was like a wall, a barrier that did not allow him to cross to the foyer and to escape to the outside. The sprinkler system was having little effect on the fire. The enormous heat was an invisible wall that was pushing him back down the stairs. His leg give out and he tumbled down the flight of steps, sending him sprawling onto the floor. A bone in his leg that was not completely healed, protruded through the skin. He heard the bottles in the liquor room exploding. Using his hands he pulled himself across the floor, but not fast enough to escape. Soon the old restaurant was engulfed in flames. Ruben did not stand a chance.

The fire trucks, with their lights flashing and with sirens blaring, raced down the busy city streets, forcing the traffic to yield out of the way. They turned off the busy street onto a less busy one, where they could see the smoke marking the location. It only took minutes before the firemen reached The Garden, but it was too late. The roof of the old restaurant had already collapsed, leaving only the outer burning walls standing. There was big sign that stood boldly in front of the building announcing the restaurant, but now it was only a tombstone for Anna's Garden and for Ruben. The firemen had hooked-up their hoses and were spraying water on the remains of the building when one of the fireman reported that he smelled gasoline. Soon it was confirmed by his fellow firemen. After a while the crowd began to disperse. The show was over, the only thing to be seen was the firemen spraying water on the remains. That was when June and Gus returned. She ran from the car towards what was their place of business, the place that her whole life had revolved around for so many years. Now it was all gone. She stood as close as they would let her. She wanted to cling to it as one wanted to embrace a dying loved one. Gus put his arm around his crying wife. "What happened?" he asked the fireman that approached them.

"Are you the owners?"

"Yes, yes, we are. What happened?" asked Gus.

Before the man could answer June cut in, "Did Ruben get out?"

"Who is Ruben?"

Frantically she looked around. She saw only strangers. "I don't see him! I don't see him!" She buried her face in her husband's chest and began to cry. "It is my fault. We shouldn't have let him come back to work."

"We had no way of knowing that it was going to burn down."

"Why did you say that you shouldn't let him come back?" another man asked.

"Who are you?" Gus asked.

"I'm Walter Schultz, the Fire Marshall." He held out his I.D. "Was there a reason why he shouldn't have been working?"

"Some low life bums beat him up. He was….is." Gus choked up. "Do you think that maybe those bastards did it? Burned down the restaurant with Ruben in it?"

"Who are those 'bastards' you are referring to?"

"I don't know. Whoever burned down our place, those are the bastards that I'm talking about. Those damn low life bastards, that's who."

"Do you have any idea who are they?"

"Those bastards who raped Hope Adamsen, that's who I think did it."

"Were they arrested?"

"But they let them go. They never even had a trial. They just let them walk away like nothing ever happened. Those low life bastards, those are the ones that I'm talking about."

"She was a waitress that worked here," June tried to clarify what her husband was saying. "The ones that work at the Coldman Studio raped her, and she committed suicide. They said that there wasn't enough evidence to charge them, so they let them go."

"She was a nice girl. She wouldn't ever lie," Gus said. "She committed suicide. Those low life bastards caused her to commit suicide. What more proof to you need? They raped Hope and they burned down our restaurant. They are bad, bad men, and something should be done about them."

"You are saying that someone started the fire?" asked June. "Then it must have been them. No one else had any reason to. Do you think that it was them?"

"It's too soon to say. We have to examine all of the evidence before we can come to any conclusion." Schultz stated.

"What evidence? It burned down. There won't be any evidence. Everything is all burned-up." Gus declared. "That is what they said to Hope, 'there isn't any evidence'."

"There will still be evidence."

"Like what?" June inquired.

"For one thing some of the men smelled gasoline."

"Gasoline?" Gus asked. "So it's true what we have been saying all along that Ruben was murdered? Someone killed him on purpose? He was a good boy. Now you are saying that some low life bastards killed him?"

"It does look like it might be the case," the Fire Marshall said.

"Whoever in the hell did it should be killed themselves, right? An eye for an eye, a tooth for a tooth?" Gus questioned the man that represented the authorities.

"I think it is best to let us handle it."

"You must see it through our eyes," June defended her husband. "We just lost both our business and an employee, a friend. Of course he is upset. You can understand that, can't you?"

"You are talking like he might have been the target."

"It was his first day back."

"Was there any reason that they would go after him?"

"He got into a fight with those low life bastards that raped Hope Adamsen," Gus said. "Those are the ones that did it."

"Did they have any way of knowing that this Ruben was coming back to work today?"

"No, it probably was a coincidence," June said. "But will you still look into them?"

"Of course," he said as he giving the grieving couple a half-hearted smile before he walked away.

Seth was in his bartender's uniform when he pulled-up to the remains of The Garden. There was one fire truck left, spraying water on the smoldering skeleton of the building, only the fire place and part of two walls remained. Along with the fire truck were two squad cars with other police vehicles. A local T.V. reporter was interviewing June and Gus in front of the Anna's Garden marquee with the remains of the fire in the background. He could hear Gus telling the reporter, "This fire was no accident, some low life bastard burned down our restaurant."

"Do you have any idea who did it?"

"Yes, we do. It was those…."

"We don't have any proof. We do have our suspicions, but we can't say," June gave her husband a forceful look. "If we tell you then we will be opening ourselves up for a slander lawsuit against us."

"So you think that you might know who did it?"

"Yes, but we will not discuss it." She pulled on Gus's arm. "We have to go now."

"You are going to walk away without telling us who burned down your restaurant?"

"You don't care if we are sued for slander or not, do you? All that you care about is that you have a good piece to put on the news. That is all, isn't it?" They walked away, leaving the reporter holding the microphone.

Seth went to them and June give him an unexpected hug. "Ruben was in there," she told him.

"He didn't make it out?" June shook her head. He looked at Gus and he also shook his head. "I heard you telling the reporter that someone started it. Did someone see him?"

"No, but the firemen smelled gasoline," June replied.

"Yes, someone burned it down," Gus declared. "Some no good God damn low life bastard set it on fire. And Ruben was in it. Somewhere under all of that rubbish is Ruben's body. May God rest his soul. He was a good boy. He was like the son that we never had. He was a good boy. Now he is gone. What can I say? He is no more."

"Are you sure that he didn't get out."

"We're sure," June answered. "If he had made it out then he would be here. He is in there, and that's his car over there. When they get it cooled down enough, they will find him."

"So he was murdered?"

"Yeah, you can say that," Gus spoke angrily. "And if I get my hands on them they will pay. The good book says an eye for eye and a tooth for a tooth and a life for a life. If I get hold of them they will pay, that's for damn sure. I will do to them like they did in the olden days, I will burn them at a stake. They will suffer like Ruben did, that's for sure. That is what they deserve, that's for damn sure. Am I not right?""

"You said them, were there more than one?"

"I don't know how many there were. No one saw them, in broad daylight, and no one has seen them. They must have waited until no cars were in sight, then they set it on fire, those dirty cowards. We think that it was those low life's that raped poor little Hope, don't you?"

The smell of the burned building filled the air as one by one the employees came. Each looked at the ruins and tried to reconstruct it in their minds. Each of them felt the loss in their own way. Some were effected more financially as others were effected more emotionally, but all of them felt a loss. They were for the most part in their uniforms, one exception was Grant. He heard about the misfortune over the radio. When he got there Seth told him, "Someone set it on fire. Ruben was inside. He didn't make it out. He is still in there." With that news he had a sinking feeling; the loss of a person that was more than a co-worker, he was also a friend. The knowing that it was in part his own fault that left him with the feeling that he had just caused the death of a friend. Years before he had sworn that he would never take another life regardless what the cost might be. Now he knew that his actions had played a part in the death of a friend. He walked away from the ones that had gathered by the yellow tape that had been placed around the crime scene. Seth followed him. He mumbled, "They did it," partly to himself and partly to Seth.

"You mean the ones from Coldman Studio?"

"Yes, of course, Coldman Studio. You were right, we should have let it go. I don't know who in the hell I thought that I was that gave me the right to go after them. We were all going to be Hope's avenging angel. Now see what it got us. Ruben is dead. He was burned to death in the fire."

"What did you do?"

"Enough."

"Enough?"

Grant looked at Seth and told him, "We set out to destroy them, as you know. I went after the one that was the photographer. He was also an artist, I let the art world know what he had done, in an effort to destroy his dream of being a famous artist. And Nicole and Desiree went after the other two men, getting them on statutory rape. And I think that they were trying to get back at us by burning down The Garden."

"Revenge?"

"They had to be the ones. Who else would do just a thing like that? It had to be them."

For a long time the two did not speak, they just stared at the smoldering remains of The Garden, each with their own thoughts. Grant with his feeling of guilt, and Seth, whose world had been turned upside down again. And now he wanted it to be returned back to the way it was, the way it was the day before, and the day before the tragedy that happened to Hope, and back to the time before the death of his family. What he was looking at might have been a reflection of the soul of the men that have done those terrible deeds.

The two were joined by Davy. Also he was in his street clothes. His usual smile that he used to greet people was gone. "What happened?" he soberly asked.

"It was set on fire," Seth replied.

"Who?"

"My guess it was the ones that raped Hope," Grant answered.

"All that they know is that someone started it. Who? No one knows. But I will put my money on him being right," Seth added.

"D-Do they know?"

"Who knows what?" Grant asked Davy.

"June and Gus, about o-ones of those rapists did it?"

"I don't know," Grant said. "But my guess is that they do. Why? I don't know. Someone must have said something to them, or they overheard us talking about it. Or maybe they just figured it out for themselves. I have no idea."

"W-We were going after th-them, but we didn't do anything."

"We did."

"What?"

"What?" Grant was trying to decide on what to tell them. He had just admitted that they did something. Should he come clean and tell them everything? "The photographer, who was also an artist, was a part of an art show. I went and told them what he had done."

"And for th-that they bu-burnt down the restaurant?"

"No, there was more."

"What?"

"Well, Nicole and Desiree went after them, trying to get them on statutory rape, and they did. All three of them were arrested, but they are out on bail."

"What happened to the girls?" Seth asked.

"They got Nicole on delinquency of a minor, she is out on bail," Grant told them. "And Desiree went back to Wisconsin, I don't think that we will see her anymore. Like it or not there is a price to pay for everything we do."

"You saying th-that Wis-Wisconsin is that bad?" Davy joked.

Grant smiled at him and said, "I'm just saying that before you do anything you should look at the downside. One must always be willing to pay the price for his actions."

"You think that we should go and tell his mother what happened?" Seth asked.

"No," Grant stated. "That's the police job. And until they find his body we won't know for sure he is in there. Let them do their job."

"I-I don't know if we should count on them to do th-their job. They didn't do th-their job when it came to Hope, did they? I-I don't see then get-getting con-convicted on th-this either, do you?"

Chapter 59 ━━━━━━━━━━━━━

"Ruben," Lucy said in a loud voice, so he could hear her if he was in his bedroom, but there was no answer. The apartment was silent. As she set her bag on the table she noticed a note from him. 'Mom, I am going to the Garden. If they let me work, I will be home later. Ruben.' She remembered that she didn't notice his car. She wasn't that concerned, although she felt that he wasn't ready to go back to work yet. She still felt that there wasn't any danger in him driving. She removed a TV. Dinner out of the freezer and put it in the microwave. As she was removing a beer from the refrigerator she heard the doorbell ring. At the door were the couple that she seen in Ruben's hospital room. She tried to remember their names but she couldn't.

"Mrs. Garcia, do you remember us?" the man asked.

"Yes, you two was at the hospital. I'm sorry, but I don't recall your names."

"I'm Dan Long and this is Emily Newman, we are police officers." He held out his badge.

She stared at them, whatever the reason for them being there she knew it wasn't going to be good. "What did he do now?"

"He was working at The Garden when it caught on fire." He could see that she had stopped breathing and her eyes widened. "He wasn't able to get out. I'm sorry."

She backed away and sat down on the couch, still staring at the man who had just brought the news of her son, her only child, the only family that was still a part of her life, was dead. This man in front of her must be an angel that God had sent to tell her that her son was now in heaven. Or was he sent by the Devil to explain that he is now and forever in Hell. Or could that be a lie, a bad joke. Or maybe a mistake. Yes, a mistake.

The body was of someone else, not Ruben's, not her son, but someone else. Another mother's son, not hers. With tears running down her face as she tried to speak, she only mumbled. She cleared her throat and took a deep breath before asking, "What happened?"

"He was in the basement when it started. He wasn't able to get out."

"Was there anyone else?"

"No, he was the only one there at the time."

"How did it start?" She saw him look away and she knew that something was wrong. "How did it start?"

"Right now that is not important."

"He was my son. Now you're telling me that he is dead. I'll say what is important or not. How did it start?"

"Arson. Someone started it."

"Do you know who it was?"

"No, but we do have some leads."

"Could it have been the ones that beat him up?"

"It's a possibility. We are looking into that possibility. I can assure you that we will find the ones that did kill your son. They will pay for what they have done, I can assure you of that."

"What I don't understand is why they would do such a thing. It don't make any sense to me. Everything was settled between them. Why do you think that it might be them?"

"They might not have known that he was in there," interjected Detective Newman.

"She is right. He was in the basement when the fire was started. More than likely the arsonist wasn't aware that your son was in the building. It was just by chance that he was there at that time. I'm sorry."

"Do you know who did this awful thing to my son? What person, what animal that would do just an awful thing as that? Do you think you know who did it?"

"I'm sorry Mrs. Garcia, but I'm not at liberty to discuss the matter. All I can tell you is that they are under investigation."

"Are you holding something from me? Did something happen that I don't know about?" He didn't answered her. "I think that I have the right to know. What happened?"

"We are still putting the pieces together."

"What happened?" Lucy demanded.

"I think that she has the right to know," Detective Newman stated.

He looked back-and-forth between the two women, than he gave in. "Desiree Adamsen and her friend Nicole Harris set them up so they could be arrested on statutory rape. It's possible the ones that they were setting up were seeking revenge."

"You saying that they were mad at Nicole and Desiree so they murdered Ruben? That don't sound right to me."

"Like what we said that more than likely they weren't aware that he was in the restaurant. They were associating them with the restaurant. It is what is call indirect aggression, they wanted to hurt them without anyone knowing or proving that it was them. And at the same time sending a message to the girls that they should not testify against them."

"How about Nicole and Desiree? Anything going to happen to them?"

"Desiree was sent back to Wisconsin. Nicole? That is still up in the air."

"So Ruben got killed and Desiree is getting off scot-free? And Nicole might do the same? That is bull shit. They should pay too. Ruben is dead and those two are running around free, that's not fair, is it?"

"Well, to what do we attribute the honor of your present company?" Dick asked as Detective Long and Detective Newman entered the studio.

"You don't have any idea why we are here, do you?" Detective Newman asked loud enough so everyone in the room would hear. All of their attention was being focused on the two police officers.

"Are we playing a game of riddles?" Dick smiled and asked her, "Did you come here to subsidize your income?"

Her face grew red, before she could come up with a good reply Detective Long cut in, "Anna's Garden burned-down yesterday. We were wondering if you happen to know anything about it."

"That's too bad, a real crying shame, but you don't think that someone here had anything to do with it, do you?"

"Of cause not, not a fine up-standing citizen as you are," Detective Long said sarcastically, "but never-the-less for our records we need to know where you guys were at say two o'clock yesterday afternoon?"

"Is that when it burned-down? I have to start paying more attention to the news."

"Yes, that is when someone set it on fire, with Ruben Garcia in it. He didn't make it out." Dick and Max showed no emotion. Lenny turned and walked to the window. Detective Long could see him lower his head. "He was burned to death. That's a horrible way to die, being cooked alive. We are going to find the cowards that started the fire. So we need to know where you were when it burned-down."

"Let's see now," Dick rubbed his chin as he pretended that he was having a hard time remembering. "Let's see, you said about two o'clock yesterday? Max do you remember what we were doing at two o'clock yesterday?"

"Wasn't that when we went to the Art Institute?"

"Yes, I do believe you are right. Matter-of-fact I think I have the receipt here in my desk. Yes. Here it is, the receipt for three tickets for yesterday. You know what is the funny thing about the Art Institute? They are every paranoid. They are afraid that someone, an unscrupulous person, might steal one of their beloved paintings. They have cameras everywhere. Did you know that you are on film before you even go inside until you leave? Almost every second that you are there you are on tape."

"I see," Detective Long confirmed. "That's very fascinating, but what I find interesting is the fact that it only records who is there, not who isn't there. Do you know what I mean?"

"Are you implying that we paid someone to set it on fire? Surely not. Why would we do a thing like that? I for one didn't have any animosity towards the place. Matter-of-fact I thought that the food was quite good even if I say so myself. Now, you think that I, or one of us, had something to do with burning down that fine establishment? I must say that I am offended. How could you think of such a thing like that?"

"I surely don't want to offend a good up-right citizen like you." Detective Long turned his focus to Lenny. "Do you have any thoughts on the subject? Any idea who would do such an awful thing? Completely destroying The Garden, hurting the people that were associated with it. But the worst thing was what happened to Ruben Garcia, the young man that your friends nearly beat to death. He had to go back to work, for he needed the money to take care of his mother. So what happened on his first day back to work? Some cold-blooded animal who doesn't give a damn about anything or anybody else burned-down the restaurant, cooking Ruben Garcia alive. That has to be about the worst way possible to die. He was still recovering from the beating. He would not have been able to move very fast. He would have tried to escape but he was trapped. The restaurant would have filled up with smoke as it had become hotter and hotter. Then the flames would have caught his clothes on fire, burning him. Have you ever been burned?"

Lenny looked at Detective Long, but he did not answer. He too felt that he was trapped somewhere between his conscience and his fear.

"Can you imagine what it must have been like to have all of your clothes on fire all at once? When they pulled his body out last night he was burned to a crisp. We had to tell his mother what happened to her son. Can you imagine the anguish she must be feeling that her son was burned to a crisp and the one who did it is still out there? She will be in agony until her son will get justice."

CHAPTER 60 ———————————

They say that the saddest thing in the world is the passing of a child, especially if he was the only child and with the knowledge that there would be never another. This was the realization that Lucy was faced with. Her hair that was always meticulous, but on this day it fell short. Her face usually had more than an adequate amount of make-up, but on this day there was none. Every line and every wrinkle were revealed, as if to bare her soul to the world. She was faced with the realization that the world had stripped her from her family, leaving her to stand alone. Ruben was her only child and now his remains had been placed on the altar by his picture. Her hour of grief was shared only by a few people that came to the funeral home. Most she did not recognize. They would study his picture then they would give her their condolences and tell her of how much that they had liked him and that they would miss him. She would thank them with a forced smile.

Her role as a grieving mother quickly was transformed into a woman who was filled with rage when Nicole and Desiree entered into her view. "What in the hell are you two doing here? Haven't you done enough?" She caught the two young ladies by surprise. "Because of you two whores he is dead. He would still be alive if it wasn't for you."

"We did not set the restaurant on fire," Desiree defended their actions.

"But you caused it, didn't you?" Lucy said between her teeth. "You were as much to blame as those bastards who did it, and now you come in here as if you were all nice and innocent."

"Believe me, Mrs. Garcia, when we tell you how sorry we are," Nicole begged Ruben's mother. "I know how you must feel."

"You have no way in hell of knowing the way I feel. Have you ever had a son that was murdered? That was burned to death in a fire? No.

You haven't. No, you don't know how I feel. I wish that it was you two who got burned-up in the fire, not my son. He was innocent. He didn't deserve that. You two did." She fell back onto her chair and she began to cry uncontrollably.

The two young women stood, looking down at the woman, knowing that they were partly the cause of the death of her son. Both of them wanted to comfort her, but they knew that it was impossible. Even though they shared in her grief, their attempt to comfort her would only lead to more hostilities. But still they stood looking at the grieving mother, until they felt hands guiding them away. It was Grant. He led them out of that room of the funeral home.

Out of a mixture of anger and grief Lucy wept uncontrollably. She sensed a man that sat down next to her. He did not try to get her attention. He sat patiently, letting her release her feelings of pain she had for the loss of her son. 'Who was this man who sat down next to her?' She wondered. There was a whole room of empty seats. Why did he choose that one? Through her tears she saw that the man that came to share his grief with her was Seth. She laid her head on his shoulder as he held her. For a long time they held each other before she told him, "They killed my son. They murdered him."

"I know."

"He died an awful death. Nothing is more horrifying then being burned to death. And they are going to get away with it. They murdered Ruben and nothing is going to happen to them."

A young man, about the same age as Ruben was, stepped next to the altar that bore the remains and the picture of the deceased. The clean shaven man wore a three piece suit. He stood there until the room became still. Then he spoke in a voice and with the mannerism of a man who was experienced in public speaking, "I was given the privilege of being the one to deliver Ruben Garcia's eulogy. At first I thought that I was not worthy of the honor, but when his good and loving mother, Lucy Garcia, asked me to give the eulogy, how could I refuse? We were best childhood friends. Due to unfortunate circumstances, we were separated. He moved away and he went to a different school. But we remained friends. As time went by, we went our own ways, but I always felt that we shared a bond that was forged by our early friendship. Due to this, I always felt that I did have an insight into what he was really like, his hopes and dreams. I know that, like all of us, he fell short. His twenty three-years were not enough time for him to be allowed to fulfill his dreams. The writer Sherwood Anderson wrote that you should not solely judge a man on his accomplishments, but also on his dreams, for his dreams reveal his true nature. I knew his dreams. I knew his true nature. And I am here to testify that he was a good and noble person. A man that I am proud to say was my friend.

"You might ask why don't people, why don't we all, fulfill our dreams? Why do we fall short of our goal? Why aren't we more successful in our professional and personal life? None of us truly reaches our potential, do we? We are like big powerful birds sitting high upon a perch ready to soar to unbelievable heights, for we all have that potential in us. The only reason that we don't succeed is we let other people put shackles on us. We all have shackles, don't we? Most of them we put on ourselves. True, we all have handicaps-some are physical, some are economical and I am also talking about society. I'm talking about how we let other people, some are our friends and some are not, but nevertheless they all do influence us. Yes, I know that we do not live on an island. Everyone influences every other person, and that's the way it should be. If we did not have it that away, then we would not have a society. We would not have a civilization. But that is not what I am referring to. I'm talking about how we let others tell us what roles we must play. We let others dictate to us, telling us what is right and what is wrong, when all along we know that we have the ability to determine what is right and what isn't for ourselves. We owe it to ourselves and to others to break loose from those shackles. For we all have the potential to soar to greater heights."

June and Gus joined the circle of their former employees outside of the funeral home. They traded hugs. "He was a good kid, a good employee," June said. "I will miss him every much."

"I pray to God that they will get those cowardly bastards," Gus expressed his anger. "If I ever get hold of them, I will… It won't be pretty, that's all that I can say."

"T-that how w-we all feel," added Davy.

"You were always good to him," Grant commented. "When you reopen, I will be glad to work for you again."

"I'm sorry, but we won't be reopening the restaurant," she told them. "The cost, even with the insurance money, is just too great. Sorry, but Gus and I decided to retire."

"So, The Garden is no more," said Seth.

"I'm afraid so. I have always seen you more like friends than employees," she said to all of them. "If you ever need a reference, you can count on us."

"You telling us that is it?" Yvette asked. "There will never be another Garden."

"That's how it looks," she said before she and Gus departed.

"Well, it looks like it's time to see if I can find another bartending gig," said Seth.

"Maybe we got what we have coming to us," Grant said softly.

"W-what d-do you mean?" Davy asked.

"I don't know what in the hell I was expecting, setting out to destroy them and thinking that they wouldn't do anything about it. That sure in the hell was stupid of us. It was as if we killed Ruben ourselves."

"W-what, what in the hell y-you talking about? We killed Ruben? No way! Th-those dirty bastards killed him, not us. May they all go and burn in hell forever. Th- they are the ones that killed him, not us."

"You can say anything you want to and you can believe anything you want to, but the cold hard truth is if we did not go after them Ruben would still be alive."

"And we would still have The Garden," added Yvette.

"And those ass holes would have got away with murdering Hope," Desiree stated. "Wouldn't they?"

"I can appreciate your feelings," Grant told her, "but it was not our place to avenge your sister. That's the law's responsibility, not ours."

"The law didn't do a God damn thing, did they?" she give a rebuttal.

"And they probably won't give a damn about them killing Ruben either." Nicole added.

"All that I'm saying is that we are partly at fault for Ruben's death," Grant restated his view.

"I don't th-think it was our fault," Davy replied.

"Well, Davy, you can believe anything that you want, but it still won't alter the truth. We are responsible for Ruben's death. Whatever you do you are responsible for your actions." With that Grant ended the conversation and they all left in different direction

"Jason says that you keep calling him Nelson," Angela brought up to Seth.

"I don't think so."

"But you do. I've heard you. You do call him Nelson. You might not realize it, but you do."

"Maybe once in a while, but it's no big deal."

"Yes, it is a big deal. It hurts him. He feels like you're trying to make him into Nelson. You can't do that. And it's unfair to him."

"O.K., I'll be more careful."

"He likes you. You are the closest thing that he ever had for a father. And we are both grateful for that, but he needs to be himself. Do you understand?"

"Sure....I do."

"No, you don't. He likes to play catch with you, but baseball is not his favorite sport. It's soccer. That's what all of his friends play. Not baseball. And he likes speaking Spanish, not English."

"This is America. We speak English here in America. It will be better for him if he learns it."

"We are Americans too. We are from the Dominican Republic. We are a part of the Americas. Just because we eat rice and beans instead of potatoes and gravy doesn't make us less of Americans."

"Okay, okay, you win. I'll buy him a soccer ball and we will play with that, and I will try not to call him Nelson anymore."

"Me too."

"What do you mean, 'me too'? I don't call you Grace. I never called you Grace. Not once."

"No, you haven't. But you're still trying to turn me into her. You want me to cook like her, dress like her. You even want me to make love like her. Last night you said that you would like to have another child, a daughter. What would you want to name her, Crystal?"

"That's not fair. My family was a big part of my life. You cannot expect me to forget them?"

"No, but you cannot expect us to be their replacement either, can you? Look, you are a good man, but you want to relive the past. We need to be part of the future, not the past. That is gone forever. You can never get it back. That is why we must end this relationship."

"What do you mean, 'end the relationship'? Are you breaking-up with me, just because I called Jason, Nelson?"

"It's more than that. I really do care for you, but I think that it is time for us to go our separate ways."

With those words Seth felt that he was being banned. Again he would be alone. No one to love nor no one to love him. When he dropped them off he watched them walk to the apartment building. At the door, before they went in, Jason turned and waved good bye."

CHAPTER 61 ━━━━━━━━━━━━

Again on a foggy morning Father Rafael took out his trumpet, put it up to his mouth and blew. The vibration of his lips against the mouth piece created the music as the wind passed through the keys of the brass instrument. The two songs that he played on that morning, they were songs of the days of reckoning. The songs were cast out into the fog that blanketed the city. Over its churches and the homes of the ones that dwell in them-their houses and apartment buildings. The fog surrounded the factories and the office buildings, leaving only the tops of the skyscrapers uncovered. It blanketed the parks that line Lake Shore Drive and spread over the lake that lay beyond.

On that foggy morning, miles from the shore the boat by the name of the Get-A-Way was bobbing on the surface of the lake. On the big boat, with beers in their hands, three that men were celebrating their release from custody. The fog was concealing them from all of humanity as if they could hide from their sins. Dick raised his beer and the other two followed, touching the bottles together. "I'd like to make a toast to good old Art, for getting the charges dropped, with the help of some well-placed campaign donations."

"For you, but not for me," Max complained. "I still have rape charges pending."

"Don't worry, he'll get you off with a lesser charge. Maybe you will get probation or some shit like that. That little bitch had a falsified I.D. There wasn't any way that you would have known that little cunt was under age. She should be the one that has her ass thrown in jail, not you. I wouldn't worry too much about it. The only thing that you should be concerned about is if something else pops up."

"Something else pops up? Like what?"

"Oh, let's say something like a little movie of you raping her sister."
Both of the men turned and looked at Lenny. "Max, how far do you think
that we are away from the shore?" Dick asked as he gave Lenny a sinister
smile.

"Shit, I don't have any damn idea, Dick. Why do you ask?" Max
replied.

"It's that three mile limit thing. You know, the law stops at three
miles," Dick said as he continued smiling at the terrified Lenny. "Actually
we are far beyond the three mile limit. We are more like ten or so. Only
thing out here is us. Probably no one in miles. So, if we, say, wanted to go
skinny dipping no one would ever know."

"That only goes if you are out in the ocean. Not on the lakes." Lenny
said, trying to hide his fear. "I, I think that we are beyond the Illinois
boundary. Maybe we should head back. We aren't allowed to leave the
state."

"Head back? I don't think so. We just got out here, away from
everything. Max, do you want to head back in?"

"What the hell for? I'm aiming to get good and drunk. Who in the hell
will know if we are past some damn imaginary state line or not."

"That's the way that I see it. Out here we are the law. Whatever
we decide goes. We are the judge and the jury, and if need to be the
executioner."

"What are you getting at?" Lenny spoke with a nervous voice.

"That day when we had that little swimming party, you do remember?
Don't you? We had those two pretty young things with us. Everyone was
wearing a swimming suit except for me. Well, I took the liberty of going
through your pockets. I hope you don't mind. You don't, do you, being
old friends and all?"

Lenny pulled out his keys and checked them. One was missing.

"I found a post office box key. I asked myself what Lenny is doing with
a post office box key. You can see how one might find that a little strange,
don't you? Why would you need a post office box? For the life of me, I
couldn't come up with a good answer. So, I took it upon myself to see if I
could find the mail box that this key belongs to." He dangled the key in
front of Lenny. "Do you know what I found in that mail box? A package,
a little package that he had mailed to himself. Yes, he did. And the cute

thing about it was that it had on it marked return to the sender. And do you know whose address was on the package that was supposed to be sent back to? It happens to be the police, isn't that right, Lenny? If you did not pay the rent on the box than it would have been sent to the police. Right Lenny, that little movie of us with that girl."

"You damn bastard!" Max said just before he hit Lenny, knocking him to the deck.

"Grab him!" Dick ordered. Max wrestled with Lenny until he was able to get him in a full Nelson. "Many times you hear me using the old saying 'Mess with the bull and you will get the horns.' Well you sure in the hell didn't listen, did you?"

"You got the chip! I can't hurt you!" Lenny cried. "Please! For God sake, don't do anything crazy."

"Poor Lenny. You are a liability, and as long as you are around we will not be safe. Isn't that right Max?"

"You got that right."

"No! No! I swear I will never, never tell. You can have my word on it. I will never tell."

"That I am sure of," Dick said as he pulled out some handcuffs. "Do you remember these? You were the one who said that we should buy them. You said that we could use them. Isn't that funny? You were right, we are going to use them."

Lenny squirmed and kicked but the two larger men overpowered him. Soon they had handcuffs on his hands and feet. "Please! Please! I beg you! Please don't!" He realized that begging was useless. "You have no right."

"No right? Max, do you think that we have the right to carry out the punishment for trying to betray his friends?"

"Of course we do. Let's throw the damn cowardly bastard overboard."

"Now, now, he might be right. He does deserve a trial. This is true. So, we must accommodate the .prisoner. After all we are civilized men, aren't we? And to approve it we will hold it right here-on this boat. Yes, we will give him a fair trial. Since I am the captain of this ship, I well be the judge. Max, you're the prosecutor, state your case."

"Yea, I'll be the prosecutor, I'll be a damn good prosecutor. Who will be his lawyer?"

"Being the judge I will appoint him to be the one to represent himself. So Lenny I hate to inform that you have a fool as a lawyer," Dick laughed. "Max, do you want to give your opining statement?"

"Sure. He is a cowardly scumbag that would turn us in to save his own damn ass. He should die."

"Umm, a very good argument. You stated your case well. Does the accused have anything to say in his defense?"

"Please don't kill me. I'm begging you. Please don't kill me."

"If the only defense that someone has is to beg for mercy then he has no defense. He must be guilty. The court finds the accused of the crime not being loyal to his friends. There is a name for that. Does the defendant know what that is?" Lenny glared at Dick as he struggled hopelessly to free himself from Max. "Does the prosecutor knows the correct name for someone that is willing squeal on his friends?"

"Yeah, we called a rat, a dirty rat."

"What is the penalty for being a rat?"

"We kill them."

"That's right Mr. Prosecutor. I believe that the correct term is exterminate. Does the defendant have anything to say in his defense?" Lenny did not reply "No defense? I am afraid that I have no choice but to have the court find you guilty as charged. And the penalty for being a rat is death. I'm truly sorry Mr. Chopin, but you have been sentenced to death. Do you have any last words to say before the sentence is carried out?"

"You bastards will never get away with this. They will catch you and make you pay. You think that you are committing the perfect crime, but you're not. They will catch you and you will pay."

"Don't you realize that this boat is named the Get-A-Way? And that, my friend, is just what we are going to do, get a way. There will be only three people who know about what is happening here, there aren't any cameras to record us, and you can be assured that I wouldn't tell. Max, are you going to tell anyone?"

"I'm no damn fool."

"And since you will be at the bottom of the lake I can count on you not saying anything either, right? So, there you have it. Our little secret will never be known."

Dick gagged Lenny and attached an old anchor to the handcuffs that were on his feet. They heaved him and the anchor upon the side of the boat. Lenny squirmed but Max held him tight. "We cannot risk you popping back up." With that Dick plunged a knife into Lenny's gut. Lenny's eyes bulged as he let out a muffled cry as blood squirted from his gut. Dick pulled the knife upward Lenny's body stiffened then he went limp, when they dropped the anchor over board. In a whip like motion it yanked Lenny's bloody body into the cold water. They watched the lifeless body descend into the abyss.

Drifting aimlessly in the fog, Seth sat in his boat, Spirit. After finishing drinking one beer he opened another bottle. Usually he would spend his times on the boat fishing, but on this day the fishing gear lay idle. On this day he had no interest in anything other than in his own thoughts. His mind kept going back to the events of recent days, bounding back and forth between break-up with Angela and what had happened to The Garden and Ruben. Among them it left him with the feeling of a great sense of loss and anger.

He always had a craving for someone to fill the emptiness that he had ever since Grace and his children had been killed. He felt that Angela and Jason might, by chance, have been the ones, the ones that could bring him the love that he so desperately wanted. In his mind he had seen Hope and Ruben in a way as replacements for Crystal and Nelson, for they would have been approximately the same age. But they are now gone, all of his family were gone. Even Angela had rejected him. She had told him that she did not want to be a part of his life anymore. She felt she would only be a replacement, someone that always would be playing the role of second best. She demanded more, and she was afraid that it would never come to her. The truth was that he felt that she might been right, Grace would always be his true love. And the burning of The Garden was devastating to him, not only in the financial aspect but also socially. The people there had become his extended family. In the funeral home when sharing the grief with others, his grief was not only for Ruben and Hope but also for his wife, Grace, and their two children, Nelson and Crystal.

He heard voices through the fog of men talking on another boat that was drifting in his direction. Even though the fog was lifting the visibility was still limited. He was debating with himself if he should start his boat up or not, to move farther away. He barely made out the silhouette of the other boat. He put down his beer and picked up his binoculars to read its name. The name on the other boat was Get-A-Way. He remembered back to the time when he met the owner, the night of Ruben's twenty-third birthday. That was the night that Hope gave Ruben his birthday cake. It was when all of the trouble started, that led to the death of Hope and Ruben, also the burning of The Garden. Now, they were in front of him. He looked through the binoculars again to verify that the two that were on the boat were Dick and Max. Should he make them pay for the deeds that they had done or should he let the law handle it? In his heart he felt that if justice was going to be carried out then it had to be by him, and it had to be then. The question was should he let the teaching of the church and the laws of man determine what is right or wrong? Or should he dismiss the teaching of the church and the rules of law in which society had decreed what is right and what is wrong? Or should he decide for himself what is right and what is wrong? This is what he was debating with himself. The image of Hope's innocent childlike face still haunted him. Her face and the face of his daughter, Crystal, keep interchanging. He also could not remove from his mind the horrifying sight of the remains of The Garden, for he was there when they removed the charred remains of Ruben from the burnt out restaurant.

He could see the two men drinking beer and laughing. With the feeling of anger and duty he felt he knew what had to be done. He had two empty beer bottles and three full ones, plus the one that he had been working on. He poured them out over the side. Then he disconnected the fuel line to the motor, and with the gasoline he filled up the empty beer bottles. He tried to reconnect the line, but he had stripped the threads. He could not keep it from dripping. After he shut off the fluid valve he ripped up an old towel and stuck part of it into each of the bottles for a wick. The two vessels were about a hundred feet apart. They were slightly swaying, back and forth. It had been a long time since he had thrown anything that distance. The two men noticed him. Through the fog, they were trying to make out if they knew him or not.

The first Molotov cocktail, that Seth threw, hit the top of the cabin, setting the wooden boat aflame. Dick grabbed a fire extinguisher and tossed it to Max. Then he rushed inside of the cabin to retrieve a revolver. He came out firing the gun. The first shot missed because he had to dodge another Molotov cocktail as he was shooting. That one sailed over the boat. The second round hit Seth in the right leg, the one that he pitched off of. It hit him just as he was lighting the third bottle. Seth grabbed his leg as he fell to the deck, holding the beer bottle with the flaming wick. As he rolled over he was able to keep the cocktail up-right. He grabbed the rail that was attached to the top of the side of the boat, and pulled himself up. He heaved the cocktail towards the Get-A-Way, falling short of its mark, into the water in front of the boat. Dick fired his third round from his bobbing boat to the other bobbing boat, hitting the Spirit's rudder shaft, breaking it in two.

Seth ripped off his shirt, popping the buttons. As he was tying the wrap tight around his leg, trying to stop the bleeding, a bullet came though the side of the boat, just missing his head. Through the pain he managed to light another one. He pulled himself up, exposing himself to Dick as he released the fourth Molotov cocktail.

Dick was trying to watch the incoming fire bomb as he was shooting at Seth. He missed his target, but Seth's did not. It hit with an explosion of fire. It drew their attention away from Seth as they tried to extinguish the flames. It gave him enough time to light another one. This one hit the fuel tank. The explosion threw the two back into the cabin of the Get-A-Way. The boat was engulfed in flames. There was no escape. Seth could hear the screams of the two men as the burning vessel began to sink into the cold water of Lake Michigan. Seth could no longer hear nor see the two men. They had vanished into the water where they were meeting the same fate as their victim had.

He dragged himself into the cabin, leaving a trail of blood. Many years before his late wife, Grace, had insisted on having a first-aid kit in the boat. Now, her insistence might save his life. He untied the blood soaked shirt from around his wounded leg. He quickly ripped open the jeans, revealing the wound. Fortunately the bullet had passed through him without hitting the bone. Like in the old westerns, he poured whiskey over the wound, causing great pain, before he wrapped a bandage around his leg.

He dragged himself back to the motor and tried to refasten the fuel line, but the threads were too badly stripped. He soon realized that trying to fix it was futile. Then he discovered that one of the bullets had broken the shaft of the rudder. He looked out where the Get-A-Way had been, but now only debris was floating on the surface.

Seth had taken the lives of two men. He had been their judge, jury and the executioner. From then on he could never see himself in the same light. The sun was burning off the fog. Around him he saw nothing but emptiness. He began drifting to where? He did not know.

Acknowledgement and notes from the Arthur

One morning while I was driving my wife, Carmen, to the doctor's office, when a thought came to me. 'If you kill someone's dreams it is like you are killing them.' It dawned on me that it could be the basis for the novel which I wanted to try my hand at writing. It would be about how the under dogs would seek out revenge against the villains after the law had failed to bring them to justice. The question was what would be the setting? Not being a historian it was an easy choice to have it be in the present day. The story needed to take place where the haves and the have nots congregate. Being a weekend bartender I realized that that it is a place that where different economical levels do mix. So the Garden was created, not a lot unlike the place where I worked on weekends, but still not the same. Working at the Willowbrook over the years I have known several bartenders and waitresses. Sure there were some that cared only about themselves, but for the most part they are good men and women, who see their co-workers as friends and are concerned with their welfare. And if one of them was the victim of a horrifying crime, and if they felt that there was not going to be justice, then they might react to it. That is the premise for the book. I must confess my lack of knowledge of the world of the pornography business, but I do have knowledge of ruthless people that would take great pleasure in doing anything that it might take for them to get what they want. They will always justified their actions regardless whatever the cost to others maybe.

Being a new writer I found that transferring the book from my mind onto paper was not working out fairly well. Using an old cliché, it was like trying to put a square peg in a round hole, I never realized what I was

271

doing wrong. Then one day I saw a young man in his mid-twenties who had long hair and sideburns with tattoos in a black Jack Daniels' T-shirt, and at that moment it was clear what was wrong. That man was obviously Ruben, not my ego. With that the pieces began to fall into place.

I know that 'fall into place' sounds like it was easy and quick, but still that was not the case. The book was something that I would work on now and then, but it was more then and less now. On Sunday afternoon at the Willowbrook, where I tended bar, I would discuss my would be novel with a customer, a lady by the name of Beverly Logan, whom everyone call Bev. Telling her what I wrote or planned to write and she would give me her feedback. On one of those Sunday afternoons she asked if I would bring her one of the chapters. The truth was that all that I had written down by that time was parts and pieces that that I jotted down in longhand. So that night I broke out the laptop, which had pretty much been idle for the two years since my family gave it to me as a Christmas present, and I started to write. If it wasn't for Bev this book would never been written it.

There were people whose brains I pick and those I am grateful to. One that I am especially grateful to is Patty Doten, a friend of the family, who proof read it for me. Another friend of the family that should get mention is Betty Sereno, who kept telling me that the book was good and I should finish it and get it published. Along with Bob Cirsrik I would like to thank him. Those and all the others I would like to thank. And now as I am writing this my wife, who is reading this over my shoulder, is telling me that I should also thank her for putting up with me while I was writing this book.